JOE KASSABIAN

COLD STEEL

aethonbooks.com

COLD STEEL
©2022 JOE KASSABIAN

ALSO IN SERIES

FRONTIER CORPS

COLD STEEL

COFFIN TROOPERS

CHAPTER
ONE

THE SHUTTLE CIRCLED our destination for hours. I watched the large, expansive circular shape of the station float under us. Its gunmetal grey structure flashed in the solar brilliance each time the sun caught it in just the right way. A never-ceasing train of shuttles ran from the station down to the surface of an asteroid, the two tethered together by long metal spikes.

"Next stop Sassoun Station" came a soothing voice from the overhead sound system.

I reached over and slid the window shade closed.

"Excuse me, My Lord?" I faintly heard someone say.

I saw a flight attendant standing in the aisleway, a large metal cart beside her. She was an attractive middle-aged woman with a tightly pulled-back brown bun. She was bowed at the waist in deference. Not to me, but to my family. I had forgotten to take my family crest off of my school uniform before I had left the spaceport on Olympus. Its golden lion shape still sat prominently over my heart. I took my earbuds out so the sounds of the Martian ska music I was listening to didn't drown out what she as trying to tell me.

"Hm?" I asked.

She bowed lower.

"The pilot wished for me to extend his apologies to you for taking so long to dock," she said, her voice shaking.

I guess not many members of the nobility ended up on commercial flights between Sassoun and Mars. I didn't want to be on this flight either. Commercial flights didn't offer stasis treatments so I had been stuck in this damn uncomfortable seat for the last three days. The cabin smelled like stale cigarette smoke mixed with the farts that only subpar economy flight food could produce.

The shuttle was packed full of migrant workers from the nearby planets. Their unfamiliar musks and strange accents all making their way to the station, hoping to get one of the jobs down in the mines. Each of them eyed me with a mix of hatred, shock, and jealousy when I boarded. I'm sure wherever they were coming from they wouldn't be allowed to share a cabin with a member of the nobility. On Sassoun we hardly had the space for such privilege.

"It's not a problem." I smiled at her. "My sister told me traffic has picked up over the last few months, so I suppose it couldn't be helped."

"Have you been away long, My Lord?"

"Four years." I nodded.

I didn't feel like being trapped in small talk with someone who was seemingly scared just to be near me, but I recognized when I was in too deep. "My sister had told me the mine has expanded since I have been gone."

She beamed. "Oh yes. House Boguni had taken great lengths to bring in workers from around the sector. We can hardly keep up with all of the flights."

I frowned at the mention of the Boguni house and I think she noticed because she quickly added, "But of course, none of this wouldn't have been possible without your father, the Duke Haduni."

The aisleway of a transit shuttle was not where I wanted to get into a debate regarding inner palace politics that this poor woman probably wouldn't even understand.

"It's fine." I smiled again. "I am glad the people of Sassoun are doing well."

I think she caught on that I wasn't in the mood for chit-chat. She shuffled back to her cart and produced a miniature bottle of gini, the regional specialty of the station. From the looks of it, it was an incredibly cheap bottle of the stuff. "*Stationer Special!*" read the label alongside a little picture of a rocket circling around the spoked outline of Sassoun Station. I would have been rude to turn it down, so I accepted it with a slight bow of my head.

"A gift from the pilot, the staff of Sassoun Starways thank you for choosing us for your travel, My Lord."

I didn't want to tell her that I didn't choose this third-rate starway to travel. Nobody with more than a handful of bits to their name would have picked Sassoun Starways. The only people who rode the rusted buckets they called transit shuttles were smugglers and migrant workers. I just didn't want to wait on Mars for another three weeks for my father to send his personal shuttle. The only thing that was worse than this shuttle, was Mars.

"Send the pilot my thanks." She bowed even lower, straightened up and fished a small molded cup from her cart, and handed it to me.

No ice, I shouldn't have been surprised. The attendant finally pushed her cart down the aisle, leaving me with my four bit bottle of gini and a room-temperature cup.

I cracked the cap on the small bottle and decided to drink it straight from the source. The red liquid hit my tongue and burned so I gutted it down as fast as I could, holding the bottle high so the flight attendant could see me do it. Nobody was going to accuse House Haduni of being ungrateful on my behalf. I licked my lips and was forced to retaste the stuff. It tasted like the synth grapes had been steeped in gasoline before it was brewed. I smiled at the attendant and she returned a toothy grin.

"*We have been cleared for landing at dock four-seven-nine. Please return to your seats and prepare for landing,*" came the voice again.

Finally. I couldn't wait to get off of this tub. All around me passengers pushed by one another to get back to their seats. More than one of them was smoking while others had the beat red eyes of dust addicts. I handed one of them the remainder of my bottle of gini. An old man with a bent back and a face like shoe leather took it from me.

"Thank you, M'Lord." He smiled broadly. "Please send my regards to your father."

The man held up the bottle and drank from it. "To his health!"

I smiled and tried not to wince when he downed the rest of it in one gulp without so much as a blink from its harshness. Once everyone found their seat a small light flashed overhead politely telling us to fasten our seatbelts.

The shuttle passed through clouds of transit craft along with the occasional massive ore freighter that stretched out for miles. They were branded with the logos of countless companies I had never heard of, each owned by one noble house or another, their crest stenciled on at seemingly random intervals. I noticed many of the freighters showed the crest of House Boguni, a black crow with unfolding wings.

The organized chaos of the shipping lane was shut away from view as the shuttle was swallowed by the cavernous halls of Sassoun's docking system. All around us, there were thousands of docks just like this one, each having to work in perfect unison with one another to bring in the countless ships that passed through station space every day. It was organized choreography at a scale so great it took tens of thousands of people working around the clock to make it work.

The shuttle shook and a loud metallic *clang* could be heard throughout the cabin. Outside, a large arresting claw had grabbed onto the shuttle to hold it in place and was now retracting it back into the station itself, out of the vacuum of the dock. Triple sealed doors opened one at a time, slowly bringing us further and further in. The last door finally hissed and retracted, revealing the disembarkation area. I had assumed flying economy would mean me flying under my father's radar. I really should have known better.

The disembarkation area was a drab, mostly rundown space. Its once carpeted flooring had been stomped flat by generations of feet and its off-white walls were now a sickly yellow from cigarette smoke. Several of the waiting room seats were broken and hadn't been replaced. In the middle of this disrepair was a full squad, of twelve fully armed men, wearing their palace guard dress uniforms. The dark yellow uniforms were decorated with all kinds of awards, medals, and ribbons. Their ceremonial rifles were laid across their shoulders at port arms, and they stood unmoving.

"We have arrived at Sassoun Station. Thank you for traveling Sassoun Starways. We hope to see you again in the future," the voice bid us farewell.

Not damn likely, I frowned to myself. I waited for the rest of the passengers to get off first. If there was one thing I hated, it was pushy people all jostling for position while trying to get their overstuffed bags from storage. The last thing I needed was to get brained by some miner's carry-on bag.

When they finally cleared out, it was my turn. The flight staff were lined up to greet me, each bowing low as I walked by. I made sure to thank them all individually as I went. When you're the duke's son, everything you do is a part of the bigger political picture. Or at least my father would always insist it was. I always hated that about living on the station. Every interaction was a finely tuned exchange, an act. You could never be sure who hated you and who didn't.

I stepped off the shuttle and the leader of the palace guard rose a foot up and stomped the ground. His means of drawing attention to himself was somewhat muffled by the dingy red carpet.

"His Imperial Lord, Andranik Haduni!" the soldier announced, I could tell by the chevrons on his sleeves that he was a Sergeant First Class.

The palace guard, all in unison, brought their rifles down from their shoulders and thrust them out in salute. Caught up in their presentation, passing civilians bowed low to me as I fought with the wheels of my suitcase across the carpet.

From behind the palace guard came a young woman dressed in a long white dress, a shawl draped loosely over her dark hair. Her soft feature cracked into a huge goofy smile when she saw me.

"Ando!" she cried.

The duke's daughter is supposed to keep herself composed at all times. She even had several attendants whose full-time job it was to make sure she didn't do anything that could be considered "unfitting," which I was sure was a lengthy list of activities. Right then she clearly didn't care, as she ran across the disembarkation platform and hugged me. I dropped my bags and caught her.

"Anahit." I smiled. "I didn't expect you to be here."

I hadn't seen my older sister in four years but it felt like it had been much longer. We had made sure to write to one another every day while I was away at school, but it just wasn't the same. Cloistered away in the drudgery of palace life, we were the only people we could vent to and not worry about upsetting some unwritten rule of noble custom or procedure. With me gone, she was forced to survive in the palace political monster on her own.

"And why wouldn't I be?" she huffed. "Bad enough you rode that roach coach here. Did one of the planetsiders give you any parasites I should be wary of?"

She laughed and motioned for one of her attendants, an older woman wearing a pantsuit, to grab my bags. I glanced down at my device.

"Because it's three in the morning, Ana," I pointed out. "Don't you have something to be planning? A wedding perhaps?"

She rolled her eyes. Ever since she was announced as heiress to the throne of Sassoun, the House Agency had been sent a deluge of marriage requests from around the Empire. My father was old-fashioned, so of course he wanted someone from one of the other prominent families to take his daughter's hand in marriage and strengthen the house's holdings. Unlike many other noble fathers, he respected his daughter enough to allow her to choose who would become her husband. Unfortunately for him, she had so far chosen nobody, much to the chagrin of the entire station government and countless families across the sector.

"A wedding," she scoffed. "You should see some of the suitors they are sending. Absolutely atrocious. Did you know some of these men still live with their parents?"

She stuck out her tongue. "They even tried to hook me up with that revolting Aren Boguni."

"The one who had a crush on you all throughout school? The one who used to follow you around like a lost puppy?"

She nodded. "The very same. He came to the palace in his dumb dress uniform and proposed right at the front door! The poor idiot started crying when I laughed in his face."

"Those Boguni think they should have claim to everything just because of their wealth."

"If only their wealth could buy them a personality. Or charm. Or looks." She laughed.

We walked through the palace guard and they pivoted on their heels, re-shouldered their weapons, and marched in two single-file lines at our sides. Eventually, the crowd of civilians abandoned their shows of respect and went about their day, giving the guard a wide berth.

"The flight attendant said traffic has picked up recently?"

"Oh." She rolled her eyes. "The Boguni have pressured Father to change the laws regarding migrant workers. Some kind of special permit system. It allowed a surge of people to be hired to work in the mines. Of course, it only benefits them. I'm sure you've seen all of their new freighters."

"I did. But how are all of these people affording the trip? Sassoun Starways may not exactly be a high-class venture, but their ticket prices are still a bit pricey for your normal planetsider looking to work in the mine."

"That Goddess-forsaken Ara Boguni," she hissed. "He opened companies in every surrounding settlement offering anyone who could work a job for six months and a ticket here. When they get here of course they learn the cost of the ticket equals to be six months of their pay, which the Boguni accountants then deduct from their paychecks. Then they are sent back to wherever they came from. Slavery with extra steps."

"Goddess above, Ana, how is that not illegal?"

Our procession finally reached the metro station. The Sassoun metro reached every one of the twelve districts that branched off from the central landing point, each sticking out like the spoke of a wheel with the central being the hub. Lines of people were waiting for one of the hundreds of metro cars. They would scan their device to pay for their fare and then would be gone in the blink of an eye. A new car would arrive only a few seconds later.

There was only one spoke that the metro system wouldn't take them to, the administrative district, home to the nobility as well as the various ministries of government that they ran. The head of the palace guard approached the metro, the crowds parting in front of him. The sergeant scanned a small device that he wore on his wrist and a moment later a special metro car arrived. It was generations newer than the rest of the cars. Flawlessly white, it was adorned with the golden eagle of the Emperor of Terra, as well as the lion and crow of the local families. Rather than being controlled by the Ministry of Public

Transportation's drone system, it was staffed by human attendants.

The door slid open and we made our way inside. Even though the ride would only take a few minutes, the cabin was lined with seats that looked downright luxurious compared to the transit shuttle I had just stepped off from. Metro attendants in starched and pressed uniforms offered me a glass of water which I took.

"Trust me, Ando," Ana continued. "I've tried to point that out to Father. However, he only sees the influx of money due to the increase of exports."

"Surely those exports only benefit the Boguni." I sipped the water and was thankful to wash the taste of cheap gini out of my mouth.

"They pay their taxes, so Father doesn't care." She sat down heavily on one of the seats.

She tried to act normal, but it was obvious the hour and her workload weighed on her.

"Say, I thought you always hated palace politics. If you're that interested in law and administration I'm sure I could change Father's mind about your future in the military."

I laughed. As the youngest child of the Haduni Duke, it was tradition for me to become an officer in the Imperial Army. As far back as anyone had bothered to write down the sons and daughters of Sassoun had served the emperor on the battlefield. After spending the last four years of my life training at Tigranes the Great Armed Forces Preparation Academy, I had no intention of breaking that tradition.

"Somehow hearing you complain about nobility and taxes is more than enough to convince me to stay my course." I smiled. "I'll tell you what, once I am promoted to captain, I'll request to come home and you can give me whatever dreadful ministry job you want."

She covered her mouth and laughed.

"How about ambassador to Mars?"

I had made no secret of my hatred for the red planet during my time at school. It had long been considered the artistic and intellectual capital of the Empire. The only thing I saw was self-important navel-gazing from high-born debutants. Nobility so far removed from any actual part of society they were functionally unemployed, nearly alien to their own subjects.

"I think I would rather join the Frontier Corps," I joked.

The metro car slowed and came to a stop, the doors slid open and the attendants reappeared. They offered another glass of water and bowed as we exited.

The administrative district was exactly how I had remembered it. The overhead day-night cycle lights were dimmed, owing to the early morning. It was chilly, the air cooled by the constantly churning climate control systems that kept the station habitable. I could taste the purification chemicals from the oxygen scrubbing network that made the environment breathable. Planetsiders thought the smell and taste were overpowering and it took them time to get used to. For me, it let me know that I was home. The crisp, fresh air of the terraformed Mars never felt right to me.

The metro station deposited us at the head of the administration spoke and we were met with more soldiers, though these were gendarmes, the main law enforcement arm of the Imperial Government. They wore brown, drab uniforms and the look was completed by their utility belts, from which hung a holstered pistol. Unlike the palace guard, these guns weren't ceremonial. They gave a slight nod as we went by.

After the reception at the disembarkation area, I assumed I would be walking into more of the same in the place that had been my home for the eighteen years prior to me leaving. Instead, the district was mostly empty other than the normal night shift workers going about their duties of maintenance, cleaning, or the like. Ana must have seen me looking around.

"Father said he wanted to come, but he's not doing very well," he said, her voice dropping low, almost to a whisper.

Our father had been dealing with a terminal illness for several years. It had just really started to take hold before I left for school. Rumors were it was the same illness that claimed our mother when I was younger. The planetsiders insisted it was because we lived most of our lives on stations, that the human body just wasn't meant for this kind of habitation. I wasn't sure if I believed them, but I did notice many more elderly people on Mars than I ever did on Sassoun.

"That bad?" I asked.

She nodded. "He can hardly leave the palace these days. He still makes his appearances when he needs to, though."

"So, it's all on you now, huh?"

"Unofficially," she added. "Though you'll be pleased to know that he is still planning his youngest a party."

She poked me in the ribs and I groaned.

"You've got to be kidding me. A party for what?"

"A celebration for your commission into the Imperial Army, of course."

"But I haven't commissioned into anything yet, Anna. I still have to take the induction exam tomorrow."

She waved me off. "That is a formality and you know it. Have you ever failed a test in your life?"

"No," I admitted.

I had always done better in school than she had. Her failure wasn't due to any kind of fault in her intelligence, but rather boredom. School work never appealed to her. She would sleep through class and then come home and try to debate with our father over civil servant pay raises or some such with such a level of expertise it shocked the people he had actually hired to advise him in such matters. She only graduated with a diploma due to the intervention of the House Agency.

"I told you. You'll be first in your class and then go on to command some armored regiment like every other child of the Haduni family. Better than those logistics clerks that come from the Boguni. Spinless even in their service to the Empire."

I didn't want to explain to her how spending years studying the complex logistical system of the Army probably did a lot of good when they returned to the station and ran their businesses. It would truly benefit my family if I went the same route, but our tradition was riding tanks into war in the name of the emperor. The skills didn't exactly transfer the same way.

Countless members of the Haduni family had been named the hero of the Empire, had streets named after them on Terra, and Tigranes the Great had even come to my father's coronation. At least that is what people tell me. All of that glory didn't amount to much when our House Agency was running up debt to a rival family just to keep up appearances.

"If only I am so lucky," I said quietly.

As we went further into the district, the boulevard was lined on either side with administrative offices, split down the middle between the two families. On one side were the various licensing and ministerial offices that made the station tick. In front of them stood statues of the heroes of the Haduni family, all of them standing triumphantly in their resplendent Imperial Army dress uniforms. Each of them had plaques at their feet, listing their accomplishments.

On the other side were the business offices of the Boguni. There was a reason why over the years they had been nicknamed the Boguni Cartel. Dozens of mining, freight, and export businesses all with different offices, names, and logos but each owned by members of the same family. It was a façade they could use to make sure if any bits exchanged hands outside of official taxation, it went directly into their pockets.

They kept up countless shell companies to give people a

mirage of competition. If a family on another planet or station, or Goddess forbid, the security services, caught on to the backroom dealing of one company, they would simply close it, change its name, and reopen it. It kept the pipeline open indefinitely and secured the Boguni family as one of the richest noble families in the entire Empire.

Instead of statues of military heroes, each head of the Boguni family had a simple bust. They wore boring business suits and ties, each of their faces frozen in a way that made them all look like they were trapped in a particularly boring board meeting. Each family had chosen how they wanted to be viewed by the public and the differences were stark. The Haduni were related to the Tigranes of Terra, though distantly, and wanted to reflect their Imperial lineage. The Boguni, rumor had it, had begun life as commoners on Luna, and only through the accumulation of money and power via an export business had they secured a noble peerage through a particularly large bribe.

They even eschewed the protection of the Imperial Army's special palace guard detachment. While the palace guard stood outside of our family home, they hired their own security. The so-called "Mining Protection Agency," an official-sounding name for what amounted to be a bunch of hired guns kept around to keep migrant workers in line. As we approached the Haduni Palace, I could see the outlines of their black dusters looking out at us from their posts at the Boguni home across the street.

In front of the Haduni Palace yellow-jacketed soldiers stood on either side of the door. Unlike the ones we had met at the metro station, these carried real weapons rather than ceremonial ones. They didn't bow to us, but rather glared, eyeing us up and down. It was clear they recognized Ana but not me. Soldiers were only posted to various planets and stations for a few years at a time, so there was a good chance none of the current guards were here before I left for school.

"Name," grumbled the soldier on the left.

He wasn't asking.

"Roman," hroaned Ana. "This is my brother, Andranik. He's the duke's son for Goddess' sake."

"You know the rules, My Lady." Roman eyed her, I had a feeling this was an argument he had frequently with her.

He looked back at me and repeated, "Name."

"Andranik Haduni," I answered.

Roman glanced down at his wrist device. A hologram list projected from it in blue letters in front of his face. He scrolled down a list of approved visitors before finding me. My name glowed and a picture appeared, showing my badly out-of-date high school graduation photo.

"Welcome home, My Lord," Roman finally said, turning to the door he scanned his device and the door clicked open.

Ana gave Roman a side-eye as she pushed by him, opened the door, and led me inside.

The palace remained unchanged. Members of the Haduni family had lived in the oversized home since the founding of Sassoun, each of them adding furniture, decorations, statues, paintings, and the like. The family that followed the last one soon found it to be in bad taste to remove the things their ancestors had hung up. It created an aura of a museum rather than a place to comfortably live. A living exhibit kept spotlessly clean by an unceasing and constantly rotating janitorial staff.

"I'll leave you to find your room. I trust you haven't forgotten where it is."

"I think I'll be fine." I rolled my eyes at her. "As much as I would like to catch up, I do need to wake up early for the exam."

"Fine." She folded her arms across her chest. "But tomorrow night you are going to tell me everything about Mars."

I yawned. "Okay, I promise."

I made my way upstairs and down the familiar hallways until I found my room. Another soldier stood in the hallway on a roving patrol. She gave a slight bow as I scanned my device and entered my bedroom. Like everything else in the house, it hadn't changed. It had not been abandoned, however, as someone was sure to leave out study material for the induction exam.

I wouldn't need it. Unlike many other Imperial Army hopefuls, I had spent the last four years preparing every day for this exam, mentally and physically. For ten hours a day, every day, at Tigranes the Great Prep we studied Imperial military history, doctrine, and tactics. We took practice exams every night until test anxiety had been purged from our minds. The cadre ran us ragged and pushed our bodies until the standard physical agility test hardly made us break a sweat.

Only the most prominent Imperial families could gain entrance into the school. Of which, the Haduni were not, no matter how much my father wished we were. Instead, he signed various lopsided trade deals with the Arshuni family of Mars in order for me to gain entry. The Haduni family's profile was bolstered by my attendance at such an important school while the Ashuni would enjoy tax-free imports for such a long time I'm sure it would only add to our family's growing debt problem.

I stripped off my clothes that still smelled heavily of economy starway and crawled into my bed, slipping into a dreamless sleep.

CHAPTER
TWO

SASSOUN WAS TOO small to host a full-time Imperial Army recruiting office. Rather, they would swing by once per year to conduct the induction exam for whoever showed up at the local high school. It didn't matter if you were a noble or a citizen, you were to take the same test. Officer candidates simply had to score higher and pass something akin to a job interview with the recruiter at the end. It was always conducted by another noble. They weren't really judging you as much as your pedigree and if your family deserved to be elevated into the Army's corps of officers.

Hopefuls from the surrounding stations and settlements too small for even a yearly visit from the recruiter all traveled to Sassoun in order to take the exam. As such, the area had become packed with human bodies of all shapes, sizes, and various regional accents. It was easy to tell who was here for the officer corps and who was there to enlist. Nobles were dressed in exercise uniforms from their local military academies where they had attended prep school. Others wore street clothes in different stages of disrepair. I noticed I was the only one there wearing the red tracksuit of Tigranes the Great Prep, a good sign for me.

What branch of service you ended up in depended on your test scores. For the Army, the highest scores meant you could pick from infantry, armor, or artillery. If you scored high enough and had the right connections, you could even commission into the Navy. The thought had crossed my mind to buck family tradition and become a pilot, though my time trapped on the starway told me that becoming a space jockey probably wasn't for me.

Everyone stood around in small groups made up of people they had arrived at the high school with. They stayed in their like groups, nobody wanting to socialize with a stationer or planetsider until it was required. Eventually, a man dressed in Imperial Army blue emerged from the inside of the high school. He was a noncommissioned officer, a staff sergeant from the look of it. His chest was heavy with skill badges and awards and his face showed deep-set wrinkles that tend to come on faster than normal with Imperial service.

"Listen up for your names!" he called out.

He read off from a list of what seemed like hundreds of names. I was the only Haduni on the list, but I did hear three different Boguni be announced. They had much of the same traditions as we did, shuffling off the younger ones into Imperial service so they could learn the ins and outs of the shipping trade on someone else's dime only to get folded into the family business cartel at the end of their five-year stint.

After everyone answered when their names were called out, the staff sergeant walked down the stairs and onto the field where we were all gathered.

"We are going to do the physical agility course first. It weeds out which of you didn't even bother to prepare for this exam and gives the ones being pressured by their families an easy out."

He walked over to where another group of blue-uniformed soldiers stood, they were low-ranking soldiers and looked annoyed they had been ordered to be there.

"The first event is two minutes of push-ups. You will line up in front of one of these soldiers and they will count out each of your reps. If you fail, don't come crying to me. I'm not going to entertain your arguments about how many you did or how the person grading you couldn't count. It's a push up, not rocket science."

We did as we were told. We stood in single-file lines without speaking, watching the person in front of us get down on the ground and do push-ups while the watching soldier loudly counted out the reps. I noticed a few of the people in front of me struggled after only doing a few, walking off with a defeated expression. When it was my turn the soldier asked my name.

"Haduni," I answered.

The bored-looking soldier glanced up from his device and motioned to the ground.

"After you, My Lord." I got down and began doing push-ups.

I had done hundreds a day while in school, for both exercise and the occasional punishment when the cadre caught someone doing something unlawful. After all of that there was no way I was going to do anything other than get the highest score I could. When I hit one hundred and still had thirty seconds left, the soldier told me to stop. The score didn't go up any higher than that.

After the push-up event, our ranks had thinned out somewhat. A dozen or so people had failed and been sent packing. They would have to wait a full year before trying again. The next event would be the pull-up. The soldiers had wheeled out collapsible pull-up bars, embedding them in the shallow synthetic dirt that made up the soccer pitch.

Again, one at a time we filed through. More people were struggling now. The accumulative fatigue of dozens of push-ups made the second event harder by design. The people who didn't train for it or weren't some natural athletic freaks, simply wouldn't be able to do enough at this point. When it was my turn, I jumped up to the bar and began knocking them out. The bar was gnarled and bit into my hands the tighter I grabbed it. I had lost count of how many I had done, but the soldier stopped me when I hit fifty.

At Tigranes the Great Prep, the cadre had stood outside of the dining facility and watched as each student did a minimum of five pull-ups before being allowed inside to eat. With every semester of school that would pass, the number of required pull-ups would increase. This same rule was put in place in front of the library, dorms, and classrooms with different exercises. The goal was, by the time you graduated, the minimum of any exercise you would do would be the maximum score on the induction exam.

Our number had dropped considerably by the third event, the hardest event of the physical portion of the induction exam: the run. We would be sent in eight laps around the school track, totaling three miles. This event was easy to train for, but many people failed due to the location of their training. If they were a planetsider, the station air might hurt their lungs or be harder to breathe, and vice versa. I was about to find this out for myself as I had not nearly enough time to reacclimate to Sassoun since I had arrived.

When I began running the station air, once so familiar, stung my lungs harshly. The Martian atmosphere felt strange to me the entire time I had been there because it was so clean and crisp. It was a natural, real space. Growing up on Sassoun meant that I had functionally lived in a human terrarium my entire life. Everything down to the air that I breathed was synthetic. It took four years, but I eventually acclimated to Mars, something my body was constantly reminded of now that I was attempting to sprint three miles with mouthfuls of polluted and recycled station air.

I coughed and sputtered as I went, still in the lead of the pack. The muscles in my legs began to burn with exertion while my lungs thirsted for clean air. I could hear the planetsiders behind me going through the same realization I was. I still forced myself to stay ahead of the acclimated stationers who were jogging without a care in the world as a matter of pride. I mercifully crossed the finish line at the fifteen minute mark and collapsed into the too-stiff synthetic grass of the soccer field.

It took me several more minutes to catch my breath. I was thankful for a small cup of water that the soldier who was grading me offered. It tasted like purification chemicals but I didn't care. The sergeant running the physical portion of the exam let us all sit around on the field until we weren't panting or sweating profusely anymore. I was sure it wasn't out of kindness, but rather because nobody wanted to be locked in a classroom with a hundred sweating bodies as they took a test.

Before we were brought into the school the sergeant ordered us to line up. We stood shoulder to shoulder in the middle of the field as a captain appeared from the inside of the school. Instead of wearing the blue of the Imperial Army, he was cloaked in brown, a member of the Imperial gendarmes. He was old for a captain, probably in his mid-fifties. He was bent slightly at the waist from a bad back, and he walked slowly toward us with his hands clasped behind him.

"Candidates. My name is Captain Vartan of the Imperial Gendarmes Corps." His voice crackled from a synthesizer, a grotesque implant stitched into his throat.

It made his words sound like a cartoonish robot from a network drama. "As you are all aware, you are about to take the Imperial Services Vocational Aptitude Battery portion of the induction exam."

He began to pace in front of us, eyeing us up and down with a bored look on his face. "Millions of citizens take this test across the Empire every year. So, it should come as no surprise when I tell you that some of these citizens decide to try to cheat on this test. I'm sure you can tell from my presence here today, that we do not take cheating lightly."

I'm sure I wasn't the only person standing there that had heard stories about the gendarmes. Admittedly, my status as the duke's son would allow me to get away with a lot. On more than one occasion growing up, Ana and I had talked our way out of legal repercussions. No low-ranking Gendarme wanted to be the one who brought the duke's children back to the district jail.

This was different, though. Sending an officer, a noble, like Vartan to threaten us told me that nothing was going to protect anyone if they were caught cheating. I wasn't going to be able to talk my way out of any suspicion like a kind of youthful indiscretion.

"The integrity of the Imperial Battery is protected under the national security act. This means we, the gendarmes corps, are charged with using any means in order to protect it from being compromised. We take this duty very seriously. Because of this, we have used various means to sus out who exactly might be attempting to bring answers or cheating devices into the official testing room. Thankfully, for you, these means are all quick and painless."

Vartan spun on a heel, more brown jacketed gendarmes appearing out of the school doors behind him.

"So, at this time you are going to remove all of your clothing and leave it in front of you. After you are fully undressed, do not touch your belongings until we tell you." He sighed, rolling his eyes. "Or the people to your left and right."

I did as I was told. The communal living of prep school had made me very desensitized about my own nakedness. Shared showers and bedrooms meant you were forced to lose whatever shame you had very quickly.

I piled my clothes in front of me and waited. gendarmes slowly made their way down the line, searching our clothes and skin. Another man used a handheld scanner, quickly running it across our naked bodies. Citizens were allowed to have implants and they were incredibly common the more money one tended to have, however you had to get them removed before entering Imperial service. The service would supply you with whatever implants they wanted you to have, nothing more, nothing less. Not to mention it would have been too easy for someone to use their neural network implant to cheat on a test.

Eventually the gendarmes found someone, their scanner beeped and they yanked some skinny girl out of line. She was slammed to the ground, screaming and crying, placed in handcuffs, and carried off. Her clothes were left behind, I assumed wherever she was being taken came with its own uniform.

A gendarme stood in front of me while another rifled through my clothes. The scanner was run over my head and I felt the warmth of its rays penetrate my skull. After a few seconds, I was given permission to get dressed again and I slipped back into my still sweat-soaked tracksuit.

Before they were done the gendarmes had found another suspect. A thickly built planetsider. He had the bright idea of scribbling a series of small notes all over his body, which were clear as day once he had taken off his clothes. Much like the girl, he was dragged away kicking and screaming.

Once the search was over, we were led inside the school. The doors were locked behind us and the gendarmes stayed behind. The Sassoun Central High School was not where I had gone. The children of the administration district had our own school. The Hayk Haduni School was staffed by the best teachers on the station and the student body was made up exclusively of the nobility.

The district spared no expense giving us the best educational experience on Sassoun. That had not been the case here at Central. The hallways were rundown, the false ceiling was missing squares, and the linoleum floor was cracked and scuffed. It looked like the school was almost in as bad of a need of renovation as the disembarkation area I had arrived in.

We were led into a classroom and locked inside. We all took our seats behind simple wooden desks, each with a sealed package sitting on top of it. The sergeant reappeared and deep down inside I was happy that Captain Vartan was not locked in the room with us, though I was sure he was waiting just outside.

"In front of you, you will find your copy of the test and a sealed pencil. When I say, open your packet and begin the test. You will not be allowed to use the bathroom, ask any questions, or talk to one another until you have completed your test and have left the room. Any deviation from these rules will lead to immediate failure and if you're really unlucky, detention by the gendarmes until they decide what to do with you. Now, open your packet and begin."

I tore open the paper packet and found my test book. It was hundreds of pages long and came with a sharpened pencil, taped to the top. I tore the pencil off, opened the book, and got to work. I did my best not to glance up at the clock to track how much time had passed. As I worked through the questions, pages blended together. The questions were a scattershot of history, political science, and general military knowledge in no particular order.

In what year was Tigranes the Great's Campaign against the Drani of Titan?

What model of destroyer is considered standard for the Imperial Navy?

Explain each rank in the Imperial Army between private and major general.

It took me about halfway through the book before I found a question that gave me pause. An essay question that demanded an in-depth explanation of the failures of the Imperial Frontier Corps during the Battle of New Beginnings. It took me the better part of an hour to craft a two-paragraph answer that I thought made any sense. I decided that was good enough and moved on.

By the time I got to the last page of the book, I was confident that I had done well. Looking at the people around me, their faces driven into the palms of their hands, some were crying, I was clearly feeling better than most. I had never failed any of the practice exams in prep school and always scored within the top twenty percent in my class.

I raised my hand and the sergeant approached.

"I said there were no questions." He grumbled.

"No, Sergeant. I don't have a question, I'm done with my test." The look on his face told me I was the first person to finish.

I tried not to pay attention to anyone else so as not to be distracted.

He raised an eyebrow at me. "Are you sure?"

I nodded and he grabbed my book from me. He motioned to the soldier at the door to move aside and let me out. I felt the eyes of the rest of the struggling test-takers following me as I made my way out.

Soldiers and gendarmes stood bored in the hallways, distracted, and playing games or videos on their devices. One of them noticed me and stuffed his device in his pocket.

"If you failed you can just go home," he said.

"I just finished," I corrected.

"Oh, well I'll be damned. Follow me then." The soldier led me deeper into the school, eventually taking me to a waiting area.

Seats lined the walls on both sides of a hallway, so far, they were all empty.

"Have a seat, someone will call for you in a bit. I'm going to judge from your tracksuit you know what comes next." He pointed to the crest of the school on my chest.

I nodded. "You shouldn't have anything to worry about. But

just mind your manners, I've heard the noble they sent out to conduct the interviews this time is kind of a hard ass."

"Thank you. Any idea what family he is from?"

"I haven't seen him. I've heard he's a stationer though." With that, the soldier turned around and walked away.

I took a seat in the empty hallway but I wasn't left there for long. A nearby door opened and a soldier stuck her head out.

"Haduni, Andranik?" she asked.

"Yes, Ma'am," I answered.

She waved me toward the door.

"Please come in and have a seat. The major will be here in a moment." She led me into an office that appeared to be a repurposed teacher's lounge of some kind.

Before I could sit, the door opened again and a man entered.

Like the soldier said, he was a stationer. A tall, lanky man with the telltale orange-tinted skin of life under the artificial sun of our day cycles. He sat down behind a desk and began typing on a device, my face appearing in a blue hologram next to him.

"Sit," he croaked.

I pulled a chair in front of his desk and sat down. When I finally got a look at his face, I realized he looked familiar. It wasn't uncommon for lifelong stationers to all look somewhat alike. There were only so many families who called the stations home and they tended to marry into one another. It was such a problem that arranged marriages with other families thousands of miles away were common in order to keep our bloodlines diverse.

"Andranik... Haduni," the man read off.

I nodded. "Yes, sir."

He leaned back in his chair, his arms folded over his chest. That is when I saw his nametag.

"A. Boguni."

Major Aren Boguni. The same man whom Ana had just sent running from the palace, crying, after rejecting his marriage proposal. Of all of the thousands of places he could have been stationed, in all of the hundreds of thousands of recruitment drives, he ended up being in charge of mine. How did I piss the Goddess off so badly to be given such terrible luck?

One of the first things I learned about palace politics was to never show when you were upset. Never let anyone know that they were getting under your skin. No matter what happens, you were at most supposed to seem indifferent to whatever bad news or barb was being thrown your way. It was meant to be a verbal parry, to buy you time to think of something to say in return. Father called it mental chess.

At the moment my face was as emotionless as concrete. It was a self-defense mechanism as my eyes locked onto his nametag and refused to look away. Aren and I had known each other for years but we were acquaintances at best. The only words we had exchanged had been in passing at one of the countless balls, festivals, and ceremonies our two families always seemed to be holding. He was ten years my senior and was considered the most eligible bachelor of the Boguni family, hence why he had spent the majority of his adult life trying to get Ana to marry him.

We didn't truly know each other, we had nothing personally against one another, but it didn't matter. Aren hated me, and I hated him just by virtue of who we were. In any other run-in with a member of the Boguni family we would almost certainly break down into an argument, or worse. But I wasn't in any other situation. He was a major in the Imperial Army and my entire future rested squarely on his shoulders. I knew there was nothing I could do at the moment to make the situation any better, so I kept my mouth shut.

My only hope was that the Imperial Army was everything that I had heard it was. Feuds between noble Families, clans, tribes, whatever were all thrown out of the window. They had to be. It would have been hard building a military if it was constantly tearing itself apart because of countless regional disputes that had no bearing on a war a thousand miles away.

"Haduni, eh?" Aren said again, his mouth tugging into a smile. "How is the duke doing these days?"

"I've heard he isn't well, sir." I swallowed. It was taking every ounce of my strength to remain stone faced. "I haven't yet seen him, I have only just returned to Sassoun."

"Ah yes." He eyed my tracksuit. "A Tigranes Prep grad. A virtual free pass into the officer corps."

I didn't respond, there was no way to answer that. I knew Aren didn't get into Tigranes Prep. He couldn't have if he wanted to. Nobody from the Boguni family had ever gotten in. It was one of countless sticking points between our two families.

"So, why is it you want commission into the emperor's army, Haduni?"

"I wish to serve Emperor Shahen, sir," I answered quickly.

It wasn't the best response, a canned answer at best, but I just wanted to get through this. He scrolled through pages of my information, somewhere I knew in the lines of text were my test results.

"You scored incredibly high in the political history section," he said, almost bored. "Did you learn much about loyalty to the Empire in your political history classes on Mars?"

I nodded. "Yes, sir."

"That is odd." He leaned forward on his desk, his eyes boring into mine. "Considering how disloyal your family is to the Empire, Haduni."

The political rules of remaining indifferent to slights and accusations had a line. Generally, that line was drawn when it came to defending the honor of your family, especially the head of your family. This went double if you happened to be the son of the ruling duke. However, I could hardly challenge an Imperial major to a duel at the moment. Furthermore, I was sure his training meant he would cut me to ribbons in short order if I had.

"Sir, whatever disagreements our families have had over the years I believe it would be foolhardy to question their loyalty to the Empire." I tried to keep my voice measured but I felt it rising with anger. "How many generations of Haduni had fallen on the battlefield in service of the emperor? Does that show disloyalty?"

He was standing now. He leaned over the desk, glaring down at me, tripoding himself over with his hands. A smirk tugged at the corner of his mouth.

"And do you believe loyalty is only measured in getting your ticket punched on some nameless planet?" He walked around the desk, getting uncomfortably close to me. "What about civil duty, eh?"

He jabbed an outstretched finger into my chest. I had no idea what he was going on about. The Haduni family funded and managed virtually every civil institution on the station.

"Picking the most capable candidate to ascend to the dukedom is one of the most important things a duke can do!" He was now towering over me, poking me repeatedly.

I was leaning back in my chair so hard the two front legs had left the ground. He had lost all sense of control. His eyes were bloodshot and wild like he was just lashing out and I had the misfortune of being around for it.

"Instead, your father sits on his little throne, rotting from the inside from whatever ailment the Goddess cursed him with, refusing to hand over the reins."

"Sir, in all due respect my father has named his successor. Duchess Anahit will inherit Sassoun in accordance with Imperial law." I decided to ignore the slight he had thrown at my father.

It was the only way I could maintain any level of courtesy. Did all officers of the Imperial Army carry themselves in such a way?

"Anahit." Aren fumed with venom. "That loathsome little harlot. My family offered her everything if she only understood how badly unprepared she was to rule and marry me, a man made for the job. If she only had as much sense as she did thirst for the cocks of your palace guard, she could see this."

That was finally it. I saw red, pushing myself from the chair. I channeled every bit of hand-to-hand combat training I had learned in school and delivered a right cross to Aren's chin. I felt a satisfying crack and his teeth smashed together upon impact. He was sent over his desk, falling to the ground on the other side, his devices clattering all around him as my file and picture flickered out of view.

The momentary flash of anger subsided and was replaced with a horrible sinking feeling. My hand stung but watching my future collapse over a desk hurt much worse. I just punched my only way into the Imperial Army directly in the face. Years of school and training thrown out of the window because I couldn't control my temper. If I was lucky, he wouldn't call for the gendarmes when he came to.

I peered over the desk and jumped back. He was staring right at me. The bastard wasn't unconscious! He was just sitting there, a little smile still played across his face. A small rivulet of blood dripped from his bottom lip. Then, he started laughing. Aren slowly got to his feet, producing a napkin from his pocket and dabbing at his bloody lip. I bladed my stance, bringing my hands up in front of my face. He was going to come at me any second and I wanted to be ready.

He laughed. "You're a stupid bastard, you know that, Haduni?"

Aren wasn't attacking me, he wasn't even preparing to fight. He just stood there, cackling at me like a madman. Did I punch him so hard I knocked a few screws loose?

"I assumed it would take more than that to get you to crack. I thought they taught all you prep losers how to keep your bearing?"

My arms dropped slightly. What was he talking about? Get me to crack?

"Goddess above." He rolled his eyes. "I can see your little brain working overtime trying to figure out what happened. I heard rumors you Haduni are all inbred and I'm starting to believe it."

I bared my teeth and lunged at him again, taking another swing. This time he deftly side-stepped my attack, pivoting slightly and sending me tumbling head over heels into the corner of the room. My head bounced off the floor and I saw stars.

"Let me spell it out for you, dumbass." He squatted down next to me. "When we heard you were coming back from school. My father bribed the Army to get me put here to oversee this recruiting drive. Now, I knew you weren't going to fail. Nobody coming from Tigranes Prep fails the induction exam. Your background is spotless and so is your family. There was no way you were going to be denied a commission."

"You lied." I coughed. "About my family's honor!"

"Of course I did!" He chuckled. "Tell me Haduni, have you ever heard of someone getting a commission after punching an officer in the face? You little shit, you think I wanted to spend the rest of my life wearing this rag and shuffling paperwork for one of my family's companies?"

He stood and gave me a kick to the ribs. My body instinctively curled up to protect itself.

"No!" he roared and kicked me again. "My future was supposed to be marrying that whore of a sister of yours and ruling over Sassoun as the first Boguni Duke!"

His next kick caught me on the top of the head. "Well, you know what? Your sister ruined my future, so I ruined yours."

"She was never going to marry you, you psycho." I managed to get out, blood filing my mouth.

He returned to his desk, righting his device, and began typing.

"Your petition for commission into the Imperial Army is officially denied." Aren walked to the door, opening it a crack.

"Come get this trash out of my office," he called to someone.

I assumed this was when the gendarmes would carry me away

to jail, and throw some charges at me about assaulting an officer. But it wasn't gendarmes, it was the black dusters of the Mining Protection Agency. They hooked me under each arm and began dragging me away, but not before Aren delivered one more cheap shot.

The blow was powerful enough to turn my world black.

CHAPTER
THREE

I WOKE up in my bed. My vision was blurry, but I didn't feel any pain. It felt as though I was floating above my bed, my skin was tingly and warm. I found the root of my current bliss in the form of a transdermal patch on my forearm. It slowly unknown and wonderful painkillers into my bloodstream.

I searched around the room, expecting to see gendarmes, waiting for me to wake up before slapping cuffs on my wrists. Instead, Ana hovered over my bedside, a look of concern on her face. A few soldiers stood guard in front of the door.

"You're awake!" she cried.

She hugged me and pain shot through my ribs. I guess the drugs weren't that powerful.

"How did I get here?" I rasped.

My throat felt as dry as a desert.

"We found you out front," she said. "A few of the soldiers said they saw some of those mining agency ghouls drop you off. What happened?"

I pushed myself up in bed, the amount of pain in my midsection told me I must have gotten worked over after I had been knocked out. I told her what happened, but decided to leave out the part where he blamed her. I didn't want her to blame herself for this. She had nothing to do with it.

"That monster," she seethed. "Backroom politics is one thing, but assaulting a member of our family? I'll order the guards to drag him out into the street!"

"You can't," I said. "You know as well as I do if our soldiers go near him, they will cut off their mining payments or stop paying taxes. They would bankrupt the family. Or worse. He isn't just a Boguni thug, he's a major in the Imperial Army. He's untouchable."

"Father needs to know about this." She pinched her chin. "Remember, this is bigger than just us. The Arshuni were the ones that did Father the favor of getting you into that school. Their good name is also sullied by this Boguni scheming."

"Could they blame us for this?" If the most powerful family on Mars turned against Father, it could mean the end of Haduni rule of Sassoun. They had the kind of power that could bend parts of the Imperial Government to its will.

"No, certainly not." She shook her head. "But they will demand a response."

"I'll give a damned response." I winced, swinging my legs over the edge of the bed.

She stifled a laugh with her hand. I wanted to be offended but I knew I hardly struck an intimidating figure at the moment.

"Leave the response to me, okay?" She patted me on the shoulder. "As soon as you are able, Father would like to see you."

She got up to leave.

"Where are you going?" I asked.

"If you haven't noticed I have several more fires to put out thanks to this little incident. I have Arshuni to smooth over and Boguni to plot against. On top of planning the Station Founder's Day Ball."

There were so many balls that were part of noble life that I had forgotten about most of them. Founder's Day marked the day construction on Sassoun was complete and the first Haduni duke took his seat on the throne. Growing up it just meant a chance to sneak a few drinks and flirt with girls from class.

She exited the room, one of the soldiers following after her, another staying behind. I got up and went to my closet. Someone had unpacked all of my bags and hung my clothes up. Row after row of red Tigranes Prep uniforms. I didn't feel right wearing them now. Not only was I no longer a student, but I also wasn't even an officer candidate anymore.

I pushed them aside and found my daywear. The usual black suit with yellow tie, a Haduni family lion pin stuck on the collar. As much as wrapping myself in several layers of formal clothing caused me pain at the moment, it was the only thing in the closet that still fit me. I was able to get the pants and shoes on, hand-made Terran leather, but the act of throwing the blazer over my shoulder caused pain to shoot through my midsection. The soldier who was guarding me had to leave his post and help me finish dressing.

As I made my way through the hallways of the vast palace countless staff and aids stopped what they were doing and bowed to me. I was conditioned to return the gesture, to the great displeasure of my battered ribs. Other people looked on in shock at my appearance. I couldn't blame them. It wasn't often you saw a member of the nobility with his nose broken and two black eyes. Nobody dared ask how it happened, but the way the palace rumor mill worked, I had a feeling most of them had already heard some version of events. I hoped whatever version they had heard, I made the other guy look as bad as I did.

Father no longer took guests. It had been some time since he had been healthy enough to hold regular court. Now, that duty fell to Anahit. Father would remain in his chambers under the watchful eye of a rotating staff of doctors and conduct what work he could from his bed. The letters I had received from him while I was away weren't even typed by him. I could tell.

Two soldiers stood in front of his chamber doors and they quickly let me inside. Father's chambers were one of the more ornate rooms in the palace. Exotic rugs made of animal skin were carpeted over the steel station floor. Art and tapestries showing previous dukes hung on the walls and a portrait of my late mother sat on an end table next to the large four-poster bed he was confined to. The room smelled more like a hospital suite than a bedroom. Antiseptic and sick permeated the air.

My father looked shrunken, his skin grey and sallow looking as if he had aged thirty years in the last four. His wrinkles had hardened and his brown eyes peered out from deep sockets. Not a hair remained on his head and even the mustache had worn his entire life was gone. He was covered up to his chin with mounds of blankets and a doctor tended to the countless lines that went from his body to a bank of machines that looked powerful enough to power most of the station on their own.

"Father," I greeted him.

He struggled for a moment, slowly pushing himself up in bed. He squinted, trying to figure out who I was, before the doctor handed him a pair of glasses.

"Andranik, my boy." He grinned. "Look at you, you're the spitting image of your grandfather before he entered the service."

I swallowed deep. The pride I could see on his dying face made me want to burst out into tears. He had wanted nothing more than for me to wear the same blue uniform as every other youngest child of our family.

"Father, I'm not sure if you have heard—" I began, but he cut me off.

He raised a withered hand up to stop me.

"The business with those rotten Boguni." He balled his wrinkled fist up and it shook. "Don't worry about that. That toad Aren might be a major in the Imperial Army, but he is still a two-bit recruiter from a nothing family."

His voice sounded hollow and dry, but it hardened as he got angrier. "I will work something out with the Arshuni. It will just take a bit longer than we originally planned."

I knew the Arshuni family was powerful, second only to the Tigranes if you believe the rumors, but I wasn't sure even they could wipe away an assault on an Imperial Army officer.

"Your Grace," the doctor cut in, looking away from the machines for the first time since I had been there. "You should be resting. Especially if you want to make an appearance at the Founder's Day Ball like you say."

He turned to me. "Apologies, My Lord. Your Grace has a hard time following the suggestions of his medical staff."

Father folded his arms over his bird-like chest. I couldn't help but smile. Even in this state, he was still the defiant man that had raised me.

"You're going to the ball, Father?" I asked.

"Of course," he rasped. "Many suitors from around the sector are coming to meet Anahit. I could hardly miss it."

I didn't want to be the one to tell him Ana was probably never going to pick a husband from the overdressed fops he was inviting.

"They will be bringing their sisters as well, Andranik," he hinted.

I had a feeling the furthest thing from anyone's mind right now was marrying their sister or daughter off to someone like me.

I smiled. "I will keep my eye out, Father."

"Your Grace," the doctor scolded, eyeing us both.

"Fine, fine," Father conceded. "I will see you tomorrow, Andranik."

I bowed and was ushered out of the room.

CHAPTER
FOUR

THE NEXT DAY was a blur of activity. The amount of work that goes into the countless festivals and balls that the palace hosted never ceased to amaze me. Hundreds of decorators, cooks, and wait staff clogged the hallways. Thankfully for Ana and me, we had no part in any of that. Instead, we were being measured for our clothes for the night.

The palace's master tailor ran a handheld scanner over my body, jotting notes down on his device every few seconds.

"We have plenty of other clothes already, don't we?" I asked her.

Our family was in dire financial straits and current events hadn't done us any favors.

"It is the Founder's Day Ball, Ando." She rolled her eyes. "Families from around the sector are sending representatives. We must put on a good face for them."

"But Ana, I thought the family was broke." She shot me a sideways glance.

The tailor stifled a laugh as he went about his work.

"I don't expect you to understand the delicate political game we are playing here, Ando, but do keep up." She pointed a finger at me as the green light of the scanner slowly went over her body. "Good relations with the other families are the key to righting the wrongs that have been committed against us. And the key to *that* is not letting them know how bad things actually are. It's politics."

"That sounds like lying, Ana."

"Like I said, it's politics." She shrugged. "Besides, it is what Father wanted."

"Speaking of Father, you know he is just going to trot you out there for the suitors."

"I am aware." She sighed. "It has been an ongoing theme over the last few years. His patience is wearing thin."

"What are you going to do? You can't sell yourself to one of these idiots just because Father wants you to." The tailor wheeled out a cart of shirts for me to try and handed me a pseudo-military-looking tunic with yellow piping.

"I have no intention of giving up what is rightfully mine, Ando. None of these pretty boys or stuffed shirts are going to sit on Father's throne." She smiled. "I will be the Duchess of Sassoun whether Father approves or not."

I snorted slightly as I failed to hold back my laughter. The tailor slapped me on the shoulder for moving while he worked.

Ana shot me a venomous look. It screamed that she was sick of being underestimated.

"And what is so funny, exactly?"

"Nothing." I smiled, again. "It's just that you've changed so much since I've been gone."

I watched her face crack into a smile for the first time in what felt like forever. Always having a face of unbroken porcelain for appearances must have gotten exhausting. She had been getting groomed for power by Father for years. She sat in on all of his meetings, councils, and business deals. Even then she was still allowed to be a kid. Having friends, going out, and enjoying life, but not anymore. My sister was a hardened political being now.

"You're right to not want to get married just because he wants you to. That throne is yours."

"Thank you, Ando." She stiffened slightly as the tailor held up a length of white silk against her back. "You may be surprised by this, but you're the first member of the court to tell me that."

"I'm hardly a member of the court," I scoffed.

"You will be." She must have seen the look of confusion on my face. "When I'm in charge I will need to surround myself with allies. I can hardly run this place with a bunch of men Father's age who only want to me marry the first noble tart that comes through the door."

"I'm hardly the political cog that you are, Ana. I've been training to be in the military, not a council chamber. I wouldn't know what to do with half of these people."

"You've learned one, you can learn the other. I have faith, brother."

Just as I was about to quiz her on just what terrible court job she had in mind for me, I was whisked away by the tailor into a side room. He made me try on the uniform that had been stitched together by a nearby machine as he took his measurements. He had settled on the blue number with the yellow piping. Several medals hung on the breast of the jacket. Awards for things only tangentially related to the accomplishments of our family. Among them was the crest of Tigranes the Great Prep. I was hesitant to wear something so close to the uniform that I had been denied due to my actions, or the crest of the school that I had dishonored while doing so.

I slipped it on anyway. I was sure Father had planned such a thing for quite a long time, assuming as everyone else had that my exam scores and commissioning were a foregone conclusion. I had already disappointed the man enough for one week, I could at least wear the clothes that he had picked out for me.

The rest of the day I stayed in my room, ostensibly to stay out of everyone's way. In reality, I just didn't want to face the palace. Unlike the early morning time of my arrival, the full staff had returned. On top of the normal help, there were the hundreds of minor nobles and ministry members that made the Sassoun Government work. By now they had all heard about the duke's idiot son attacking an Imperial Army major. I had no intention of showing my face until I at least had the civility of the ball to protect me from their gaze.

I passed the time reading *A History of Imperial Armored Warfare Vol. II* and sipping on a small bottle of gini I kept in my desk. Unfortunately, no matter what I did, I couldn't focus on the book. It was one volume in a ten-part series and I had read them all more times than I could count and I had them nearly memorized. They were my favorite.

Subconsciously I think I fell in love with the books because I knew one day it was going to be me in those pages. Excited kids and historians alike would be reading about my exploits. I was destined to cut a dashing figure in Imperial field grey, riding upon my tank as I stormed across whatever battlefield I happened to be on. My loyal crew and I staffing our armored behemoth together, working like a finely tuned and deadly war machine to crush the emperor's enemies.

Instead, I was sitting in my room half-drunk on several-year-old stale gini reading a dog-eared book for the thousandth time. The realization dawned on me that I would never be in this book. Nobody would ever write about me nor would the emperor ever be regaled with stories of my heroics. I would never wear Imperial blue, field grey, or anything other than this higher quality counterfeit that my father had commissioned for me to wear.

A knock on the door distracted me from my own thoughts and I tossed the book aside. When I got to my feet I wobbled slightly, realizing that I may had drunk more than I thought I had during my self-imposed exile. The door opened a few seconds later to reveal Ana, dressed like a duchess should be, in a flowing gown of gold and blue, a house crest pinned over her heart. On her head, she wore the laurels of the heir apparent.

"Have you been drinking?" she asked, her nose wrinkling at the smell in the air.

I cursed the struggling air scrubbing systems of the station for lagging behind on this particular day.

"It's a ball." I scrambled to cover myself. "You know I hate these things. It helps steady the nerves before the inevitable barrage of questions. This year more than most."

"Fair enough. I normally do the same thing before council meetings" she admitted. "It really helps dull the various passive-aggressive comments Father's cabinet throws my way. Goddess, I cannot wait to fire them all."

She smiled at the thought. "Are you ready? It is almost time for us to make our entrance."

The pomp and circumstance of the Founder's Day Ball, or any ball for that matter, was more important than the actual thing being celebrated. First, the invited nobles must enter the palace ballroom and take their seats, which were strictly assigned by the rank and importance of the family. Each was announced by the doorman, with the least important going first. This led to a comical situation where the least powerful noble's presence was announced to an empty room.

After this came the ruling family, with the duke being presented last. Even though in our situation several of the families were more important than we were. Father was simply being given the courtesy as the ruler of the station. If it was our turn to make our entrance that must have meant almost everyone else was already seated in the ballroom.

"I guess." I sighed. "Let's get this over with."

"Don't look so glum," she snickered. "Father has probably already chosen a spouse for you too."

"Ugh."

We walked quickly through the hallways. As we left the living quarter section of the palace and into what was considered government workspace, the area transformed. In the living quarters little was done in the form of upkeep other than just surface cleaning and the rugs and paint that covered the bare metal walls and floor were showing their age. Since these were our private quarters, there was no reason to keep up appearances.

The government workspace consisted of the various meeting and ballrooms so numerous I lost count. No expense was spared in keeping these areas at the cutting edge with constantly rotating art, sculptures, and other bits and bobs of culture all done to insure that on any given visit to the palace the area anyone not part of the dukedom's royal family would not see the same décor twice. An artificial space created for other people within our own home. A terrarium within a terrarium.

As we crossed over through the lacquered double doors we stepped onto the spotlessly clean carpets and were greeted by guards in their blue dress uniforms. Servants rushed back and forth carrying platers of food and drink from the kitchen to the ballroom. The smell of roasted meat with all the fixings wafted through the air and made my mouth water. I suddenly remembered that I had hardly eaten since I had returned and my appetite was coming back with a vengeance.

The commander of the palace guard stood in front of the ballroom doors. He was an older man, a captain somewhere in his mid-fifties, wearing a drooping mustache over his lip. The captain had commanded the palace guard for as long as I could remember, it was hardly a glorious military assignment but it was regarded as an easy and honorable one. Seeing us approach, he glanced down on a wrist-worn device, the day's schedule and guest list dancing above it in a hologram.

"Lord, Lady." He nodded at us. "Are you ready?"

"Yes, Captain," Ana said.

The captain glanced down at his device again and lowered his voice.

"If it makes you feel any better, none of the Boguni showed."

"What do you mean?" I asked.

"Not a single member of the Boguni family answered their invitation, My Lord."

"Why would we invite them?"

"Politics," Ana pointed out. "You invite every noble family even if you hate them. Because it isn't an invitation as much as it is a summons. A summons they ignored completely."

I noticed her anger flare as she spoke.

"Do not stress, My Lady, I am sure His Grace will have an answer for their disrespect."

Ana bit her lip. "Right, I'm sure he will."

The captain opened the door to the ballroom. Inside long synth wood tables lined the room, and at each one sat a different family. At some tables, there were only a few people, at others dozens. Against the far wall on an elevated platform at the head of the room was our table flanked on either side by our house colors and the Imperial standard.

The captain stepped in and bowed deeply, announcing in a booming voice.

"Lord Andranik Haundi and Lady Anahit Haduni!" The room got to its feet, erupting into applause as we walked by.

I didn't recognize any of the faces looking back at us. I didn't have any close relationships with any of the children my age before I left for school. Something about being the duke's son made forming personal connections hard when you're always taught that if someone was trying to get close, they were only trying to use you for something.

Ana seemed to know them all. Waving to many of the people our age and shaking hands with the elder statesmen as she went. I saw more than a few men attempt to greet her by kissing her hand only for her to grip their hands tightly in a formal, business-like handshake. The refusal was obvious to everyone. That was not why she was here.

We reached our table but remained standing. Customs dictated that we would have to wait to be seated until Father made his entry. I hadn't seen him since our brief meeting the night before and the condition I saw him in led me to believe he wouldn't be able to attend at all. Before I could ask Ana, the doors were flung open again.

"His Grace, Duke of Sassoun, Samvel Haduni!"

I couldn't believe my eyes, but there he was, standing in the doorway. Father stood, guards on either side, and was propped up slightly with a cane. The color had returned to his face and while he was still thin, he looked lively. Other than the gait of an old man which required him to shuffle slowly, it was as if he was an entirely new person.

"Unbelievable." I gasped. "How?"

"His doctor is very good," Ana whispered. "Every so often he can be given a drug cocktail that gives him some of his energy back for a few hours."

Father didn't get a round of applause, instead, he was greeted by row after row of bowing nobles. Even those of higher standing, which was many of them, rendered him the respects he was due.

"Long live Duke Haduni!" called out someone.

The rest of the crowd echoed the call and someone followed it with, "Fifty more years!"

Father, more alive than I had seen him in years grinned ear to ear, waving with his free hand. He made it to our table and took his seat at the head of it. With that, the rest of the ballroom sat back down.

A man wearing white robes rose from a table near the door. It was the station Bishop Levon Ter-Avonian. Bishop Levon was an old man, probably near the same age as Father, and had been the Bishop of Sassoun for as long as anyone could remember. He had to be helped to his feet by his two assistants, clad in black. The Bishop had grown too frail and old to even hold up his thurible any longer. Instead, one of the assistants swung it back and forth for him by a chain, and a trickle of smoke petered out as they marched toward our table.

"Old Levon still hasn't retired, eh?" I whispered to Ana.

She covered her mouth, suffocating her laughter.

"He'll die before he passes on his office." She rolled her eyes. "He hardly even conducts service anymore at the temple."

I vividly remembered him falling asleep during a baptism service before I left. He had to be nudged awake by one of his assistants so he could speak his part of the rite.

"Why doesn't someone just fire him?"

"When is the last time you've ever heard of the Holy See firing someone?" She laughed. "They would let a corpse preside over a temple if it had enough dirt on the All Catholicos. And from what I've heard about All Catholicos Vazh, there is more than enough dirt to go around."

Bishop Levon had finally shuffled his way to the front of our table, turning to face the rest of the ballroom. Even his act of turning around required assistance from one of the two black-cloaked men. I had a hard time seeing Levon being a political cutthroat behind the scenes of the church, whose notorious bickering put even the noble houses to shame.

Like most nobles, I wasn't exactly a faithful person. Belief was something reserved for the people left wanting. I observed the major church holidays as everyone did, but only then because there was always some palace function to celebrate them. My mother had been the only pious person in the entire family and had made the church an integral part of Sassoun's daily life and culture, something my father had never attempted to discourage after her death. I had heard that the other planets, even Terra itself, were not nearly as adherent to the faith.

"Holy Mother Goddess," Levon croaked.

His voice was hardly a whisper and I struggled to hear him. One of his assistants reached over and pressed on the implanted voice amplifier that rested just beneath Levon's sagging neck skin.

Only after that did his crackling, computerized voice reach the entire room. "We come to you offering thanks and felty for your everlasting love on this day, the founding day of our glorious Terran Empire.

"We thank you for allowing your shining light to bask upon our Emperor Shahen, as he strives to rule over this vast ocean of stars in your name and your name alone. We ask for your blessings for the people of Sassoun Station and your rays of holy light to warm our leader, Duke Haduni in these times. In your name, we pray, amen."

We all repeated "Amen' in a low voice.

The assistant held up the thurible and it wobbled back and forth by its long chain, puffing smoke. Bishop Levon brought his palm over his heart in the symbol of the sun and everyone followed his lead. Eventually, he began to slowly make his way back to his seat.

With the blessing finally out of the way, long lines of servants made their appearance, each of them carrying oversized platters of food and drink. A large reflective platter was placed on our table by a man wearing white gloves. He removed the platter's cover, revealing a glistening round of meat surrounded by a bed of vegetables and potatoes. My mouth began to water just looking at it. A servant began to cut the meat into thin slices while another rounded the table, pouring deep red colored gini into our glasses.

"Would you look at you two," Father beamed at us.

His newly rejuvenated features were foreign to me. The last time he had looked so alive had been when I was a child.

"I could say the same, Father." Ana's eyes followed her plate as the servant placed it down in front of her.

"I don't know what you mean." He winked, knowingly. "Anahit, I have seen many well-dressed suitors in the crowd."

"Oh, I've seen them. Small men with smaller minds, Father. Not a single one fit to be called the Duke of Sassoun" She waved him off.

Father laughed so hard and loud it startled me. A day before, such an outburst would have cracked one of his ribs. He motioned for one of the servants to fill his glass. He drank deeply, his lips turning dark red from the gini.

"Ana, I know I have been pushing you to find a husband. A bit too hard, I'll admit," he began.

Ana immediately attempted to cut in, she probably knew where this conversation normally led, but he held a hand up and she backed down. Her face began to change colors with rage as the last topic she wanted to talk about was raised once again.

"But, I want you to know, it was never because I thought you were not suited to be the heir." He leaned forward, placing a hand on Ana's. "In fact, you might be the most qualified heir in the history of the station."

"What about you, Father?" she asked, her face returning to its normal color.

"As an heir?" he chortled. "I didn't know my ass from my elbow. Your mother was my rock. If it wasn't for her, I don't know I would have made it the first few years before someone tried to take the throne by force!"

His laughter continued. "That is why I wanted you to find a husband, Ana. Not because I wanted some man to take power. Goddess above, I can't imagine you'd ever let someone do such a thing. But because I know what it's like to have the weight of the station on your shoulders. You'll never feel more alone than when you are duchess. I want you to have someone like I did. Someone to lean on, to support you when times are bad."

"I'll get married someday, Father. But it'll be someone I choose, and it won't be for political power. It'll be for love, like you and Mother." She smiled, gripping his wrinkled hand. "And besides until then, I'll have Ando here with me."

"If you're sure about this, I support you, Ana. I'll call off the wolves, but once I'm gone there will be a line of eager suitors from the palace gates to the spaceport for you to deal with." "They can keep waiting." She gave his hand a squeeze.

The two locked eyes and I could tell at that moment, Father had never been prouder of her. He pulled his hand away and held his glass back out to the servants.

His glass filled to the brim he took it in his hand and rose to his feet.

"Lords and Ladies, thank you so much for joining us here today on this blessed day!" he said, his voice louder than it had ever been before. "There will be time for pleasantries later and I will let you return to your meals, which smell just incredible by the way."

He raised his glass toward the servants. "You have truly outdone yourselves this time. But first, I must ask everyone to drink to my daughter, Lady Anahit."

He turned toward her, his glass up. Ana's face rapidly turned bright red.

"May no man ever tame you. To the future Duchess of Sassoun!"

"To the future Duchess of Sassoun!" the gathered nobles echoed.

My voice joined in as I thrust my cup into the air. Wine splashed out and Ana watched in embarrassment as the entire ballroom drank to her. The gini had to be some of the best I had ever tasted and I held out my glass to the servants for more before sitting back down.

"What's wrong?" I goaded her with a nudge of my elbow.

She was never much of a drinker and had left her glass untouched, instead sipping from a bottle of water.

"I cannot describe to you the awkwardness of a room of people who don't like you, cheering to your name." She frowned. "Every single one of these insignificant little worms only came to try to pair me with their idiot sons. I'm like meat at a market."

"Didn't you hear what Father said? Let no man tame you. Could he have told all of these losers to shove off any harder?" I said, my words slurring slightly.

I was already becoming light-headed and my skin tingled. I couldn't believe the drink was hitting me so fast. Drinking was strictly against the rules in school so maybe I had become a lightweight over the years.

She sighed. "It won't matter. They'll keep coming."

She sipped her water. "I have an idea."

She suddenly perked up. "You already have the education and training. Why not be the commander of the palace guard? Then you can personally make sure none of these angry little men try anything."

"What about the captain?" I asked, my tongue was getting heavy and my vision fuzzy.

Whoever had brewed the gini certainly had a heavy hand. "He has been here forever, I couldn't possibly take his job."

"He put in his retirement packet last week, actually." She winked, knowingly. "It seems he has purchased a small piece of land somewhere on Calisto, far above his paygrade may I add, and intends to start a farm."

"What are the odds of that?" I laughed just a little too loud.

Ana's playful expression changed to one of business.

"My offer is serious, Ando. I will need someone I can trust by my side. I would hardly be the first duchess to die a mysterious death in court and I have no intention of being murdered by some hired Boguni thug. I need you."

I took another drink and swished the gini around in my mouth. It was starting to taste foul.

"Then you will have me, Ana." I nodded. "After all, where else would I go?"

My stomach began to do twists and turns and I decided that I was going to forego dinner. I wasn't sure if it was from all of the gini on a mostly empty stomach or my body still readapting to the station, but I was feeling like someone had just pulled me out of the trash chute.

The key to any palace ball was to look for a good time to exit when nobody would notice you were gone. Soon, a band would enter, I was sure, and after we would start pairing off for dances. Father would take the first dance with Ana, per custom, and I would probably get sent to dance with someone's daughter who remembers me, but I've never heard of them before. I would suffer through the first song then excuse myself, probably to use the bathroom or something. Then, I would make my escape back to my room.

As if on cue, the band entered. They wore deep red jackets of the Olympus City Band, I assume brought by the Arshuni family as a symbol of goodwill. Sassoun had many of its own band assemblies, but nothing quite like Mars. I wasn't sure if they were any better, talent-wise, but from an importance standpoint, your palace function always looked better when you imported something from the cultural capital of the Empire.

The band leader struck up a slow song, the *Ballad of the Imperial Stars* if my memory served me correctly. I always tended to zone out during our music history class. Father pushed himself to his feet with his cane and took Ana by her hand, leading her out to the ballroom floor. For a man near death only just the other day, he could still move on his feet. At least until the drugs wore off.

I also made my way to the dance floor. The polished marble tiles seemed to swirl under my feet and I could feel my pulse pounding against the sides of my skull. Had I really drunk this much? I saw an outline of a woman in a blue dress approach me. She looked about my age, and I assumed she was meant to be my partner for the dance. I squinted at her, unable to focus. The colors of her skin and dress melted together into a strange kaleidoscope as my vision began to blur.

I tried to say something, but my tongue wouldn't move. It was cemented to my teeth, unable to break free.

"Are you okay?" I think I heard her say.

Her voice sounded like it was yelling up at me from underwater. Distant and distorted. I tried to speak again, panic rising in my chest like a hot knife, but nothing came out. Finally, my legs gave out and I collapsed. I knew I landed hard on my side but I didn't feel anything. A strange numbing feeling, like pins and needles, flooded my body and the last thing I saw was my father.

He was laying on his back in the middle of the ballroom, a crowd of people running to his side.

CHAPTER
FIVE

I AWOKE WITH A START, sitting bolt upright so quickly the nurse tending to the intravenous lines that led to my arms jumped back in shock. I was in my room, and a small group of medical professionals in white coats surrounded me. An armed palace guardsman stood in front of the door, a small carbine in his hands.

The nurse that I had spooked quickly came over and placed a hand on my shoulder.

"Please, lay back down," she said, trying to soothe me.

"What happened?" I gasped, my throat bone dry.

The nurse glanced over at a doctor. I noticed it was the same doctor that had been treating my father the day before. He cleared his throat.

"You were poisoned, My Lord."

My head began to swim. I was poisoned? Why would anyone try to kill me?

"Thankfully," he continued. "The assassin was not targeting you, or the dose would have been much higher."

"They weren't targeting me?" I repeated.

The doctor sat down on the edge of my bed, his features softening.

"No, My Lord." He shook his head. "It is clear they were targeting your father, and also probably Her Grace, Anahit. But alas, your sister doesn't drink at public functions and they poisoned the wine."

His words slowly worked into my ears and I felt my heart leap into my chest. He called Anahit *Her Grace*. Did that mean...

He saw the realization dawn on me.

"I'm sorry, My Lord. Your father was poisoned as well. In his current state, there was nothing I could do to save him. It was just too much for his body to handle."

I balled my fists and my fingernails dug into the palms of my hands. My eyes began to burn with tears, but I fought them off. It wouldn't have been proper. I tried to say something, but my throat had grown thick.

"Who did it?" I managed to get out.

"We don't know at this time. It is being investigated by the gendarmes, My Lord. I am sure they will inform your sister of anything they uncover."

I bit my lip so hard I thought I could taste blood. I may have not been an investigator with the Imperial gendarmes, but there was no doubt in my mind this had to have been the Boguni. I motioned to the guard at the door.

"Are you under orders to keep me in this room?" The guard snapped to attention and saluted me.

"No, sir. It is customary that when a soldier of the guard is in hospital, they are never left alone."

A member of the guard? I had a foggy memory of Ana saying she would make me captain of the palace guard. I guess that meant she went ahead and did it while I was unconscious.

"Good. I'll be seeing the duchess now. Do I have a uniform or something?"

"My Lord, I must insist you stay and recover a bit longer," the doctor urged.

I shot him a fierce look.

"And I must insist you get out of my way." The guard approached, laying a dark yellow uniform at the end of the bed, along with a pair of boots spit-shined to a mirror finish.

The doctor frowned but relented. I assumed he had been worn down after having to deal with my father. I wasn't exactly sure what authority a guard captain had and I didn't want my first use of it to be threatening a doctor.

I got dressed, finding the uniform to be a perfect fit. The uniform came with a pistol belt, polished black, with a small compact sidearm secured in a holster. I buckled it around my waist and made my way across the palace, leaving the medical staff to clean up after me. The guard in the room followed after me, I still wasn't sure if I trusted him about not being sent to watch me. It also dawned on me that I knew nothing about palace security, which was now apparently my job.

"Any word on who did this?" I asked the guard.

He shook his head. "No, sir."

I noticed the various statues that lined the hallway were cloaked in black, covering them to observe the legal mourning period of one month after the death of a duke. "The palace security detachment doesn't handle investigations."

"But you know who did it, right?" I pressed him. "In your opinion, I mean."

"The Boguni, of course, sir," he admitted. "I assume the same as you."

"What can you tell me about their Mining Protection Agency?"

"I can tell you they are little more than hired guns. They have money, but we have official resources and the gendarmes have to screen every single one of them before they are given a firearms license on the station."

"I thought nobody with a criminal history could get one of those."

"Oh, you can't, sir. But none of them are from the station, most of them are planetsiders, you can tell just by looking at them. All of them are registered as being born on Sassoun, though. Their identities clear a background check, but I've seen some of the tattoos they have. If you were a family with as much money as the Boguni, it wouldn't be too hard to get a fresh identity with a clean for someone you wanted to hire for a specific job."

We passed a few more guards who saluted as we went.

"They have been getting bolder in recent years too," he continued. "Their hired thugs have been caught getting a little too close to the palace on more than one occasion. And since the palace is as old as the station, there are more little nooks and crannies than we can keep an eye on. I wouldn't be surprised if they knew more about the palace grounds than some of our guards."

"Hypothetically, it would be very easy for one of these mercenaries to sneak in here and drop some poison into the gini."

"*Hypothetically*," he stressed. "Yes."

We approached the duchess' office. Massive wooden double doors with intricate lion carvings working their way up both sides met in the middle, where there were two golden lion-shaped door handles. Guards stood outside, saluting me as I approached.

"Is my sister, I mean, the duchess, in her office?" I asked.

One of them nodded. "Yes, sir. But she is in a meeting with the commander of the gendarmes."

I leaned toward the guard who had followed me from my room. I told myself I should probably get the man's name at some point.

"Does that mean I can't go inside?" I whispered.

The guard coughed, which I recognized as a poor attempt at covering a laugh.

"Sir, you are the commander of the palace guards and the

duchess' brother. Nobody can stop you from doing anything you want."

The guards at the door seemed to know what I was going to do next and simply stepped out of the way. Ana's office had remained unchanged from the way Father had left it. I had no idea when he had last used it, since he was confined to his bed for months, if not years. He had been notorious for not allowing cleaning staff into his office in the past, not wanting to give them access to possible confidential information. There had also been more than one occasion where a spy had disguised themselves as palace help, snooping around behind locked doors. His paranoid streak was justified every once and a while, but it meant his office was always filthy.

The bookshelves that lined the wall were cluttered and dusty. The busts of previous dukes were covered with black cloth in mourning but I had a feeling underneath they would have been wrapped in spiderwebs. A golden rug covered the bare metal floors but the years of foot traffic had soiled it to the point it resembled the color of dehydrated urine.

Ana was speaking to an older man in the brown uniform of the gendarmes. He was stooped with age and wore a chest full of medals, his pointed facial features reminded me of a vulture. Ana was seated behind her large desk, with her beat red eyes set by dark rings. It looked as if she hadn't slept in days and spent much of that time crying. The Gendarme commander glanced back at me but continued speaking.

"As I'm sure you're aware, Your Grace, we are looking into every lead." He sounded deeply uninterested in the conversation they were having while Ana looked like she was trying her best to just remain seated, her face changing color rapidly with her rising temper.

"General," she fumed, breathing out of her nose. "There is no question who did this, the only real question is why you and your vaunted men have not arrested anyone."

"Your grace, if one so wanted, they could take such words as an accusation."

But he didn't sound offended. I could have sworn I saw the flash of a knowing grin across his wrinkled features.

"The only way anyone could have heard such an accusation is because they know it to be true," Ana snapped. "I'll be having the security services look into you and your connections to the Boguni family, General. Pray to the Goddess they find nothing. Now, get out of my office."

"Your grace!" the general barked, finally reacting.

I had heard rumors that the gendarmes had a tendency to be run like personal armies by their individual commanders. The commander would fall under the influence of the richest Imperial family of wherever they happened to be stationed, using their men and their official capacity to act as a cudgel against the family's enemies.

The Imperial security services had no such reputation. Known to be cruel and ruthless in their rooting out of corruption, especially that of Imperial officials, falling under their gaze was the last thing anyone wanted, even if you were innocent. The security services operated under the ideology that they would rather destroy one thousand innocent people than let one guilty person go free. The general's voice dripped with fear.

"General!" I yelled. "The duchess has asked you to leave. Now do so under our own strength before the guards do it for you."

The old man's features contorted and twisted as he fought back what he really wanted to say. Our eyes locked and I could feel an intense hatred coming from him. He glared at me the entire time he made for the exit, only breaking eye contact when he walked by me. The door was closed behind him, and a heavy lock clicked into place.

With the general gone, Ana got up from her desk and wrapped her arms around me. That is when I finally broke. Tears poured out of me in deep, heaving sobs. My tears began to wet Ana's expertly arranged hair, and I finally pulled myself away after a few moments. I wiped my face on my sleeve. We couldn't spend our time mourning our father like commoners. We were Haduni.

"Was that what I assumed it was?" I managed to choke out.

"Yeah," she sniffed. "The gendarmes were put in charge of the investigation, namely General Poroshkin."

She glared at the door as if the general was still standing in front of it. "Mysteriously, he has found no evidence implicating the Boguni family in any of this."

"Is there anything the palace guard can do?" I asked.

"No." She shook her head. "I have already ordered that nobody without explicit permission be allowed into the palace until further notice. The general's mood will get worse when he finds out I actually alerted the security services yesterday. I just wanted to watch him squirm."

"I understand why you would want to alert the security services, but could even they go after the Boguni? They have to have some very important friends, more than one of which is probably close to the emperor."

Ana sighed, sinking back into her chair. It was a battered synth leather number that looked old enough to have seated several station rulers over its lifespan.

"I can't think of anything else to do, Ando," she admitted. "They have our backs against the wall in every conceivable way. The only thing we can hope for is maybe at least one Imperial institution can't simply be bought with coin and influence."

"Order the palace guard to arrest them," I said. "The crime happened here in the palace, it is under our jurisdiction."

I wasn't sure if that was true or not, but it sounded right in my head.

"What are you going to do?" Ana laughed. "Burst into their palace and shoot it out with their protection agency?"

"If we have to, yes," I nodded. "The protection agency is mostly just hired thugs, chasing after a paycheck. They kick around migrant workers down in the mines and collect debts from merchants. They are hardly soldiers."

"This could go very wrong, Ando."

"Force of arms is the only advantage we have on our side, Ana. If the security services show up and end up on their side, we'll have nothing. If we have to act before they get here. You made me the guard captain because you said you trusted me, let me do this."

She leaned back in her chair, deep in thought. After a few moments of biting her lip, she nodded.

"Okay," she said. "But if anything goes sideways, get out of there. If my brother leads a hit squad into the Boguni palace and kills half of the family, there is no way I could spin that. You're going to *arrest* them. Understand?"

"Of course, Your Grace." I bowed.

CHAPTER
SIX

THE AUTOMATIC LIGHT cycle had dimmed to darkness a few hours before we gathered in the palace courtyard. I asked the guard who had been following me, whom I learned was named Yevon, to pick the best guards in the palace. Though in order to make sure the mining agency didn't catch wind of anything, it had to be people already on the night shift. The night shift, I learned, was where the veteran guards dumped the newest recruits.

That meant our mission would rest on the shoulders of a bunch of green palace guards, led by me, someone who didn't technically have a single day of military training or experience. It didn't matter. I would kick open the door to their palace alone if it meant getting revenge for my father.

I pulled a folded-up piece of paper from my pocket. The warrant of arrest for Aren Boguni signed by Ana, the highest authority in all of Sassoun Station. I unfolded the paper and read it.

The Office of the Dukedom of Sassoun Station hereby orders the arrest of the following individual:

Aren Boguni, Major, Imperial Army Recruiting Command.

The above individual is wanted for questioning regarding the murder of his Imperial Grace, Duke Samvel Haduni, five hundred and Sixty-fifth Duke of Sassoun Station. Any who holds this warrant is authorized to detain the above individual using any means necessary.

Signed,

Her Imperial Grace, Duchess Anahit Haduni, Five Hundred and Sixty-sixth Duke of Sassoun Station.

I stuffed the warrant back into my pocket. In front of me, three yellow uniformed guards stood in the synth grass courtyard. They all held small carbines, as well as their standard issued sidearms. The guard detachment had no battle armor to speak of and looked slightly ridiculous, kitted out for combat with only various medals pinned to their chest for protection.

"Captain?" coughed Yevon.

I realized I had been standing there for a few minutes lost in thought. I wasn't entirely sure how to tell them why they were there.

"Right, sorry," I said. "Gentlemen, I have been given a warrant by the duchess for the arrest of Aren Boguni. It is our job to bring him back to the palace dungeon for questioning regarding the murder of my fa—"

I stopped myself. "The murder of our late duke, Samvel Haduni."

Yevon had been in the office when this decision had been made, but the other two guards gave each other panicked looks.

"My lord, Captain," one said with a shaky voice. "Are we to fight the mining agency?"

"Her Grace doesn't want us to turn the quarter into a warzone, however, if we need to defend ourselves during the enforcement of the warrant, so be it."

"You're all trained soldiers in service of Emperor Shahen," Yevon scolded them. "Start acting like it!"

"Yes, Sergeant!" yelped the other two guards.

"May the Goddess watch over all of us in our duties," I said, making the symbol of the sun over my heart.

Yevon halfheartedly followed suit while one of the other guards kissed a pendent and held it to their forehead.

"Follow me."

We exited through a side gate, walking by two other guards. The streets of the quarter were deserted as they normally were at this time of night. I marched straight across the expanse, tunnel-vision on the front gates of the Boguni palace, only a few short strides away.

I was stopped by the front gate, a giant wrought-iron beast of a thing that closed off the entire front of the Boguni palace area. The Haduni palace was open to any citizen of the Empire and was meant to look welcoming, current situation notwithstanding. After all, it was more a place of governing than an actual residence. The Boguni palace was built to be as standoffish as possible. To be looked at from afar by the people, to remind them they were being looked down upon.

"You lost?" came the voice of a black duster-wearing agency man from the inside of a guard booth.

The booth sat on the left side of the gate, the man sitting inside looked bored, glancing up from a magazine.

"Open the gates!" spat Yevon. "In the name of the duchess!"

"You piss jackets authority ran out when you crossed the street," laughed the man. "Get lost."

I reached into my pocket and slapped the warrant against the booth's glass.

"I am Captain Andranik Haduni and have a legal arrest warrant signed by Her Imperial Grace Duchess Anahit, I command you to open these gates or may the Goddess be my witness we will open them ourselves!"

Yevon wasted no time. Charging around the booth, ripping the door open and shoving the agency man out of the way. The man stood out of the way, wide-eyed, as Yevon fiddled with the controls until eventually, the gate began to creak open.

"Keys," Yevon demanded of the man, his hand out.

"Fuck you, buddy," the man cursed.

Yevon looked at me, and I nodded. Yevon slammed the butt of his carbine into the man's face with a sickening crunch. Blood sprayed from his ruined nose and he collapsed to the ground. Yevon straddled the downed man and rifled through his pockets until he found his keycard. He also relieved him of his sidearm and strapped a pair of handcuffs around his wrists, leaving him prone on the ground.

I laughed. "You're good at this."

"I did ten years in the regular army before I was transferred to the guard detachment, My Lord Captain." He smiled, stuffing the downed man's sidearm into the back of his pants. "You'd be surprised how often you have to rough up your own soldiers when they get too much liquor in them."

He approached the front door and swiped the stolen keycard over the security system. It buzzed and the front doors clicked open.

I crossed the threshold into the Boguni palace, not knowing what to expect. The lights dimmed and everything was cloaked in darkness to the point I could only just make out the room I was standing in. Gone was the traditional look of our palace. Sleek modernist design choices made the entire place look more like a hospital than a home.

For a moment it seemed like the palace was barren or everyone had retired to their beds for the night. Then I heard what sounded like laughter from somewhere down the hallway. Yevon took the lead, his carbine in his hands. I fell in line behind him and the other guards followed after us.

Another mining agency man sat at a guard post up ahead of us. Luckily for us, he seemed fast asleep, drool pooling at the corner of his mouth. Yevon pointed to one of the guards and ordered him forward. The guard crept up on the sleeping man, reaching into his belt he produced a small yellow rod I knew to be a neural disruptor. In school, we learned if you cracked someone with one of those, they would be knocked out cold by a burst of electrical energy.

The disruptor let out a high-pitched whine and the sleeping man collapsed to the ground. A guard quickly slapped a pair of restraints on them before disarming them and turning their radio off. We inched forward through the darkened hallways, the portraits of various Boguni business owners staring down at us.

The laughter turned to conversations. I couldn't make out the individual words, whatever they were saying was muffled by the distance between us.

"Hey!" I heard someone call out.

We froze in place. "Who in the hell are you?"

A man in a black duster had appeared from a side door, walking right into our path. He must have been a roving guard. The agent dropped a plate of food he was carrying and reached for his sidearm.

I reached to the pistol on my hip and fumbled with the holster, its safety latch keeping my nervous hands at bay. Yevon fired first, catching the man in the shoulder, the impact sending him spinning around awkwardly to the ground.

"So much for staying quiet," he said. "We should hurry."

We took off at a run, sprinting down the hallway, passing by the wounded agency man who was writhing on the ground. The once lively conversations in the nearby room became panicked shouts as we got closer. They all would have heard the gunshot. Yevon picked a door, swiped the keycard, and entered.

Inside was a sitting room bar combination area. An overly fancy chandelier hung down from the arced, painted ceilings. Its hundreds of tiny plasma candles lit a room that had around a dozen people in it, I recognized most of them to be members of the Boguni family.

"What is the meaning of this!" challenged an old woman sitting on a loveseat.

"Aren Boguni!" I bellowed in a shaky voice I struggled to steady. "I am Captain of the Sassoun Palace Guard and have a warrant for your arrest, signed by Her Imperial Grace, Duchess Anahit Haduni! Surrender yourself!"

That is when I saw him, Aren, still wearing his army uniform. It had been unbuttoned, and his tie undone. He had a glass of gini in his hand and was sitting nonchalantly at the bar.

"You have no jurisdiction here you puffed up little shit," he said, dismissively, climbing to his feet.

Yevon pointed his carbine at him.

"Turn around and put your hands behind your back immediately!" he commanded.

"Get out of my house!" screeched a voice from the gallery.

"Shut up!" demanded a guard.

I was losing control of the situation, though I wasn't sure if I ever had it in the first place.

"Aren, you're wanted in connection to the murder of my father, Duke Samvel Haduni. You know as well as I do any warrant signed by the duchess of this station is as good as an order from the emperor himself and we are well within our rights to use any means necessary to bring you in."

I began marching toward Aren when out of the corner of my eye I saw another agency man appear from a side room. He was pulling a scatter gun out of his duster.

"Gun!" I cried.

I ripped my sidearm out of its holster and fired once, blowing the man's jaw off. A gunshot sounded from near the bar. I turned in time to see Aren, holding a pistol and firing. Yevon went down, blood spurting from a ragged throat wound.

"Fall back!" I ordered and we began retreating back out of the room.

I fired blindly over my shoulder as we ran. I saw several of the occupants of the room drop lifelessly, caught in the crossfire. Another guard was hit in the leg, yelping in pain as his knee buckled in a way it wasn't meant to. I got clear of the room, spun around, and fired the last round from my pistol, catching Aren in the arm and sending him ducking behind cover.

"Surrender Aren!" I called out.

Another shot slammed into the wall next to my face

"You're fucking dead!" he hissed. "You'll never get out of here alive!"

"The only thing you're doing is catching more murder charges you stuck up prick!" I yelled back.

The last guard standing handed me one of the sidearms he had taken from the downed agent.

"Are you really so dumb to think the gendarmes are going to come for me?" he laughed. "Who do you think pays for their vacations? Their bonuses? Their fancy new homes?"

Another shot skipped off of the metal floor by my feet. "Let me tell you what tomorrow's headline says. Haduni's reject son breaks into Boguni home, and is killed in a shootout by Major Boguni in self-defense."

I knew it. Ana's suspicions were right, they owned the damn gendarmes. If their hooks were in that deep, they could own the security services too. If they walked away from this room, they would get away with killing my father. I wouldn't let that happen. I looked at the other guard, sweat dripped down his face and his pupils had narrowed down to pinpricks.

I nodded. "Let's go."

I took a deep breath, swallowed down my rapidly thumping heart, and spun into the room. As soon as I did, a shot burned across my face. I cried out, jumping for cover behind a nearby couch. A dead man lay splayed out across it. The guard charged ahead, shooting at Aren who was hunkered down behind the bar.

Aren brought up his pistol, firing several well-aimed shots toward the attacker. The poor man dropped mid-stride, collapsing on top of himself. He gave me the opening I need to squeeze off a shot at Aren while he was exposed. The pistol recoiled, letting out the stench of burning powder of an old slug thrower. My shot found purchase, tearing through Aren's neck, and spraying blood across the mirror behind him.

I advanced on him, my gun still up in front of me. Blood dripped down the mirror and coated the countless bottles of expensive liquor that were lined up under it. I could hear him taking deep, wet, mouthfuls of air. Like a dying fish after being dragged out of a lake.

Aren lay on his back, his hands clasped over his neck wound. Blood bubbled up between his fingers and pooled in the back of his throat. He mouthed words but no sound came from him other than gurgling. I reached over and fired three more times into his chest, before my hand finally gave out, dropping the stolen sidearm onto his body.

I sat heavily on one of the barstools and noticed my breathing was so rapid it nearly drowned out the thumping in my temples. The room around me had been a party only a few seconds ago, and now I was the only person still alive. It stank of burning powder and a copper smell I couldn't identify.

Footsteps began to approach, dozens of them. I could hear the crackling of radios and the hushed commands of soldiers as they grew nearer. Flashlights broke the darkness of the hallway and eventually barged into the sitting room. Panicked eyes looked over the scene and finally found me sitting at the bar in my blood-stained palace guard's uniform. I had owned it for only a few hours.

Hands, I don't know how many, grabbed at me, shoving me to

the ground face first. I saw the twisted, dead facial features of Yevon staring back at me as I felt the cold steel of handcuffs snap over my wrists.

The windowless cell I found myself in was freezing cold. I had been brought so far into the depths of the gendarmes' headquarters I lost track of how many different floors I was brought down. By the temperature of the place, I assumed I was on the last layer of station metal before the dark void of space.

My breath clouded up in front of me as I let out deep, gasping sobs. There was no light cycle this deep into the station's structure and I had quickly lost track of how long I had been locked up. Occasionally a small trap door would open and a plate of food would slide in. It was formless, tasteless mush fit only for someone in the situation in which I found myself.

I was certain when the door opened, I would be staring into the face of a gendarmes executioner. There was no reason to doubt what Aren said before I had killed him. To make things worse for me, if the gendarmes really were that crooked, they would want to dispose of me before the security services showed up to poke their nose around a small civil war between noble houses. They could blame me for everything, shove me out of an airlock, and keep the security services from looking too hard at their bank transactions.

I heard the door click and it swung open. The light, piercing to my unattuned eyes, caused me to wince and blink away.

"Haduni," a voice said. "Andranik Haduni?"

"Yeah," I answered, when I cracked my eyes just a sliver, I could see the outline of a man standing in the open door.

"Come with me," the voice ordered.

I stood up and they reached forward and clamped handcuffs around my wrists. The man shoved me forward down a wide hallway where I passed dozens of other cell doors just like my own. The sounds of whimpering and crying could faintly be heard all around me.

"Where are we going?" I asked.

I was jabbed in the back with something.

"No talking," the man snapped. "Take a left here."

I did as I was told and eventually came to another door. Inside was a small windowless room, a table in the center with a chair on either side of it. I was told to sit down on one side, and the chains of the handcuffs were looped around a hook at the center of the table, pinning me to my spot.

"Wait here. Someone wants to see you," they said before turning around and leaving.

A second later a thin woman entered. I had never seen her before but she was obviously a high-born official of some kind, with the expensive clothes to match. On their collar there was a lion pin, showing she worked for the family.

"My lord." She bowed slightly before taking her seat.

"I'm sorry ma'am, but I don't think we've met."

"No, we haven't," she said curtly. "I am Her Imperial Grace's chief of staff."

"Is Ana okay? Why hasn't she visited me here?"

"Her Grace is fine, physically." She frowned. "Politically, not so much. As you can imagine her brother leading a hit squad into the palace of another noble family and killing six members stains her reputation somewhat. The security services are involved."

I bit my lip. "So, what happens now?"

"We are still working on that. But, as you can imagine, Her Grace can't be seen with you."

"I understand." I nodded. "What can I do to help?"

She reached into her purse and produced several pieces of paper, sliding them in front of me.

"My lord, you're the only survivor of what occurred in the

Boguni palace. That means we can create our own narrative on this before the security services come in and... make you talk."

I scanned over the paperwork in front of me. It was a confession. A long screed about how the entire plan was my idea, independent of that of the palace guard and especially the duchess. It had been written by someone who had a shocking familiarity with my handwriting.

"I'm a scapegoat?" I hissed. "They'll fucking kill me!"

I pounded a fist on the table. The chief of staff nervously glanced at the door.

"Have some self-respect!" she scolded in a harsh whisper. "Do you really think your sister is going to leave you here to die?"

"She might not, but you would."

She folded her arms over her chest. "If it was up to me, I would have forged your name, My Lord."

"Why are you here?"

"You need to get something straight. My job is to protect the duchess, full stop. However, Her Grace insists that we protect you as well. So, here I am."

"And your plan to help me is to send me up the river?"

"Listen." She closed her eyes, breathing through her nose in order to gather her composure. "You sign the paperwork, it gives Her Grace total separation from your actions. This will give her the freedom she needs to save you. Nobody is going to want anything to do with her if she is connected to a political assassination and under investigation by the security services. You just need to trust her."

I looked down at the confession, taking up a pen in my hand. Could she be screwing me over? It was more than possible. I didn't even know if Ana really had anything to do with this and I wasn't falling into some inter-palace political trap. Even if it was, it wasn't like I didn't deserve it. Then, what difference would it make? If she was stabbing me in the back, I was dead, if she left me to the security services, I would be tortured, and then I would be dead. My only hope of walking away with this was trusting her. I signed the paper.

The chief of staff snatched it up and stuffed it back in her purse.

"When will I hear from you next?" I asked as she started to get up.

"You won't," she said. "You just confessed to six counts of murder, My Lord. As the chief of staff of the duchess, I can't be seen with you anymore."

I tried to get up, but the chains holding my wrists to the table pulled me back down.

"You—" I spat through clenched teeth.

She cut me off.

"No member of the administration can be seen with you, understand what that would look like. We will send a neutral party and hopefully get you far away from here. Until then just sit tight and don't talk to anyone. Got it?"

I started feeling tears burning up in my eyes and fought them back. I didn't want anyone to see me crying in jail, least of all her. She didn't wait for my response. She was out of the room seconds later and the gendarme reappeared to escort me out.

I began counting the days based on the meals that were slid under the door. They never changed. I knew once I saw the same three meals, a day had gone by. By the time a week passed, I had eaten so many of the same plates of food I had memorized each and every tasteless bite they offered. Reconstituted egg product for breakfast, rice and a lump of some kind of synthetic protein for lunch, and starch-based potato supplement for dinner swimming in a broth whose flavor I couldn't quite place. Thankfully I was allowed outside, still in handcuffs, once per day and given a few minutes to shower. The water was as bone-chillingly cold as my cell.

Eventually, the door was opened again and I heard the same voice.

"Haduni."

I squinted at the light. "Still me."

"Don't get smart with me," the voice growled.

"What are you going to do?" I asked. "Throw me in jail?"

He ignored me.

"Get up," he said and I did, holding my hands out in front of me so I could be restrained.

I was led back to the same room but wasn't strapped to the table this time.

I remembered the words of the chief of staff. Nobody from the administration would be coming to see me again. How long could that go on? I tried not to think about the time it would take for a sextuple murder to cool down enough for me to be allowed to go home. Where else could I go?

The door opened a few moments later. A short, stocky man with dark skin and a shaved head appeared. He wore a dark green uniform and a matching green beret was pulled over the right side of his head. He carried a stack of paperwork under one arm and a cup of coffee in the other.

"My Lord," he greeted, bowing slightly.

He slid the cup of coffee in front of me and took his seat. The smell of the drink wafted up to my nose and I wanted to float away in its wake like something out of a cartoon. I hadn't smelled anything so amazing in what felt like a month. He motioned for me to take the cup and didn't hesitate, drinking it down greedily.

"I am First Sergeant Samsan Abovyan, from the Sassoun recruitment command."

"Recruitment command?" I asked, looking at his uniform. "Who are you recruiting for, First Sergeant?"

"For his Imperial Majesty's Frontier Corps, of course." I had heard of the Frontier Corps like most people, but I had never seen its troopers before.

They were normally relegated to the fringes of Imperial space, far away from polite society. I had heard rumors their recruits mostly came from the lower populations of Terra and the desolate farmlands of the harsher Imperial worlds. I had never seen their distinctive green uniform in the halls of Sassoun before.

"I wasn't aware Sassoun was home to a Corps recruitment command center."

"That's because there isn't. I was dispatched from Olympus."

"You came from Mars just to talk to me?" I raised an eyebrow. "Why?"

"You have missed out on... a lot." He sighed. "So, let me fill you in on a few things. After your little shoot-out—"

I interrupted him. "—You know about that?"

"Everyone knows about that," he said flatly. "Duchess Anahit spent virtually every minute and every ounce of her political credit since trying to find a way to save your life. I'll spare you the details of the politics since I don't think I understand it all either, but she found a way."

"Do I want to know?" I groaned.

"She married Hayk Arshuni, the second son of the Duke of Mars. Obviously, because of... uh... your *situation*, she wasn't exactly in an advantageous position for negotiations."

I took a deep breath. I knew after signing the confession I was going to have to deal with some things I was uncomfortable with personally, I had no idea it was going to force Ana to do something so drastic. At least she didn't marry a Boguni. I considered that a win, no matter how small.

"And?" I sighed. "You wouldn't be telling me all of this if it ended there."

"Well, your family is now a branch of the Arshuni entirely.

Hayk took the throne as ruling Duke." I could feel the tears coming back.

She had given it all away. Everything she had fought to keep for herself and our family was gone. Signed away to protect me. He must have seen my expression drop as he reached into his pocket and held out a small cigarette case, offering me one. I turned it down.

"It's not all bad news." Samsan lit a cigarette and tried to reassure me. "Lord Hayk isn't such a bad guy. Not exactly a looker though."

He blew smoke out of his nose and the grey cloud gathered above our heads in the small room. "But I guess that part doesn't matter much to you. What does matter is that Hayk's oldest brother, Vaz, is on the Imperial Privy Council. He was able to use that influence to get you a special commission into the Frontier Corps based on your previous commissioned service."

"My previous commission?"

"You were commissioned Captain of the Sassoun Palace Guard, were you not?" he asked, flipping through some papers. "By order of the duchess herself."

"Well, yeah," I stammered. "But for less than a day."

He smiled.

"Well, luckily for you the Privy Council wasn't informed of that before giving me this."

He slid me a piece of paper which read:

By order of the Imperial Privy Council,

His lordship, Captain of the Sassoun Imperial Palace Guard Detachment, Andranik Haduni is hereby offered the position of Lieutenant within the Frontier Corps, Armor Detachment, for a period no less than ten years.

Signed,

His Lordship, Member of His Imperial Majesty's Privy Council, Vaz Arshuni.

"Ten years?" I looked up from the paper.

"Ten years in the green is certainly a better option than those security services dudes I saw out there." He thumbed over his shoulder. "Some real grim-looking bastards, they are. I imagine whatever they have in mind won't leave you alive within the week."

"And the Frontier Corps will save my life?" Panic rose in my voice as I imagined the security services men waiting for me outside.

At this Samsan laughed. "What you have is as good as an Imperial Pardon, signed by the damned emperor himself. Any of those security services thugs touch you while you're holding this, their own comrades will be coming after them next."

He stubbed his cigarette out on the table, leaving a small black burn. "That being said, I'm not going to sit here and lie to your face and say the Frontier Corps is going to save your life."

He pointed down to the ground and hiked up one of his pant legs, showing the metal skin of a prosthetic. "The Frontier Corps offers you a life, My Lord, but it probably won't be a long one."

I took the pen, sighed, and scribbled my name at the bottom.

Samsan smiled, sarcastically bringing his hand up in salute.

"Welcome to the Corps, Lieutenant."

CHAPTER
SEVEN

SOMETHING IN THE DISTANCE BEEPED. An annoying, repetitive sound that wouldn't go away no matter how hard I tried to ignore it.

"Hey, Ando!" someone said and tugged on my pant leg. "They are trying to get ahold of you."

I finally relented, opening my eyes, and accepting that I wouldn't be allowed to sleep anymore. I leaned forward in my tank commander's seat, perched above the rest of the turret crew. Rubbing my eyes, I looked down at the person waking me. My gunner, Corporal Anush Krekorian. She was a corps veteran from somewhere on Luna. She was street scum through and through with a tapestry of tattoos and scars across her body that proved it.

"Did the Krag attack us yet?" I moaned.

"Nope," she laughed. "Gor and Nayiri were trying to get ahold of you."

"Why didn't they ping my SEED?"

"They did," she pointed out. "You turned it off again."

Gor had a tendency to constantly blast messages to my neural network SEED that was implanted directly into my brain. It made trying to sleep off the prior night's drinking a real pain in the ass.

I yawned. "Oh right."

I opened up the neural heads-up display and flicked the "on" button.

"*Was one of you trying to get ahold of me?*" I sent the message directly to their minds.

"*Meet me outside,*" came the voice of my troop commander.

She did not sound pleased. I sighed, disconnecting my headset and stretching my beret over my bare head.

"In trouble again, sir?" asked the man to my left.

He had the floor panels of the tank lifted up and was working grease into a fixture with a hand pump. The thick substance clung to his hands and stained his tanker-issued khaki overalls.

"I don't know Suren."

Suren Qasabyan was the best loader in the squadron and was built for the job with arms like tree trunks from years of working in the mines on Mars. Unfortunately, the same life experience that gifted him the ability to throw cannon shells around like they were toys also left him functionally illiterate and a little slow on the uptake in most situations.

"Well, good luck, sir!" He smiled a vacant smile. "Goddess bless."

"Thank you, Suren." I reached up and unlatched the tank commander's hatch, throwing it open.

The cool, fresh spring air rushed into the cramped confines of the turret. My augmented, corps-issued eyes automatically adjusted to the brightness of the sun. I grabbed both sides of the opening and hoisted myself up and out of the tank.

I was greeted by the rolling green hills of Gandak. It was the most beautiful place I had ever been in my life, though some of that glow was starting to fade after being here for five years. It was one of probably hundreds of Imperial agricultural planets with every square-inch dedicated to bio-enhanced farmland, tended to by millions of settlers.

Of course, the throne never dispatched the Frontier Corps to a planet that happened to have a friendly populace and nice weather without a good reason. Around two hundred years before, the Imperial Army had taken the rock from a race of aliens we called the Krag. They were huge, brute like creatures that had barely discovered guns by the time we showed up. The Army won easily on the field of battle, but the surviving Krag retreated into a network of tunnels and caves that had been their homes for who knows how long before we got here. It made rooting out the last of them virtually impossible.

Generations of Imperial settlers had been here ever since. Though they lived in fear of constant attacks from the lumbering monsters whenever they crawled out of their caves to strike. Or, at least that is what I have been told. In my five years on the planet, I had never seen a Krag. Instead, we spent our time patrolling thousands of miles of farmland, all in an effort to make the settlers feel safer.

"Morning, sleeping beauty!" a voice yelled up at me.

When I peered over the side of my tank, I saw the lanky form of Captain Naryiri Gnuni. She was a low-ranking noble from someplace Luna I had never heard of. She commanded our mechanized infantry platoon and had recently become our troop commander. This little arrangement meant we had been working side by side for years. We had come up through the ranks together, until recently when she was promoted to captain while I, expectantly, was not.

"Yeah, yeah." I waved her off, slowly clambering down the side of my tank, passing by the barrel of our cannon that had the name 'Daredevil' daubed down its length with red paint, and met her on the ground.

"You know the colonel's orders say no officers can turn their SEED off, right?"

"Well, if the manufacturers of the thing they stuck in my damn brain didn't want me to turn it off, they wouldn't have given it an off switch, would they?" I shrugged. "Anyway, what did I miss?"

She rolled her eyes, after several years of working with me, she was used to my shit.

"The mech boys and I scouted out around here." She forwarded a map to my SEED and it floated in front of my eyes in 3D. "Made it out to farm ninety-six, section four-hundred. A bunch of farmers were really scared, said whole swaths of their crops had gone missing over the last week. They suspect the Krag are raiding again, bringing in food for the coming winter."

"What kind of crop?" I asked, fishing for a cigarette tin I kept in my chest pocket.

"Some Khdzor trees I think, why?"

"That's why," I laughed. "The farmers skim those off the books and distill it into booze. They sell it on the black market before the Imperial farm managers come around to collect the crops. You're telling me you've never drank any of the khdzor liquor?"

"No." She folded her arms. "You drink enough of it for the both of us."

I wanted to be mad about that jibe, but she wasn't wrong.

"What makes you think it was actually the Krag?" I flicked a lighter and the tip of my locally produced cigarette crackled.

The settlers blamed the Krag for everything. Every time a crop shortage happened or a missing person was reported a farm manager would report to our base and swear up and down the Krag did it. They had become something of a local ghost story.

"Nothing, Ando. But the colonel wants us to go check it out, so we are going to go check it out. Remember? It's our job. We're corpsmen. You of all people should want to stay on the colonel's good side." I chuckled, smoke rolling out of my nose.

"I think we both know that's impossible."

"Yeah, well, either way, I'm on his good side and I plan on keeping it that way at least until I'm a major and I can catch a transfer out of his damn unit. So, get your track jackers ready to roll in five minutes." I straightened up and gave her a lazy salute. "Oh, fuck off, Ando."

She gave me a playful shove and I climbed back up the side of my tank. I reached back down into the turret, grabbing my head-set. I slid the familiar stale sweat-stained thing over my head and keyed the switch behind my right ear.

"*Eagle*, this is *Daredevil*," I said. "You there?"

"Hm?" responded *Eagle*, the name of the tank commanded by Senior Sergeant Gor Titizian.

Gor's voice was on the other side of the radio but sounded like he wasn't in his tank. I looked out to where he was positioned a few hundred meters away and saw a crowd of settlers around his tank, all of them looking like ants next to the immense war machine.

The settlers had baskets of black-market items balanced on their heads. We were paid in the Imperial standard currency, the Terran Bit. On settler planets they were paid in the local script, backed by only the word of the Imperial duke that governed the planet and totally useless everywhere else. That meant they could never pay for a ticket off the rock with their useless local money, which was by design. So, once they realize how terrible settler life was, they would try to get into any side hustle that would allow them to make real Terran bits to facilitate them leaving as soon as possible.

The easiest way to do that was skim things off of the top from whatever industry they ended up working in and selling it on the black market at a discount to the local garrison, who were paid in real money. Unfortunately for them, they got assigned to the settler world garrisoned by the Frontier Corps, and we got paid half as much as the Imperial Army. Their hustling would have to go on for a little bit longer than normal as long as we were here.

"Gor." I rolled my eyes. "Stop trying to buy a wife and mount up, Captain wants us to roll out in five."

"I couldn't afford a wife even if I wanted one," he grumbled.

"What?" I joked. "No husbands on discounts this week?"

"Nothing that caught my eye. So, what are we doing?"

"Captain wants us to chase some ghosts a couple of farms down from here so she can impress the colonel."

"You know I can hear you when you're on the radio, right?" hissed the static distorted voice of Nayiri.

"Of course I do."

"In the name of the damn crown, just mount up, would you?" she asked, exasperated.

"Yes ma'am!" Gor answered immediately.

I climbed down back into my hatch, checking the machine gun that was mounted in front of me as I went. I brushed off some dust that had gathered since we had been sitting there and found the ammo in perfect order.

"Why don't you answer me that quickly, Gor?" I complained.

"Because, the troopers respect me, Ando," countered Nayiri.

I heard laughter over the tank's internal comms.

"Hey!" I yelled over the internal network, "is that true?"

"Sir, I've been with you for four years!" beamed Suren. "You're like family."

"Have to agree," Anush said. "Like family I can't get rid of."

"And you, Davit?" I asked our driver.

He was locked away in the driver's compartment at the front of the tank. We went days or sometimes weeks without seeing him. He was a strange, deeply religious man from the bowels of the Terran mega city.

"Well, sir, Captain Gnuni is a very solid officer," he answered.

I slouched into my seat, reaching up and closing my hatch with a loud bang.

"Ah just shut up and drive the tank, Davit."

The crew began to laugh again as the engine turned over and rumbled to life.

CHAPTER
EIGHT

THE TANKS FELL BEHIND on the Gandak ring road. The mech boy's armored personnel carriers were much faster by design. Their job was to be our eyes and ears, to stir up a hornet's nest before running back to the protection of massive two-hundred-millimeter cannons that could hit a Krag in the face with a shell at three miles, if they ever showed themselves anyway.

"You know," Anush said, her face pressed to the sight of the tank's cannon, hands-on the controller of her gunner's station in front of her, slowly guiding the turret back and forth. "I bet if any of these Krags existed anymore we would have a better chance finding them if we could actually leave the ring road every once and a while."

The ring road was the only road on the entire planet, cutting through all of the arid land and to the spaceport to facilitate easy transportation of goods off-world. Everywhere outside of that road had been turned into farmland or was a dense range of mountains and thought to be useless for the one purpose of the entire planet: to supply food to other settlements.

"Could you imagine how mad the duke would be if we tore through his fields with a couple of tanks and APCs?" I laughed.

"Doesn't he want us to kill the Krag?"

"Anush, I promise you he couldn't care less about the Krag."

"What do you mean, sir?" Suren asked.

He hung halfway out of his hatch, mounted machine gun in his hands and staring off into the distance.

"Is this one of those things you only understand if your brain has been poisoned with politics?" Anush added.

"Kind of." I nodded. "You see the duke complain to the colonel that people are complaining to him about all this business with the Krag, real or not. Then, the colonel sends us to go chase after them, which as you all know we fail to find them. However, If we did, we would kill them on the spot. On the off chance we find and kill them, the duke can say the Krag have been defeated. When we enviably fail, he tells everyone he is doing as much as he can, but those damn Frontier Corps troopers aren't doing their job. If we succeed he gets the credit, if we fail we get the blame. It's a win-win no matter what for the duke."

"That sounds like we lose either way," she complained.

"Of course we lose either way," Davit pointed out. "We're in the Frontier Corps."

"That's right." I pulled down my tank commander's periscope, searching for the heat signature of the mech boy's carriers.

I only saw the glowing grey darkness of endless farmland and the black strip of road ahead of us.

"Hey, Anush, where the are the mech boys?"

"Lost sight of them about twenty minutes ago," she said, nonplussed.

I rolled my eyes and retreated to the neural menu of my SEED.

"Hey, Nayiri. Slow down, would you? We can't keep up."

"Don't worry about it," the captain responded, I could hear the gloating in her voice.

She always prided herself in the speed of her carriers. I hated the little shoebox-looking *Ganymede* model carriers. Sure, they were fast, but if push came to shove and something actually shot at us, I'd much rather be comfortably behind the foot of uranium-reinforced, Luna-manufactured, composite armor of my Mark X *Solaris* main battle tank.

My SEED pinged once again and a location overlooking a nearby farm was circled on the map in my neural heads-up display.

"You won't catch up to us at this rate. We are going to go check out the farm, if anything pops off, we are going to pull back to the position I sent you. You and Gor set your tanks up there and watch our backs."

I sighed, rubbing the weeks' worth of beard growth that had sprouted on my face since our patrol had begun. This was why she had gotten promoted over me. Even after five years of never seeing combat, she never once strayed from corps standard regulation tactics.

"All right," I said. *"Have fun out there."*

I switched from the SEED to the tank's internal radio. "Hey *Eagle*, this is *Daredevil*, sending you our overwatch location so we can protect the captain while she drives around in circles."

"Better her than us," he responded.

"Where are we going, sir?" Davit asked.

"Hold on," I said, forwarding my SEED overlay to the tank's internal computer.

Davit dutifully piloted the tank to the area that Nayiri had ordered us to. I pulled myself away from my periscope and poked up through my hatch. She had sent us to a small hill that over-looked one of the thousands of farms whose name and number I hadn't bothered to look up in the directory. I pushed myself up onto my hatch in a sitting position and stared off into the distance.

Lush, green farmland as far as I could see, broken only by the two-lane track of the ring road. I reached my arms above my head, stretching my back and hearing it pop several times.

"Settle in for the long one," I said over the internal comms, watching the sun slowly dip beyond the horizon. "You know how the captain likes to be thorough."

"You know, sir," Anush said. "You might get promoted if you tried that."

"Says the eight-year corporal," I retorted.

The other two crewmen cackled. "If they accounted for accumulated arrest record when it came to promotions, you 'd be a sergeant major!"

"I'll have you know I'm such a good corporal that the Corps has felt it necessary to promote me to this rank twice."

"You're my favorite corporal," Suren added.

Anush smiled. "Thank you, Suren."

"Well, then you're just such a good corporal you can have first watch. Two up, two down. You all know the rules."

"You're going to make two of us stay awake for this shit?" Davit complained.

"What can I say?" I grinned as the sky above me turned dark. "I like to be thorough."

CHAPTER
NINE

MY TURN TO sleep went by uneventfully and unfortunately quickly. I was kicked awake by Suren, who took my place on top of the turret, rolling himself up in a blanket before quickly falling asleep. Davit stayed down in his driver's hole in case we had to make a quick getaway while Anush dozed off behind the controls of the main gun.

I settled into my worn tank commander's seat and pulled the periscope down in front of my face. I flicked the vision from a sickly green night vision to a hazy grey thermal. It was late enough now that the fields were empty, the armies of settlers being allowed to return to their dorms for the night.

I reached into the bag that I had mounted to the turret wall next to me, fishing out a device I had managed to buy from a settler a few years before. It was the size of my hand and its screen had a spider crack in the corner of it. But it was able to link into the local network decently enough that I could watch reruns of old dramas to keep me awake during my watch shift.

I flicked on a rerun of some war movie. The Imperial Army did battle against an unspeakable alien race that somehow threatened the safety of Terra, despite living on a planet a million miles away.

I unscrewed the top of one of my extra canteens and poured a measure of khdzoor liquor into a metal cup. I sipped on the sweet brew as some tentacled monster was bayoneted on the screen in front of me.

Out of the corner of my eye something moved in my periscope. The orange-red outline of a person crossing a field in the distance. Some poor bastard must have gotten sent out to work in the middle of the night. Then it slowly it hit me.

Settlers don't work alone, especially not out in the middle of the night. At the minimum they would be overseen by a supervisor.

And that looked like a *really* big settler.

I dropped my device back into my bag, thrusting my face into my pericope view. The field was empty once again, returning back to its dull grey cold standard. I sighed, deciding I had maybe been hitting the khdzoor a bit too hard. I should lay off this stuff when I'm on patrol. Who knows what those farmers cut into it while they were distilling. My brain could be getting turned loopy from paint thinner or something.

Then I saw it again.

A tall humanoid form, lumbering across the field. They pulled a cart behind them, flanked by two more shapes. Then more of them appeared. Thirty or forty of them, marching in a line. As my eyes settled on them my SEED implant began to process and slowly, red squares outlined their body. The neural implant registered them as enemies. They weren't human.

I quickly thumbed the radio and screamed, "Battle stations!"

All around me the crew jumped up from a deep sleep, confused. Suren dove back into the turret, shirtless. Drool was still plastered down the side of his face.

"Priority traffic!" I called over the radio. "I have a platoon-sized enemy force at my location. Command, where are you?"

"They must have slipped behind us!" Nayiri cursed. "*Daredevil*, engage and destroy!"

"Yes, Ma'am. *Eagle*, do you see them?"

"I got eyes on," Gor responded.

"Load frag!" I ordered.

Suren immediately spun, hitting a knee-level switch with his leg. The blast doors behind him slid open in an instant and he grabbed one of the forty-five shells that had been neatly stacked within. He swung the hundred-pound shell deftly in his arms and rammed it home into the breach, which automatic slammed shut. Suren then reached over, grabbed a giant arming lever, and pulled it up, activating the main cannon.

"Up!" he yelled.

The turret whined as Anush brought the cannon on target.

"Holy shit is that really them?" she gasped.

"Goddess curse them!" Davit spat.

"Shut the fuck up!" I snapped. "Do you see them?"

"Aye, sir!" she confirmed. "Enemy identified!"

I swallowed hard and my mouth went dry.

"Fire!" I ordered for the first time in my life.

"On the way!" Anush cried.

The cannon boomed, the beach recoiling all the way to the back of the turret. The shell casing clattered to the floor and the smell of burning powder filled the small space. The tank rocked back onto its rear sprocket and something in the distance exploded.

I checked my periscope. Anush's shot had landed directly in the middle of them. Their hot blood glowed brightly in my thermal vision but still, others appeared. *Eagle*'s cannon erupted and placed their shot, by the looks of it a high explosive shell, in their midst. Fire bloomed from the ground and another dozen of them evaporated. The survivors began to retreat, leaving their cart behind. I kicked the back of Anush's seat.

"Co-ax," I ordered.

"Roger, switching to co-ax."

A loud metallic click could be heard as her gunner's controls switch from the main cannon to the coaxial machine gun that was mounted next to it. She fired a long burst from it, churning through ammo so fast the gunfire sounded more like a buzzsaw.

Glowing tracers stitched across the fleeing Krag. They stuttered and twitched with the impacts, but remained on their feet, leaving trails of blood in their wake as they ran.

"Did they just shrug off machine gun bullets?" I exclaimed.

Gor and his crew must have seen what happened because they launched another high explosive shell at them. The last of the Krag vanished in a shower of blood and fire.

The silence of the night quickly returned to the spontaneous battlefield and it finally dawned on me.

We did it.

CHAPTER
TEN

NAYIRI'S mech boys led our triumphant procession back through the gates of Camp Piroth, the Corps' main garrison on Gandak. When the gates of the camp opened, we saw the streets lined with corpsmen, spraying beer and wine up at our vehicles. They cheered and played music and danced. For the first time since I had been on the planet, the Frontier Corps had met with the enemy, and we had won.

I sat halfway out of my hatch not bothering to keep my emotions in check. I smiled and waved to the gathering of corpsmen. Suren sat cross-legged on top of the turret next to me, a huge grin on his face as always.

"I didn't know we were so popular," he said.

"Didn't you hear?" Anush said over the internal comms. "We're conquering heroes."

For the first time since I had known her, she wasn't being sarcastic. Before our drive back to camp, she had carved several hash marks into the armor next to the cannon's mantle. She was proud to be the tank's gunner and to show everyone that as a crew, we were blooded.

"We owe our victory to the Goddess, it is not our own," Davit chimed in.

"Shit," Anush laughed. "She may have blessed me with these hands, but she also blessed me with the free will to use them to become the best damn gunner in the corps."

I joined in with her laughter. I could picture in my head how mad such a comment would make Davit, stewing in his driver's hole, surrounded by a dozen or so sun pendants.

"I'll pray for you," he mumbled.

"Yeah, I bet you will," she mocked. "Hopefully she will make you a better driver."

Davit was one of the best drivers in the Regiment and she knew it. But she also knew he prided himself on that fact more than someone as pious as he probably should have been. Laughing at one another and prodding at our personal weaknesses was what passed for both a sense of humor and a hobby in the tank. Living in such close quarters, it didn't take long for each of us to learn what pissed off the other. Not even my elevated social standing saved me from constant ribbing, though sometimes I wish it would.

Davit didn't take the bait but the turret crew giggled amongst themselves anyway, me included.

"*Hey Ando.*" Nayiri's voice crawled across my brain. "*Got word from the colonel. He wants to talk with us. We can assume it is about last night.*"

"*Last time he wanted to talk to 'us,' he just yelled at me for an hour. Is this about me or us?*"

"*Well,*" she said. "*You were the one who saw them.*"

I groaned.

"*So, is this a good thing or a bad thing you think?*"

"*When was the last time the colonel wanted to talk to you for a good reason?*" My face dropped into my hands.

She was right.

"What could he be mad about? We actually found the Krag, Shit, I found the Krag, and we killed them!" A corpsman chucked a can of beer up to me. I caught it and cracked it open. I allowed myself a sip before handing it down to Anush.

"Honestly, I have no idea this time Ando. Make sure you make yourself look presentable."

"Yeah, yeah." I looked down at myself.

We had been on patrol for two weeks and I hadn't bothered changing into a clean set of overalls. Tankers as a whole had something of a reputation, mostly earned, for being dirty all of the time. Locked away in our vehicles for days, weeks, or months at a time we were left with few options and little time to take care of our personal hygiene. It didn't take long for a tank crew to resemble a strange gathering of vagrants before too long.

Amongst ourselves, this was obviously accepted. Unfortunately, the colonel was well known to be something of a dandy. He expected the nobles under his command to always look ready to walk into a ballroom no matter if they just woke up or returned from a battlefield.

As the tank slowly made its way down the road I climbed onto the turret and grabbed my duffle bag from the storage rack. Digging around inside of it I found my rumpled green corps-issued dress uniform. It and I were splashed with a cascade of champaign as I crawled back into the turret.

"We did good, right?" Suren asked me. "This means the colonel is finally going to promote you, right?"

"I would bet not, Suren." I sighed, unzipping my overalls and stripping down to my underwear.

The same realities that made our ignoring of personal hygiene norms acceptable also went for a total lack of shame. I slipped on my green uniform, looking every bit as if I had just pulled it out of a duffle bag after two weeks of storage.

"You look like shit," Anush said.

I grinned. "So, better than normal."

There was nothing I could do about the accumulation of stubble on my face, as out of regulation as it was. I hadn't brought a razor and even if I had, carving my face into bloody ribbons looked less professional to me than a few stray hairs. I bent down and brushed the gathered dirt and dust off of my boots and called it good enough, just in time. The tank came to a halt, pulling into the camp motor pool, alongside dozens of other tanks, carriers, and trucks.

"Good luck, sir," Suren chirped.

I nodded at him.

"Make sure our ammo and fuel get refilled, all right? I don't need another reason for the colonel to climb up my ass."

I looked at Anush, as a corporal, she was the tank's second in command and when I was gone, normally getting yelled at by the colonel, it was her responsibility.

"Yeah, I know." She waved me off. "Just don't get relieved of command, will you? The next noble they send us will probably be a dick."

"If only I would be so lucky," I joked.

I climbed down from my tank, meeting Gor and Nayiri. Nayiri had changed into her dress uniform as well, while he still wore his overalls. Gor, looked every bit the senior noncommissioned officer he was. Short and powerfully built with wrinkles so deep-set into his face they looked like they had been carved with a chisel.

"You're going with me?" I asked her.

She sighed. "The message said he wanted to see both of us. So, whatever ass-chewing you get, I will too."

The short man laughed. "And you, Gor?"

"Oh, I'm not going. I just came to wish you luck." He gave me a slap on the shoulder. "Don't get fired."

"Thanks."

Nayiri and I walked through the crowded motor pool as the

crowd that lined the camp roads began to find their way inside. Troopers dismounted their vehicles and joined the party that had engulfed the camp. I didn't see any other officers in sight, instead, noncommissioned officers stood by and let the corpsmen cut loose.

We walked by the cookie-cutter prefabricated, stackable dorm units. Hundreds of them lined the streets on either side, home to a Regiment of the Frontier Corps. The dorms had been there since the planet was declared secured a few generations before and their best days had long passed them by. They leaked when it rained and were drafty when the wind picked up. It was, however, better than living in tents like I had heard some units did for years at a time.

Regimental headquarters was a massive building, at least for the planet. It was a prefab unit, just like our dorms, but from a different mold. The cracked and flaking paint that covered its corrugated steel walls was even the same color.

Nayiri was walking as if we were late for something, powered by the gendarmes that stood outside the doors so fast they couldn't even ask us for identification. The building was full of officers from every troop and squadron. Headquarters smelled exactly like every other military building I had stepped foot in since I had taken the green of the corps. A strange mixture of lemon-scented cleaner and stale cigarettes that warped together to cling to every surface, no matter what anyone did.

It wasn't uncommon for the headquarters to be packed full of people at any given time. But after five years on this planet, there were no new faces to learn. Once the Frontier Corps dumped you somewhere, generally speaking, you were never going to leave it. In another five years, I could ask for my release from the Corps and there was a good chance I would just get some minor position in the local government.

That is why the hairs on the back of my neck began to stand up when I saw countless new faces in the halls. Not only the green jackets of the Frontier Corps, but the blue dress uniforms of the Imperial Army and the white of the Imperial Navy. This was never a good sign.

"What in the name of the Goddess is going on here?" I gawped at them.

"I don't know." Nayiri eyed a Navy Commander as they walked by. "But I think we can be sure this has nothing to do with the colonel being mad at you."

"I'm not sure if that's a good thing or a bad thing anymore."

"Me either, Ando."

We got to the meeting room where I stopped dead in my tracks. Standing in front of the door was the form of the colonel, Colonel Kuril Boguni, commander of the sixteenth Frontier Corps Cavalry Regiment was glaring at me. Like most stationers he was tall and lanky, he looked like he had been handsome once, but decades in the Corps had turned his face into worn leather.

The man hated my guts and I couldn't blame him. I had murdered six members of his extended family. The Goddess had blessed me with luck so terrible I had ended up under the command of the one member of the Boguni family in the entire Frontier Corps. Out of tens of hundreds of millions of possibilities, I ended up here.

Regardless of how I ended up in this green jacket, I did my utmost to be the best officer I could be when I reported for duty on Gandak. I made sure my troopers were trained and proficient in our tank and I spent hours making sure I knew my tank inside and out. I poured long nights into memorizing the Imperial armored tactics manuals to the point Nayiri hired me to tutor her.

None of that mattered, and Colonel Boguni made sure of it. No matter how well my tank crew did during evaluations, we were always scored the lowest in the Regiment. Over the years, everyone around me got promoted while I was left behind. Even the troopers under my command caught flak for daring to exist near me.

Nobody had ever been promoted under my command. Even if Anush could stay out of trouble long enough to finally become a sergeant, she would have been rejected due to having my stink on her career. I wasn't sure why the colonel didn't just kill me. Just shoot me in the back when nobody was around or something. I guess if I ended up dead everyone would have known it was him immediately.

After a few years of having to deal with the colonel's harassment, I figured out it hurt a lot less if I was drunk. The less I tried to shine as a good officer, the more he left me alone. His mission was to make my career, my entire life, miserable. It was my way of showing him that he had won. At least he had stopped making me clean the latrines.

"You're late!" the colonel seethed.

Nayiri jumped in front of this bullet for me.

"My apologies, sir." She bowed. "Our detachment's return was slowed due to making contact with the enemy."

The colonel frowned.

"Ah yes, that whole business." He rubbed his chin. "I heard it was Haduni's tank that opened fire."

"Yes, sir," I beamed.

I was sure he couldn't somehow make this a bad thing. Nobody else had been able to find and kill the Krag in years and it was my crew that finally did.

"That explains why the duke was complaining about several millions worth of damage being done to the crops." The corner of his lip curled into a smirk. "Couldn't your gunner hit their target, Haduni?"

I bit my lip, trying desperately to hold back what I wanted to say, to scream in his face. Suddenly, I wished I had killed more members of his family.

"Sir." Nayiri knew this exchange wasn't going to a good place and cut in. "What is going on?"

"Ah." He nodded. "Some big announcement is going to be held in the regimental meeting room. I'm not sure why, but it involves every commander from this sector, from every branch of the Imperial Military."

He glanced down at his watch. "Speaking of which we should be going."

No shit, you already took your time yelling at me for being late, I thought to myself.

At the door was a stern-faced Frontier Corps sergeant major. She had to be in her late sixties at this point with a shaved head and the build of a Terran. She pointed to a bin next to her.

"All devices have to go in there. Nothing that can connect to the network is allowed inside," she scolded.

The colonel looked down at her. "Under whose orders, exactly?"

The colonel was used to people shrinking from his gaze, but she didn't. She stared right back at him, her grey implanted eyes burning a hole into the colonel.

"His Imperial Prince, Field Marshal Tigranes," she spat, before adding, "Sir."

The colonel caved, deflating and hanging his head. We all fished our devices from our pockets and dropped them into the bin.

"Of course." The colonel read her nametag. "Sergeant Major Petrosyan. Tell the field marshal I send my regards."

She didn't respond. As we walked into the room, I felt a pressure in my skull for just a split second and my network heads-up display vanished from my eyes. The meeting room had been set up with anti-neural barriers. Not even our SEED implants were allowed to be used in here. What were we walking into?

The meeting hall had seating for five hundred people and it

had been reduced to standing room only. The seats had all been taken by the Army and navy officers along with their bloated entourages. We corpsmen knew where we stood in the Imperial pecking order, but coming into our garrison and forcing us to stand was just salt in the wound.

We joined our regimental command group who had gathered together, awkwardly standing in the corner. I noticed more than one set of eyes glaring at me. I wasn't sure if it was for my appearance or because I had apparently singlehandedly destroyed millions of bits worth of farmland.

"Evening, gentlemen," I said, trying to break the ice.

They ignored me.

Sergeant Major Petrosyan entered the meeting hall, now flanked by gendarmes. They closed and locked the doors behind them as she approached the platform at the front of the room. The crowd had been at a dull roar as hundreds of hushed side conversations blended together to create an incomprehensible noise. As the sergeant major took center stage, everyone fell quiet as all eyes were on her.

"Ladies and gentlemen," she began, her voice being amplified by a throat-mounted microphone. "Please rise, for his Imperial Majesty, Prince, Field Marshal Narek Tigranes."

Out of a side entrance came the man I had only read about in history books. His heroic defense at New Beginnings, the taking of the Galar worlds, there were so many things I couldn't even remember them all. I had even heard rumors that he started off in the Frontier Corps and ended up being transferred into the Imperial Army because someone in the government thought piling so many awards onto a corpsman was in bad taste.

I knew him to be close to eighty years old, but he hardly looked it. His face had been raked by intersecting scars and wrinkles and his once brown hair was snow-white, but he strode to the stage as confident as any young officer I had ever seen. His sky-blue uniform was resplendent with more awards than I could count, but he wore his most important one, the *Hero of Terra* medal, around his neck.

The people who were sitting shot to their feet and everyone clicked their heels together in unison, creating a sound akin to a gunshot. Each of us bowed as low as we could, though we were restricted by the available space. Tigranes waved us all off, a broad grin across his face. I had always heard he wasn't one for the games of rank and privilege, I supposed being the emperor's brother would do that to a man.

"Please, be seated."

Those that could, did.

He smiled. "I'm sure this meeting comes as a surprise for most of you, especially the sixteenth regiment, stationed here on Gandak. I would first off like to thank Colonel Boguni and his troopers for allowing us to crash their garrison for the time being."

He said "allowed" like the colonel had a choice in the matter.

"It is an honor to host you, your majesty!" Colonel Boguni said, bowing once again.

"But as you can imagine—" Tigranes continued without acknowledging the colonel, which made me smile.

"—I did not decide to call all of you to this lovely little planet for your company, as much as I enjoy it. But the emperor has dispatched me to this sector to create a task force."

A hologram flickered to life behind him, bathing the entire wall in blue light. After a few moments, it showed Gandak and its surrounding worlds, labeled "Sector Five Sixty-three." Each planet's garrison was in a column next to their station's name, with a long line of units under it.

"On the fringes of this sector, there is a small planet called Barda."

As he talked, the hologram map zoomed in, millions of miles away, to a small, white planet. We routinely had to go over star maps for our sector, just in case something went sideways and the surrounding garrisons would have to deploy in response, we were expected to know where we could go. I had never heard of Barda. It wasn't on any star map I had ever seen before.

"It's a frigid little place from what I've learned from our partners in the Navy and their topographical survey teams." Tigranes was now pacing back and forth as he spoke, the frozen planet's hologram floating behind him. "This tiny snowball is home to a couple of hundred-thousand people, miners and the like. Under normal circumstances, none of us would have ever learned about this place, its people, or its Goddess-forsaken weather. But, ladies and gentlemen, we are not under normal circumstances."

He stopped pacing, turning to face the gathered Imperial officers in front of him. His affable demeanor was gone.

"As of six months ago, we have lost all communication with the Barda Government. This is not uncommon, as anyone who has been stationed on a remote planet knows. Solar storms and the like play havoc with our communication lines. However, that is when one of our asteroid listening stations picked up this transmission."

The hall's sound system crackled to life and the harsh, distorted sound of an orbital recording filled the room.

"To the people of Terra," it began, the voice sounded like an older man with the inflection of a high-born individual who spent years in the Empire's best schools. "The man calling himself emperor is a false prophet! The light of the Goddess has left the Terran throne, led astray by the heretical church of Vazh!"

The recording hissed and broke up into an incomprehensible mess.

"Soon, the Holy See of Barda will spread its burning, cleansing light across all of humanity! Submit yourself to the glory of the Goddess and you have nothing to fear!" cried the voice, before cutting out entirely.

The hall erupted into shouts of outrage. Several officers quickly made the symbol of the sun over their hearts. Even Nayiri whispered a prayer to herself. Tigranes held up his hands, trying to silence everyone so he could speak.

He raised his voice, "I am as outraged as you are, I assure you folks, our Imperial security services have already discovered the source of this recording."

The map behind him flickered and changed to the picture of someone. An old man in the robes of a Bishop of the church.

"Bishop of Barda Grigori Ter-Kanayan, High Priest of the Barda Monastery. Until recently, considered a loyal man of the Goddess. That was until we looked back into his history." The picture behind him changed. The man I knew now to be Grigori standing next to a much younger looking All Catholicos Vazh, head of the Church of Terra.

"Thirty years ago," Tigranes continued. "When the Bishop Council of the Imperial church got together to elect a new All Catholicos, the vote came down to His Holiness Vazh and Bishop Grigori. As we know, His Holiness was chosen. The two men had what appeared to be serious political disagreements about the future of the church and instead of staying within the Holy See of Terra as His Holiness's second, Grigori exiled himself to Barda where he ran the small monastery there."

"Now, we can take a few things from his transmissions. He is clearly announcing the creation of a new Holy See, the so-called Holy See of Barda, with himself as its leader. Normally, we would discount such things as the ravings of a mad old fool and simply remove him from his position. But we must look at the bigger picture. Outside of this message, we have heard nothing from the Dukedom of Barda's government or its Imperial Army garrison. If they could, or wanted to, there are countless methods with which they could have reached out for help or to warn the Imperial Government."

Tigranes have us a hard look. "The only logical assessment of this situation is that the rightful government of Barda has been sidelined, and this heretic Grigori is leading a rebellion against the throne. This, ladies and gentlemen, is what I am forming a task force to defeat. We are to land on Barda as soon as possible and restore Imperial control over the planet without delay!"

AFTER TIGRANES GAVE us our orders, the camp erupted into chaos. Troopers of all ranks rushed back to their dorms to pack as many things as they could before the shuttles came for us.

I jogged back to my small room in one of the dorm blocs and began to frantically pack. Due to space being a premium aboard the ships of the Imperial Navy we were all limited to just one duffle bag apiece. My dorm was filthy. Unlike most officers, I never tasked a trooper to be my personal servant and my mess had begun to pile up. It wasn't that I felt like I was above such things, I really did miss the palace staff, I just didn't want them to discover my dorm had become a graveyard of empty bottles.

I kicked the bottles aside and began shoving clothes into my one allowed duffle bag. It dawned on me how strange it was that I could fit so much of my life into one single bag after so many years. After my clothes were packed, I found a box, full to the brim with paper letters. Due to the restrictions of Corps life, we weren't allowed to use the Inter-Imperial messaging network due to the risk of men and women attempting to reach back and make contact with people from their old lives. Being nobility I had my ways around such things.

During my first two years in service, I wrote endless letters to Ana. Palming off a few bits to some couriers amongst the transport ship crews was easy enough. They were hardly the most honest people in the Navy. However, no matter how many letters I wrote, they were always eventually returned, unopened. I shouldn't have been surprised. Service in the Frontier Corps for most people means you were functionally dead to anyone who had known you before you took the green. I just didn't think it would mean that for me too.

I left the box on my small bed, deciding I didn't need to be reminded of that particular kind of heartbreak. I closed the door of the small room, maybe for the last time

"All set?" I heard Nayiri behind me.

She lived in the room next to mine and had packed barely half of her bag.

"Yeah, I think so," I said, shouldering my bag.

She looked into the room and whistled at the sight, but decided not to rib me for it. The small mercies of privacy.

"Nervous?" I asked her.

"My first real war command and we are putting down a crazed church leader on a frozen shit hole." She sighed. "I bet the Corps garrisons in the rest of the Empire don't have to put up with shit like this."

"What? You wish you were going off fighting aliens somewhere?"

"Of course. That is why I took the green in the first place. Not to shoot other humans."

I raised an eyebrow. "I thought that was because your dad wanted you to marry some inbred hick to shore up his gas extraction business."

"Okay, fine," she admitted. "But once you're in the corps, you want to go do corps stuff. And corps stuff is war."

We made our way down the dorm stairs and back toward the

motor pool where we were to wait for the Navy shuttles.

"Maybe you." I shook my head. "I'd be fine riding out my ten years here. It was perfect until the other day."

"You mean when you actually saw combat?" I nodded.

"It ruined the mood of the place."

"I thought you said all you ever wanted to do your entire life was lead a tank into some triumphant war somewhere."

"Sure, but that was before." It was all I ever went to school for, but the less I thought about that the better.

That was a completely different life than the one I am living now. "But that was until I saw how the Empire really works. Our victories out here don't mean anything. At the end of the day everything is decided by two-faced, corrupt assholes who will sell out their own families if it makes their stock portfolio go up."

"But enough about the colonel." She joked and we both laughed. "Listen."

She turned to me, deadly serious. It was never a good sign when she made sure to talk to me away from the rest of the troopers. It wasn't a friendly Nayiri to Ando talk, but a Captain Gnuni to Lieutenant Haduni talk.

"We are about to go to war, real war. Not this garrison patrolling shit. I need to know your head is in the game."

"You know it is," I said, not entirely convincingly. "Is everything all right?"

She shifted uncomfortably, her eyes darting back and forth. In front of the troopers, she was a badass, take no shit commander. She had to be for their sake. Nobody wants to look over and see their commander unsure or afraid of something. I was really the only person she could open up to without breaking the façade.

"This is going to be a real war," she said, her voice lowering.

"Yeah, you said that already."

Her frustration rose. "Most of the time you don't make captain in the Corps without seeing combat first. But we got stuck out here and now I'm in charge and somehow you're the only one with any experience!"

"I'd hardly consider what I did *experience.*" I tried to reassure her. "Is it combat if they don't shoot back?"

Thankfully that one got her to smile. "You got promoted for a reason. Now you just get to prove it."

"Thanks, Ando." She took up her bag again, stopping one last time. "What did it feel like, combat I mean?"

"I don't really know," I said. "My brain kind of turned off and we just kind of did things without thinking about them. I didn't feel... anything."

So much had happened since we had gotten back from the patrol, I hadn't had time to process anything. I took solace in what I remembered from church. Aliens weren't to be considered life to regret taking. They were parasites that needed to be destroyed so humanity could prosper. But I knew that was a cop-out. I'm not religious, so why would I take comfort in religious teachings now? I should have felt something. I think that bothered me more than anything else.

I was thankful to see the long shapes of navy shuttles slowly floating through the clouds. Just what we needed to quickly change the subject. She looked as happy as I did for a way out.

"We should get going then," she said.

I nodded, reshouldering my bag. I pulled out my cigarette case.

"One for the road?" I handed her one and she took it.

We shared a lighter and she took a deep pull, smoke curling out of her nose.

"It's going to be a long road."

CHAPTER
TWELVE

IT HAD BEEN SO LONG since I had stepped foot on one of the Navy's spaceships, I had forgotten how much I hated them. They stank, they were cramped, and they were always too cold for comfort. How naval personnel stayed cooped up in them for sometimes years at a time, I'll never know.

People often made jokes about how tankers, or track jackers as the grunts liked to call us, were a lot like the Navy. Trapped in metal boxes for days or weeks at a time, slowly developing our own cultural norms away from everyone else. Part of that was true, but at least we could open our hatches and get some fresh air. Within only a few hours of being locked into the hold of a spaceship, I felt like the walls were closing in.

The *TSS Erebuni* was seemingly custom-built to be my personal nightmare. It had been originally used as a grain hauler, making long trips from agricultural settlements like Gandak back to the core worlds. Eventually, after several decades of that, the Imperial Navy decided they could buy it from whatever family conglomerate on the cheap and convert it to ferry men and machines.

The conversion was rough at best. Overworked ventilation

systems struggled to keep up with the influx of human bodies. Everything smelled like dust, burning oil, and stale breath. Every sleeping bay had a thick miasma of body odor that would never fade, clinging to the very metal of the ship itself.

I could feel the vibration of the ship's engine no matter where I went. It was always there, buzzing at just the right frequency that you could feel it under your skin. For those unaccustomed to the annoyance, it would cause your joints to ache, your ears to ring, and play absolute hell on your intestinal tract. The Navy guys jokingly called this wonderful side effect the 'star shits,' and would giggle as we ran back and forth from our cots to the latrine trying desperately to stave off disaster.

This was only made worse by the food. In the Corps our cooks would cook three decent meals a day, it was nothing to write home about, but it tasted okay. That was assuming you weren't on patrol. If you were, then you were dependent on the corps-issued food, stabilized, survival ration, or FSSR. It was often called a lie in three parts. It wasn't food, it wasn't stabilized, and you couldn't survive on them. Most of the time I just shelled out some bits to the settlers for a home-cooked meal. Neither of these things were options on the *Erebuni.*

It seemed the act of eating aboard a ship was strictly for the purpose of nourishment, taste wasn't something that survived the trip into orbit. We filed through their chow hall where disgruntled cooks in white uniforms ladled a tasteless mess into bowls for us. Each meal was calibrated to give us the calories we needed to survive the trip, and nothing more. We would have been worried about the constant hunger pangs if the mush diet didn't pair with the engine vibrations to tear through our insides faster than a tank shell through armor.

"I take back any complaints I ever had about Gandak," I moaned.

I was laying in my cot, staring up at the identical one above it in between bouts of orbit-induced diarrhea.

"I miss it already."

"I thought we were normally put in stasis for interplanetary travel," Gor added, his voice weak. "Did they decide that was finally too good for the corps, too?"

It was no secret that everything the Corps was given was hand-me-downs or rejects from the Imperial Army. My carbine even had the name of some old, long-dead soldier stenciled onto its butt-stock from around eighty years ago. Even then, we were still normally afforded the comfort of stasis.

"I already told you." Nayiri burped, fighting back another wave of sickness. "Only the long haulers have stasis pods in them. If you go somewhere in the sector you have to ride one of these boats."

She paused to force something back down. "At least the Army is in here with us."

Across from the thousands of corps' bunks were the Army's. They had ditched their blue dress uniforms for the standard field grey, almost blending into the dull colorless walls of the ship.

"I can't believe we have to share bunk space with them," I added.

"I'm sure they feel the same way," Nayiri pointed out.

"How in the hell did we end up sharing an operation together anyway? Wouldn't some high-up Imperial officer hate the idea of standing shoulder to shoulder with us?"

"Who is higher ranking than the emperor's brother?" she countered. "Besides, what else was he going to do? Wait six months for army reinforcements to finally reach the sector? We are already here, might as well use us."

"That's the kind of practical thinking that normally gets you in trouble," Gor scoffed.

I thought for a moment what rank I would be if I wasn't from a minor stationer family. Then I reminded myself my minor family didn't even technically exist anymore.

"Uh, sir?" Davit appeared at the end of my bunk.

Like most tankers, he was short and stocky, though his stocky shape had turned more to heavyset after years of easy living on Gandak. He wore three different sun pendants around his thick neck and I noticed he had begun growing out a thin mustache. He spent so much time in the driver's position away from the rest of us I occasionally forgot what he looked like.

"What's up, Davit?" I pushed myself up to my elbows as my stomach did backflips on itself.

"You might want to see this."

Davit led me through the warren of bunks, which soldiers and corpsmen had done their best to turn into their own little spaces by hanging up blankets to act as barriers. The area had been turned into a strange tapestry of thousands of green standard-issue wool blankets all held in place by a rat's nest of string, attached to any bit of the ship that they could be tied to.

I could hear the crowd before I could see them. Hundreds of soldiers and corpsmen gathered in a circle, hooting and cheering at something that I couldn't see.

"What in the name of the Goddess is going on?" I asked.

Davit pushed through the crowd, pulling me with him until we got to the front. The crowd had an opening in its middle, forming a rough circle. In the middle, Suren stood shirtless with Anush at his side. His hands were taped up with white strips, and he was smiling from ear to ear like he was having a grand old time. A soldier stepped forward, his hands taped up much the same way. He was almost the same size as Suren. A much smaller soldier was next to him, whispering into his ear.

"All right, gentlemen," Anush announced. "You know the rules, no weapons, no biting, and no nut shots. The fight ends when one of you hits the ground. Any questions?"

"You better pay up when we finally put your boy down," seethed the smaller soldier.

"That's what the last three said." Anush laughed. "I'm starting to think you soldiers are all as soft as baby shit."

"Watch your mouth, gutter trash!" the soldier spat. "Are we doing this or not?"

"Hope there's room in the med bay for this one." Anush nodded at Suren and he slowly made his way forward.

He and the soldier circled each other for a moment before the soldier lunged at him. In the blink of an eye, Suren sidestepped the attack and blasted the soldier in the side of the head with a single punch. The man dropped to the floor with a sickening thump. The crowd erupted into cheers and boos along service lines.

"There goes another one!" Anush gloated, beginning to make her way along the crowd, her beret in her hands, collecting Bits begrudgingly from the losers.

The soldier who had bet with Anush was getting madder and madder, a group had gathered around him.

"No!" the soldier shouted. "Don't pay that bitch or her retarded sidekick!"

I swallowed hard. Things were about to get way uglier. Anush stepped in front of Suren, her fists balled. Our crew was as close as any group of people could be, but Anush and Suren were as thick as thieves. We all knew Suren had his issues and we looked out for him, but Anush protected him as if he was her little brother. Insulting him in such a way wasn't going to be ignored.

"Pay up," she growled. "And I'll let you leave."

Someone pressed up against me from behind and I saw Gor and Nayiri had joined us.

"Is she using Suren to shark people again?" Nayiri sighed. "Last time she did this he nearly killed a villager. That boy doesn't know his own strength."

"It's not his fault," Gor said defensively.

"Either way, it looks like it's about to go sideways," I pointed out.

"We can't have our best loader get smashed up right before we land." Gor frowned. "We should stop this."

He marched out into the middle of the fight circle, mustering his most commanding voice.

"That is enough!" he boomed, mustering his best command voice. "Disperse this instant!"

"Fuck off!" the lead soldier spat, I noticed one of the men who had come to back him was holding a knife. "We don't answer to you!"

"Stand down boy, or I'll show you how we deal with insubordination in the corps!"

The soldier didn't know it, but Gor had just threatened to kill him. The crowd's mood had shifted. During the fights they had intermingled, jostling for a good spot to watch the show while arguing with each other over odds. Now, they had slowly begun separating themselves into camps. The green uniformed corpsmen squared off on the other side of the grey soldiers.

"How about we do the emperor a favor and gut you and the rest of you inbred rejects. I get my money back and we don't have to sully ourselves by sharing a billet with you."

"Should we do something?" I asked, turning to Nayiri.

She had slipped on a pair of brass knuckles and wasn't paying attention to what I said.

"Hm?" she asked, stretching out her arms.

I rolled my eyes and regretted not carrying a weapon like seemingly everyone else was. The only thing I had was a lighter in my pocket, I wrapped my fist around it and waited.

The fight started as several soldiers attempted to jump Suren, afterwards it felt as though the crowd itself lurched forward to attack. So many corpsmen surged in I had no choice but to go with them as a grey mass lunged at us. Soldiers and Corpsmen crashed into one another. Cries and curses flew as I swung blindly at the grey shapes in front of me. Something hit me in the side of the head and I saw stars.

I stumbled back, regaining my balance just in time to see Anush jamming a knife into the face of the soldier who had insulted Suren, she dragged it back and forth, drawing a horrific gash. He screamed and spasmed in agony as his eye was reduced to ruins. Next to her, a corpsman had an ugly divot punched into his skull by a hammer-wielding soldier.

I jumped back into the fray and landed a solid right hand across the jaw of a soldier, sending them sprawling to the ground. Before I could find my next target pain surged through my body as a combat boot planted itself firmly in my groin. My legs went limp and I collapsed onto my knees. A soldier with sergeant's stripes reared his foot back for another kick when Davit appeared, body tackling them to the ground.

"Break it up!" a voice screamed.

The hold doors opened and gendarmes in riot gear poured in. "Stop at once!"

The sickening crackle of a stun bolt flared and several armed corpsmen seized up and collapsed.

"Get on the ground right now!" the lead gendarme commanded.

I decided I had been beaten enough for one day and quickly sat down. Most troopers had a lifetime of dealing with the cops under their belt and knew better than to disregard their orders. Soldiers, with their life of privilege had a much different relationship with law enforcement. They probably had cousins, brothers, and friends within the ranks of their local police departments, some of them probably had jobs lined up for when their contract ran out.

They were the cudgel of the Empire, used to make sure the

people who were down, stayed down. The gendarmes apparently shared their sentiment, immediately closing in on the corpsmen, raining blows down on them even though they had complied with their orders. Soldiers stood around laughing as they watched, some began to join in now that the tables had been turned.

Two gendarmes grabbed Anush and began dragging her away. I jumped to my feet.

"Let go of her!" I demanded.

I turned to the rest of the corpsmen. "On me!"

I ran forward, the first gendarme I hit didn't see me coming, my fist smashed off of his hard plastic helmet. Before he hit the ground corpsmen had grabbed him, wrenching his baton out of his hands. Another gendarme was overcome and dragged down, beaten by dozens of troopers.

The soldiers, seeing their advantage slipping, decided to make a run for it. Suren grabbed one of the men, hoisting him up by his leg, and hurled him at the gendarmes that were carrying Anush. They collapsed into a pile and she broke free, running back toward the group.

Their element of surprise was ruined, and the gendarmes decided to beat their retreat as well. Laughing corpsmen released the cops they had captured, but made sure to keep their weapons and armor. They scampered back toward the door in their underwear, embarrassed.

Anush stumbled back toward me. Her lip was busted and her nose canted off at a new, ugly-looking angle. She cracked a smile, jangling her beret which was heavily laden with bits.

"I told you that these soldiers were softer than baby shit."

CHAPTER
THIRTEEN

AFTER THE FIGHT, the hold had been militarized. gendarmes in riot gear patrolled between the Corps and army bunks. Crossing the line without permission would result in a quick and violent introduction to their batons before being dragged off to the ship's brig. More than one late-night tryst was ruined by the vigilant eyes of our new guards.

The fight, considered normal corps and army affair, caused much pearl-clutching amongst the naval command on the ship. Apparently, a fight that filled the sick bay with stab victims was not par for the course in the Imperial Navy. They demanded strict and merciless punishments for everyone involved, which led to a strange and rare moment of solidarity between the troopers of the Corps and the soldiers of the Army.

When the gendarme investigators came into the hold to start asking questions, nobody told them anything. Corpsmen were used to blanking the cops, however to the high-born and privileged soldiers, not complying with police demands was something new for them. However, they knew if they opened their mouth and ratted on the corpsmen, Anush and the others had more than enough evidence to take them down with them. A game of mutually assured destruction. The gendarmes were greeted by dozens of troopers and soldiers, their faces beaten to a pulp, all proclaiming they didn't see any fight at all.

That temporary alliance didn't mean we wouldn't go at each other at the next possible chance. On top of our baseline hatred for one another, there were now countless scores to settle. I could think of a newly minted one-eyed soldier who would have it out for Anush and Suren. Most commanders didn't care when the services tore each other apart, but I had heard rumors that Field Marshal Tigranes had personally ordered the gendarmes to keep us apart, if only to make sure he still had a task force to deploy to the battlefield. It was probably a good call.

Eventually, as we got closer to planet fall, we were ordered to go into the supply hold and get issued our *Imperial Extreme Cold Weather Suit Type One-Hundred*. It was the standard-issue bodysuit given to anyone being sent to any planet that was considered cold enough to deserve such a thing. The type one hundred was a thick single piece bodysuit that regulated the wear's body temperature through a series of bio connectors.

Because of the personalized bio connector system required time to adapt to individual bodies, Field Marshal Tigranes ordered everyone in the task force to begin wearing their type one hundreds immediately. They were constricting and oddly formfitting, leading to most people simply wearing their standard uniform over it, if only to protect their shame.

We also learned that because they wrapped around our entire bodies, even simple acts became a chore. After the third or fourth time having to squirm my way out of my bodysuit to take a piss, I decided I hated the damn thing. The one time the Imperial Government issued the same equipment to both services it was the worst thing they had ever given me.

"Junior officers!" I heard a voice call out.

I looked up from my device and tuned into the *Imperial Armed*

Forces Network as it was showing me some terrible game of Blitz Ball from Luna. I wouldn't have cared about the outcome if I hadn't bet on it. With us on lockdown, there wasn't much left to do with our time other than gamble on meaningless things and try to sleep.

"I think that's you, Ando," Gor added.

I set down my device when it was clear that I was going to owe someone more money than I had.

"Yeah, yeah." I stood up, flexing my knees in my still too-tight bodysuit.

I made my way to the door of the hold, having to point out the lieutenant's rank on my collar before the gendarmes would let me through. After being looking over for entirely too long by a gendarme that didn't look a day over eighteen years old, I found Nayiri and a collection of other officers as they were led out of the hold.

A naval officer dressed in white led us through the bowels of the *Erebuni*. Its cramped gangways all looked identical to me. One gunmetal grey length after another, punctuated by a bulkhead door with a small nameplate on it. Occasionally, we passed by groups of naval crewmen who quickly jumped out of our way, bowing low as we went.

We were eventually deposited into a briefing room. It was much smaller than the meeting hall back on Gandak but that didn't stop them from packing the same amount of people into it. Tigranes didn't debase himself by riding aboard such a cramped ship. I wasn't sure what part of the fleet he was in at the moment, but I didn't blame him for not wanting to put himself on the *Erebuni*. Instead, standing in front of a briefing table was Colonel Boguni. I took some measure of glee seeing he seemed to be as uncomfortable in his bodysuit as I was.

"Ladies and gentlemen," he began. "His majesty, Field Marshal Tigranes has given us wonderful news."

"The attack has been called off?" I whispered to Nayiri and she gave me a poisonous look.

She hadn't been too pleased with me ever since I found myself in the middle of the brawl. I didn't understand why because in the middle of the maelstrom I was certain I saw her strangling an army captain with a belt.

"We are to make planetfall tomorrow, orbital time zero six." He turned to the table, pressing a few buttons, and a map of what I assumed to be Barda flickered into view.

A featureless expanse of snow and ice presented in brilliant blue. "The task force is to land here."

An area was highlighted in red on the map. "Once our landing area has been secured, we are to advance overland toward Barda Prime, the only settlement on the planet."

"Sir," a lieutenant colonel spoke up. "Do we have any word on possible enemy forces we will encounter? After all, who could this mad man rally to his cause?"

A muffled laughter filled the room.

"Scans of the planet have been inconclusive," Boguni cut through the laughter, unamused. "However, the garrison of Barda was made up of six regiments of regular Imperial Army soldiers. Since they are no longer in communication with the government, we can assume one of two things. One, an insane old bishop and a handful of his followers overpowered nearly ten thousand soldiers, or two, the garrison has joined him in whole, or in part."

The laughter was gone now. We exchanged nervous glances with one another. Why in the name of the Goddess would six regiments of high-born soldiers throw their lots in with a maniac like Grigori?

"I know which one sounds more likely to me," Boguni continued. "I cannot begin to fathom why so many once-loyal subjects turned their backs on our Empire. Maybe they all lost their minds on such a miserable little snowball of a planet. However, if the regiments turned on us, they would know how to obfuscate our orbital scanning reconnaissance. We will have to do recon the old-fashioned way. So, Captain Gnuni—"

He nodded at Nayiri. "—make sure you link up with the Army scouting detachment, I have a feeling you will be working with each other a lot. You're in command of scouting until further notice."

"Yes, sir," Nayiri said, glancing over at her army counterpart.

I noticed the thin army captain was sporting a black eye.

"Sir." A major raised his hand. "If our scans are inaccurate and Barda only has one settlement, why doesn't the fleet just shell it from orbit until this Grigori and his fake church surrender?"

"I asked the same thing," the colonel admitted. "Field Marshal Tigranes insisted that no harm was to come to the settlement. Various ministries would make even his life a living hell should we blow up the mining infrastructure of Barda. Our plan is for none of that to matter, however. Our hope and the hope of the field marshal is that we will make our landing and the soldiers who have joined this rebellion will immediately surrender upon seeing its consequences. What happens to them next is up to the security services, but we don't need to tell them that part."

"And, hypothetically, they don't surrender. Then what?" commented a sour-faced army captain.

He shared the expression with most army officers, none of them were pleased about listening to a corps colonel. Unfortunately for them, their higher-ranking officers were on the nicer ships with the field marshal and weren't about to slum it with us on the *Erebuni*, leaving Boguni the only one who could brief them.

He motioned to the map. "When we land, we will organize our forces here."

The formation of the task force was a textbook one. Our tanks and Nayiri's mechanized infantry and scouts up front and the slower infantry behind us. Though I noticed there was an added detail, all of the Frontier Corps units were on the front line, with the Army behind them. This was despite the Army outnumbering us nearly two to one.

"Grigori has clearly lost his mind, but we cannot ignore the fact he could be supported by several well-educated military officers, maybe even including the garrison commander. They'll certainly react by doing everything they can to keep us away from Barda Prime and their assets. This will most likely lead them to defending our advance here." He pointed again. "On the Barda plains. A wide flat expanse, perfect for our armor. Nowhere for them to hide."

Boguni was smiling now, completely convinced of the assured success of the plan. The fact that he almost certainly had nothing to do with its creation did something to temper my doubts.

"You all have much to do to prepare for planet fall so I will leave you to it. I'll see you on the ground!"

He was probably expecting a resounding "yes sir," or something like it. Instead, he got a few disgruntled army officers simply turning around and leaving. The rest of us gave him a halfhearted salute. His clear displeasure at the collective passive-aggressive disrespect was my favorite part of the brief.

"Can I trust you get your crews together without them getting into a fist fight?" Nayiri frowned at me as we made our way back toward the hold.

I looked around and the only people around us were army officers uninterested in our conversation.

"Hey, I saw you in that fight too," I countered.

"Everyone was in that fight, Ando. We didn't have a choice once Anush started it!"

"Started it?" I scoffed. "She was defending Suren, you heard what that grey shirt said. He got what he deserved. That army puke started it by not wanting to pay up after he lost a bet."

"Anush is always starting problems You know eventually that is going to come back on you, as her officer." She folded her arms. "Then what are you going to do?"

"I don't know." I threw my arms up. "Not get promoted again?"

My shouting had gotten the attention of the passing officers.

She lowered her voice. "Is that what this is about? You're letting your troopers act like idiots because you got passed up for captain again?"

"You think I still care about that?" I asked. "I accepted years ago that was never going to happen. It doesn't matter if I'm the best officer in the regiment or the worst, I won't make captain as long as that pompous ass is my commander."

"Yeah, you're probably right," she admitted.

"Anush might be a bit of a drunken prick. Davit might be a sanctimonious, judgmental asshole with a sex addiction, and Suren is... Suren. But you can't look at me with a straight face and say Anush isn't the best gunner in the entire regiment, Suren can't sling shells faster than anyone you've ever seen, and Davit can't fix anything that breaks down on those rickety shit buckets." A smile tugged at the corner of her mouth.

"Does Davit really have a sex addiction?" she asked, suddenly curious.

"Yeah, he's in debt up to his eyeballs with the flesh peddlers back on Gandak. I've been paying them off to make sure we didn't find him dead in a ditch somewhere." I shook my head, noticing her change of tone. "What are you getting at?"

"Our crews have spent more time drinking, screwing, and punching one another than they have fighting. That goes for my grunts as well as your tankers. I don't know if you were paying attention in there, but we are about to get into some serious shit, Ando."

I shrugged. "The colonel might be an idiot, but he could be right about them surrendering."

She laughed derisively. "Would you throw your entire life away by rebelling only to surrender yourself to the security services without a fight?"

I didn't want to tell her how close to home that one hit for me. "They might as well shoot themselves in the face and save them the time and the cost of a bullet. They're regular army soldiers with regular army equipment, trained and led by their own officers. They are going to fight and fight hard. I just don't know if we are ready."

Nayiri was an incredibly talented officer, but you could never convince her of that. Other officers didn't constantly doubt themselves like she did. But that was because they were too stupid to realize they were incompetent. She was too smart for her own good, always over thinking and reanalyzing everything she either thought about or did. It had a tendency to turn her into a neurotic mess and occasionally had to be talked down.

I shook my head. "It doesn't matter if we aren't."

She eyed me like I had just insulted her.

"It... doesn't matter if we aren't ready for war?" she asked slowly, as if the words didn't make any sense to her.

"No, not really," I repeated. "Planet fall is tomorrow. No matter how much you worry about it we won't be any more ready than we are right now. I have faith in my troopers to do the right thing when the metal meets the meat."

Well, I have faith in most of them, but I would only admit that to myself.

"You sound strangely confident." She sighed.

I gave her the biggest smile I could muster. "Of course I am. You should try it sometime."

She had no idea I was lying through my teeth.

FOURTEEN

"DAVIT, RUN A SYSTEM CHECK," I ordered through the internal comms. "I don't want to find out our turbine doesn't wind up when we hit the ground."

"Yes, sir." He sighed.

We both knew he had already checked over the tank a dozen times.

"Suren, is the ammo secure?" He gave me a thumbs up.

"Aye, sir!" He patted the blast doors with a meaty paw.

"Anush—" I began.

"Yeah, yeah cannons locked in place," she said, interrupting me.

The tank shook as the maintenance crew of the *ESS Erebuni* locked the arresting rocket system in place. Infantry would find themselves loaded into drop ships, but tanks weren't afforded the same luxury for combat landings. Naval loadmasters slapped an array of automated rockets onto our frame. One set would fire to get us into the gravitational pull of the planet with the coordinates of our landing zone being pre-programmed into its internal guidance system. The second set of rockets would stop us from slamming into its surface at the speed of sound.

I looked down at a checklist the loadmasters had handed to me. Nobody in the regiment had done a real landing before and we hardly had the time to practice one on a nearby moon as was standard. Instead, I was given a handwritten checklist and warned if I missed a single step, we would all plummet to certain doom. Comforting.

"Sealing the tank," I said, scrolling through the neural heads-up display until I found the button.

I mentally engaged it, and felt a quick, sharp hiss of air rush through the turret as it rapidly pressurized. "Confirm your hatch is sealed."

"I'm good," Davit answered.

Suren knocked on his hatch with a fist.

"Good," he said.

I reached behind my seat and found the three-point restraint that had been installed while the *Daredevil* had been in storage. Without it, we would ping pong around inside of the tank as we blew through Barda's atmosphere at such a speed we would be reduced to a soup-like homogenate by the time we landed. I brought the straps over my shoulders and clicked them into place between my legs.

The crew was normally talkative even in the most boring times, annoyingly so if you weren't used to them. Now, we had all fallen silent. I was sure Davit was repeating countless silent prayers. Suren sat locked into his loader's seat staring into the space between his boots. I kept reading over the checklist, trying not to imagine how hot the tank would get before we would all burn to death of the thermal shielding they had installed on the outside failed as we burned through Barda's sky.

Anush had a small bag on her lap and was rummaging through it, eventually producing a small flask. She uncorked it and took a swig and handed it to me.

"One for the road?" she said, her expression still twisted from the harshness of whatever was in the flask.

"What is it?" I asked, taking a whiff.

I recoiled away in horror. It smelled like a chemistry experiment gone to hell.

"Not sure," she laughed. "Exchanged a few of the bits I won for it from the Navy dweebs. It's strong enough to take your mind off the fact we are about to be fired into space though."

"Good enough for me." I sighed and took a drink.

The substance burned my insides like I had just guzzled liquid fire. I coughed and sputtered as it assaulted its way through my guts. Then I finally handed it off to Suren, he tipped it back and didn't flinch. He licked his lips and handed it back to Anush.

The tank rocked and a few empty bottles rolled across the turret floor. I looked in my periscope and saw we were being hoisted into launch position. A giant black mechanical claw had gripped onto the loading frame that held the arresting rockets in place. The massive claw made the one-hundred-ton tank seem like a child's plaything and we were slowly floating through the loading bay of the *Erebuni*. Another tank was behind us, another claw holding it up. I could tell from the name on the cannon that it was Gor's *Eagle*.

"I think we're next." I swallowed.

Anush immediately downed the rest of her flask.

"Tank *Daredevil*," came the voice of the *Erebuni* loadmaster over the tank's comms. "Prepare for launch in five, four, three..."

My brain blanked out the rest of his counting and my stomach leaped into my throat as the launch rockets kicked on. Even through my sound-canceling headset, the roaring of the rockets was deafening. I leaned over and cradled my head in my hands, pressing the headset harder against my ears in a vain attempt to keep the burning rush out of my head. The blinding light searing through my periscopes and my implants raced to shut it out.

A momentary weightlessness came over me and my body floated above my seat, held only in place by my restraints.

"Ugh," Anush moaned. "I'm too drunk for this."

She retched.

"Don't you fucking do it!" I screamed.

But it was too late. She vomited. In a normal situation, it would have splashed onto her and her alone but in the zero-gravity of our current existence, it exited her mouth and began to float around the turret in thick, green globs. One floated near my face and instinctively I swatted it away. It splashed onto my hand, warm.

"Ah!" I screeched. "What the hell is wrong with you?"

"I get orbit sick," she burped. "I thought drinking a bit would help my nerves."

She hurled again, this time thick waves of greenish-brown vomit came out. Suren squirmed and wiggled in his restraints trying to move out of the way as it slowly floated toward him, but to no avail. As the remains of the wave floated up toward me the tank shook and the second-stage rockets kicked on.

The weightlessness rapidly transitioned to a crushing top-down pressure. It felt as if the tank itself was collapsing onto my chest. Anush's vomit, which had gathered into something resembling a strange multicolored cloud at the top of the turret, turned into a torrential downpour, splattering onto us.

I didn't have the presence of mind to be revolted as we broke through Barda's atmosphere. The restraints bit into my shoulders and groin. The dull pressure slowly built into a burning pain as the tank began to violently shake. My eyes rattled in my skull until my corps issue implant blanked out, reverting back to my unaltered vision, turning everything into a blurry mess of incomprehensible colors. I couldn't hear anything other than the sound of *Daredevil* slowly puncturing through the layers of Barda's sky. A tearing, burning sound that I couldn't compare to anything else I had ever heard before.

I began to scream. I yelled and howled until my throat went raw. I screamed and screamed as my brain went wild with the feeling of my own skeleton attempting to burst out of my skin and escape my current hell. This must have been what it felt like to break up in the atmosphere. Scattered to the wind in thousands of tiny pieces never to be seen again.

And then it was over.

The pressure came off of my chest and my vision returned to normal as the smell of burning plastic wafted into the turret. I realized I had been intermittently screaming and holding my breath for who knows how long. I took big gasping breaths, not letting the new stink flooding the tank bother me. The same couldn't be said for all of the vomit stains streaking my bodysuit and uniform.

"What is that?" I sniffed the air.

"One of the loadmasters warned me about that," Davit said. "The thermal shielding burns off as we make it through and it stinks to high hell."

"You okay, sir?" Suren asked. "I heard you screaming."

I cleared my throat and shifted uncomfortably in my seat. I didn't think anyone heard me.

"You must be mistaken. That wasn't me." Anush began to shake as she fought back laughter.

"Hey!" I spat. "What are you laughing at? You made the entire turret smell like a damn dive bar!"

"I thought I smelled puke." Davit giggled, no doubt pleased with the isolation of his driver's hole in the front of the tank, away from the mess.

My implants flickered back to life and I quickly scrolled to the map of the landing zone. On the heads up display we were represented by a yellow triangle. The rest of the task force showed up as blue triangles, all of us slowly floating through the air. Nayiri and the scout detachment had already made it to the surface and I could see them spreading out to secure where the rest of us were supposed to land.

"This is Captain Gnuni." Her voice rippled across my brain, she was broadcasting to everyone within range. *"Be advised, we have enemy forces closing in fast on our location. I recommend all landing forces to hit the ground ready to fight."*

She was greeted by a chorus of voices. I wasn't familiar with any of them, so I assumed they were from the Army.

"This corps bitch thinks she can tell me what to do?" spat one.

"I'll wait until the real scouts tell me something, stay off my SEED," complained another.

"Contact!" shouted a voice. *"This is Captain Adnuni, I can confirm multiple enemy contacts in the landing zone!"*

I took from the lack of complaints launched at Adnuni that he was an army scout.

"Davit!" I called into my headset. "Prep the engine. Landing zone is hot."

"Yes, sir."

"Suren, load high explosive." He unbuckled himself from his restraints just long enough to go to work.

Dropping the breach with one arm, he reached over and unlocked the blast doors with the other before pivoting around and heaving the man-sized shell into the open cannon. The breach slammed shut, and he locked himself back into his seat for landing.

"Anush, as soon as the tank touches the ground, unlock the turret, not a moment sooner."

"On it."

I scrolled through the tank commander's heads-up display until I found the screen for my machine gun control module. I flicked it from "safe" to "arm" and I heard power hum through the machine gun controls. Ammo automatically began to cycle from its storage rack, up through the feed chute, and into the gun mounted above my head.

Warning lights began to flash across my eyes.

"Warning. Warning," droned a strangely calm feminine voice.

The tank's network warning system haunted the dreams of every tanker. Her voice would scream at you when fuel was low, with the air intake was clogged, or even when the parking brake wasn't set correctly. The voice yelled at us so often we nicknamed it 'Bitching Betty' and we always gave her plenty to complain about.

"Landing in two minutes."

Out of my periscope, I saw something bright blink in and out of my vision.

"Did you see that?" a panicking Davit asked.

I brought my scopes around and saw whatever it was crash into the surface of Barda, which was rapidly coming up at us.

"Looks like someone's rockets failed." I shook my head.

It could have been any of us. When you drop a few thousand people out of orbit the success rate was never one-hundred percent. From the wreckage I couldn't tell if it was a dropship or a tank, I just hoped it wasn't one of ours. I made the sign of the sun over my heart.

"Put it out of your minds, we don't have time for that right now. Prepare to land!"

The rockets flared one last powerful blast and the tank crashed into the ground. My restraints grabbed onto my shoulders and slammed me back into my seat. Davit switched the turbine from idle to full power and it rumbled to life. The arresting rocket frame disengaged and fell to the ground.

"All stations, all stations." I broadcasted through the network. *"This is Daredevil. We are planet side."*

"Good!" shouted Nayiri. *"You're our first armor on site. Get over*

here!"

My SEED blipped, updating her location.

"All right, Nayiri needs us, let's roll," I said.

Suren unbuckled himself from his restraints, hand still on the cannon's arming lever and ready to go. "Davit?"

"Engine is good. Status green."

"Anush?"

"The turret isn't unlocking," she cursed. "The damned load-master must have put the lock on wrong."

She punched the release button a few more times. "Never let a fuck'n orbit dork touch your tank. Never!"

"Calm down, I'm on it." I unlocked my hatch but it wouldn't open, slowly the tank hissed as it equalized pressure.

"Uh, sir," Anush said, panic rising in her voice.

"I'm going, just give me a second." I rolled my eyes.

"No!" she screamed. "Not that you damn idiot, enemies!"

I glanced over from the hatch to my periscope and my implants flashed red, outlining hundreds of enemies in front of us. Shots rang off of the tank's armor and a rocket shrieked overhead. I dropped back into my seat, grabbing the commander's gun controls, and thumbing the arming switch.

"Can you fire the cannon with the turret locked?" I asked.

"Sure, but I can't aim the damn thing if I can't move the turret."

"Sure you can." I smiled. "Davit, I'm sending you the feed of the main cannon sight. Pivot steer us on target."

I scrolled through the heads-up display and forwarded it to him.

"You're kidding me." Anush sighed.

I pushed my face into my periscope. "Quit complaining and just get it done."

Infantry dressed in white great coats and face masks scrambled about, setting up crew-served weapons. From such a position they would be able to pour devastating fire onto our troopers as they tried to land. Davit engaged the tracks, right and left churning into the frozen ground independently, turning us in place until the cannon's sight lined up on them.

"Enemy identified!" Anush cried.

"Up!" yelled Suren, arming the cannon.

"Fire!" I ordered.

"On the way!"

The tank rocked violently as the cannon spat fire, its length recoiling back into the turret. The shell exploded amongst the enemy infantry, throwing what remained of them through the air. The surviving soldiers fanned out, continuing to pour fire onto the tank. They would have known our turret was locked for the landing and watching us having to pivot and steer toward them would have clued them into our newfound handicap. Spreading out limited our main gun's effectiveness. They were good.

"Shit," Anush said, recognizing the same thing.

I grabbed my controls again, flipped the sights to my machine gun, and squeezed the trigger. Bodies twitched and exploded as they were punctured by high-caliber bullets. I swept the crosshairs across them and the snowy white ground quickly became stained with red.

"Suren, get up top," I ordered.

"Yes, sir!" He nodded and threw his hatch open, a process made much easier by the fact the pressure had finally been equalized.

He grabbed his mounted machine gun and began spraying bullets in the same direction as I was. The loader's gun had to be fired the old-fashioned way, without optics armed only with his corps-issued implants, unlike mine, but at the moment any kind of fire going out was an improvement.

"Rocket team!" Suren screamed and my implant outlined what he saw.

Three soldiers had set up a tripod-mounted rocket system,

locking the launching pod into place. I knew that weapon. An Imperial *Pilum* tandem rocket system that would punch through our tank as if the armor was made of paper.

"Kill them!" I said.

The ground in front of them erupted as Suren tried to walk his fire onto them but he was too late. I was too slow getting my gun on target and I watched the rocket pod spit fire as the hypersonic rocket left a trail of melting snow it its wake.

"Hold on!" Davit jammed the tank into gear and we lurched back so violently my face bounced off of the periscope mount.

The *Pilum* ripped over the front of the tank, so close to the driver's hatch Davit probably felt the heat from it. The rocket team was caught in the open and reloading now and I churned them into a paste with a burst from my gun. Their packs loaded onto their backs exploded into a brilliant fireball.

A voice I didn't recognize burst across my brain. *"Daredevil!"*

I glanced at the heads-up display and saw an army tank had landed next to me. It was labeled *Wrath of Terra*. *"Get on line with me, let's take the fight to these damn traitors!"*

A dropship had landed next to them and infantry rushed out into the frozen wasteland. They had hunkered down next to the *Wrath of Terra* seeking cover from the incoming fire.

"Roger." I nodded. *"My turret lock is stuck, we are down to secondary weapons at the moment."*

"That's fine. What can you expect from those old buckets?"

The *Solaris* model of main battle tank I was sitting in went out of use for the regular army at least thirty years before. They had moved onto the *Terra* model. The armor was mostly the same, but the cannon and various network upgrades made it feel like I was riding in a relic of another age. The corps did its best to bolt upgrades onto them as they went, like making our networks compatible with one another, but there was also so many new coats of paint you could slather over something as old as a *Solaris*.

"Davit, on line with the *Wrath*," I ordered. "Suren stay up top. Anush switch to coax and do what you can."

"Ready," I told them.

"Let's give 'em hell!" the voice roared and their tank gunned it.

Davit followed suit and the *Daredevil's* turbine screamed. The infantry behind the *Wrath of Terra* sprinted to keep up with us as we advanced. Their cannon boomed and a formation of enemy troops evaporated. I grabbed my controls and sighted in on a machine gun team that was about to open fire on the now unprotected troops behind us. They were gone with the squeeze of the trigger.

"Rocket team!" they warned.

My heads-up display blipped and outlined a target off to my right. I quickly spun my gun over and fired off several bursts until I didn't see anything moving. Empty shells rained down from Suren's hatch as he hammered through hundreds of rounds per minute at the enemy. He occasionally was forced to duck down inside as incoming fire snapped around his head.

"Warning!" Bitching Betty chirped. *"Deploying countermeasures!"*

The smoke trail from an unguided rocket sailed toward us and the tank's automatic defense system came to life, shooting the rocket out of the air. Another rocket exploded on the front of the tank, a cascade of fire washing over my sights and throwing Suren back into the turret. He landed in a crumpled pile on the floor.

"Shit!" Davit cursed.

"Are you hurt?" I asked him.

"No!" he said, coughing.

The smoke from the explosion must have leaked into his compartment.

"Felt like they just hit me in the face with a hammer and I can't see anything. I think they blew off my vision lens."

The corps, and more than a few overzealous mechanics, had done what they could to squeeze effectiveness out of the *Solaris'* battle systems. But our counter-measure array could still only handle one incoming rocket at a time. Even then, it had to be one of the more slow-moving ones. A *Pilum* would have cut right through them. It shouldn't have surprised me that these regular soldiers, traitors or no, knew how to defeat a defense system as old as ours.

"You'll be fine. Just keep going straight," I tried to reassure him. "Suren, are you okay?" He was picking himself up off of the floor of the turret and rubbing his face where a cut had opened under his eye.

"Yes, sir!" I lined up my crosshairs on another group of enemies and pulled the trigger.

Five of the six soldiers were killed within seconds but the sixth scampered away as my gun jammed. I pulled the trigger again only to hear an empty clicking noise as the mechanical firing device failed.

"I'm Jammed!" I spat, kicking the back of Anush's chair in frustration.

She shot me an angry look over her shoulder as her machine gun burned through ammo, empty shells clanging off of the floor. I reached up and punched my hatch open and was greeted by a burst of frigid air. It was so cold it burned my skin and made my eyes water. I retreated back into the turret to pull up my bodysuit's integrated hood and face mask and they immediately autoregulated the temperature to something slightly above freezing.

I reached up again and ducked as a bullet slammed into the turret right next to my face.

"Suren!" I yelled over the howling of the wind and deafening scream of our engine. "Cover me!"

He swung his gun over toward me and fired across the turret to my right. He scared them off just long enough for me to stick my head up. Looking over my gun I immediately found the problem. An incoming enemy bullet had slammed into the feed chute, deforming it to the extent that rounds weren't able to pass through it without getting caught on it. I wouldn't be able to fix it without taking it apart and beating the hell out of it with a hammer until it was flat again.

I ducked back into the turret and found my carbine, strapped to the turret wall next to my seat. I grabbed it and pulled the charging handle back. I couldn't remember the last time I had actually fired the damn thing and was hoping I would never need to. Nobody becomes a tanker to fight it out with a damn rifle.

I popped back out, flipping the carbine to automatic and began blindly firing off into the distance, sending the rebels scattering but hitting none of them. Rifle marksmanship was never a strong suit of mine. Our advance crested a small hill where we came across the enemy camp. A few dozen small tents and crates of supplies, all set up and laid out in standard Imperial Army regulations. It was crushed under our tracks as we went.

Thankfully, our charge had seemed to break them. They were running back into the distance, but to where, I had no idea. Nothing but a desolate frozen wasteland as far as I could see was in their path and we gunned them down as they ran. I dropped the magazine from my carbine and fished my hand into a bandolier that dangled just below my hatch, finding a new one. My hands were shaking so badly that it took me several attempts to line the magazine up with the well, and I slapped it into place. By then it was too late, none of the enemies were left alive. Their corpses were left dotting the distance, marking how far they would go.

CHAPTER
FIFTEEN

NAYIRI LAUGHED. "So much for them surrendering, eh?"

We were gathered with the other officers around a heat generator. Our bodysuits were doing their best at keeping the cold out, but were succeeding mostly at simply ensuring we didn't freeze to death when we were outside of our vehicles. Comfort was not the order of the day. Exposed to the cold, the inter-service rivalry faded away as we all crowded far too close to one another around the heater.

"How many do you think it was?"

I had my hood and face mask pulled up nearly to my eyes but I was still shivering from the cold. Somewhere in the Imperial chain of logistics, someone had carried a one over to the wrong place or something, and not nearly enough chemical heaters had been sent down to the surface with us. Another officer brought up the idea of starting a fire, but nobody had seen a single tree or anything else anywhere in sight to burn. The entire planet seemed to be a flat, dead expanse of nothingness.

"Two or three platoons?" Her hands were so close to the heater they were almost touching it. "They must have come to the same conclusion as we did about a landing zone. Put a small scout force out here to make contact with us when we did, send word back to Prime I'd bet."

"But anyone they stuck out here was going to die. They couldn't exactly retreat, could they?"

"Maybe they're true believers in this whole Holy See of Barda Shit." She shrugged. "Or maybe their commanders suck."

"I know which one I have my money on."

I was trying to tear open the mylar package of my FSSR but my gloved hands were having a hard time gripping it. After a few attempts, I gave up. Speaking of bad commanders, Colonel Boguni appeared amongst a crowd of other officers, all corpsmen. He was wearing a great coat over his bodysuit and a wool hat that made his head look three times larger than normal.

"Gnuni, get your troop over here," he said, his words muffled by his mask.

I groaned, not wanting to leave the heater, but I managed to pull myself away.

Boguni led us back to the command area. Carriers and transport vehicles had been arrayed in a circle to give them some level of protection in case the rebels wanted to come back. One of the carriers looked like it had been modified, instead of a turret where a weapon would be mounted, an extension had been slapped into place. It had the end result of making the vehicle look like it was pregnant.

The back doors were open the inside had been transformed into a command center. Membrane screens lined the walls and a holo-table was bolted to the center of it. A dozen soldiers were hardwired into the network, cables going from the transmitters to the base of their necks. Their eyes rolled into the backs of their heads as they processed thousands of messages and requests.

Boguni walked over to a machine that was slowly churning out paper notifications and tore one off, handing it to me. I took the paper and read it to myself.

Senior Sergeant Titizian, Gor.
Corporal Hovhannisyan, Alexander.
Trooper First Class Hakobyan, Tatul.
Trooper Manukian, Ani.
"What is this, sir?"

"A death notice," he scoffed. "You must have not noticed due to being too comfortable over there by the heater, but *Eagle* didn't make it."

He was rubbing his hands together in an attempt to keep himself warm. The task force had landed in a scattered pattern over several hundred miles and there were at least three other camps like the one we were in here. I had assumed he had fell in with one of the other command groups. Did this mean...

"Don't blame yourself." Boguni sighed. "The Navy's loadmasters weren't too experienced when it came to using the tank arresting system and a lot of them were attached incorrectly. Some of the damn things snapped off in orbit, those crews were lucky though. Rescue teams were able to go out and bring them back in. In *Eagle's* case, the thermal shielding failed as it broke through the atmosphere. Cooked like a chicken in an oven before they crashed."

He whistled.

I felt a chill run down my spine. I had assumed Gor was alive and well. Sitting around a heater like I was, maybe a little bit angry that he couldn't constantly be staring over my shoulder like the mother hen that he was. Instead, he died in the worst way imaginable. He didn't even have the privilege of dying on the battlefield. He and his crew burned to death, miles above the surface of this Goddess-forsaken planet.

I made the sign of the sun over my heart and said a silent prayer. I wasn't religious. I wasn't even sure if I believed the things old Bishop Levon told me when I was growing up. I just knew I really wanted to in the moment.

"Unfortunately." Boguni's voice pulled me away from myself, if only for a moment. "Due to the losses in our armored component, we are going to be folding a few of the units together. So, Captain Gnuni, you'll be getting the three carriers from Charlie Troop. Their commander went the way of poor Gor, so now they're yours."

"Understood, sir." Nayiri jotted notes down on a small device. "Will we be getting any replacement tanks, sir?"

The troop had been reduced to only two tanks, Gor and I, due to many of the other old *Solaris* tanks breaking down to the point even corps mechanics couldn't keep them running. We had been waiting for replacement parts for months before the field marshal came through and snapped us up for his task force.

"Normally, we would be able to fix the *Eagle* and just train a new crew, but as you can imagine... that is impossible in this case. When I asked the Army commanders, they weren't exactly forthcoming with replacements, but we did get a volunteer." He checked his device. "A Lieutenant Arshuni and the *Wrath of Terra*."

"A regular officer volunteered to work with us?" Nayiri raised an eyebrow. "Since when?"

"I think Haduni can fill you in with that little detail, Captain." He left that to hang in the air, turning toward one of the holo-tables.

He typed a few things into it and a map appeared. I wasn't sure why that was really needed as it seemed like the entire planet looked the exactly same from what I saw.

"So, as you know our drop went to hell in a handbasket. Field Marshal Tigranes wants us to reorganize our forces so we can continue our advance." He had a few lines and circle on the map that meant nothing to me. "In order to do that successfully, we need to push out units to insure these rebels don't try to hit us while we are split up."

He zoomed into a small ridgeline, it was the first terrain

feature I had seen so far. "Captain Gnuni, you're to take your troop to this point. The elevation will give your tanks a good vantage point. Once you have that set up have Arshuni command the vehicles and take your scouts out in this direction."

He drew another line going toward Barda Prime. The fact that the random army officer we hadn't met was immediately put in a senior role was not lost on me.

"Yes, sir." Nayiri saluted, Boguni returned the gesture and we left the area.

She nudged me. "So."

I already knew what she was getting at.

"The Arshuni thing, right?" I sighed. "Technically, we are related. Probably distant cousins somehow."

"The sister thing, huh?" She remembered a story I had told her years before. "Sorry to hear about that."

"It's been years, I'm over it." I lied. "On the bright side, we ended up next to them during planetfall. Their crew is solid."

"And—" She stopped for a moment, struggling with words all of a sudden. "I'm sorry about Gor. I know you two were close."

"Thanks. They were a good crew." I bit my lip under my mask. "How did your people fair?"

"We had a few wounded. The worse off was one of the new recruits. The idiot didn't buckle their restraints correctly and bounced around inside of the drop ship like a ping pong ball. He didn't die, but he probably wishes he had."

As we got closer to our troop's area the sound of banging metal got louder and louder. Whether it be from bad luck or some other reason, our vehicles had gotten hit hard during the drop and ever since troopers had been hard at work trying to fix them. Many had been damaged in some way or another either from enemy fire or free-falling several dozen feet due to faulty arresting systems. If it wasn't for the fact that Nayiri's mech boys rode in drop ships, separate from their carriers, dozens of them probably would have been dead on impact.

Anush and Suren had my commander's gun system disassembled on the top of the turret and Suren was hammering away at the feed chute.

"Any luck?" I called up to them.

Suren shook his head in between hammer strikes.

"No good, boss." He set the hammer down. "If I keep smashing it, it'll probably snap in half."

I climbed up the side of the tank and onto the turret to examine their work. Suren had mangled the chute, not fixed it.

"Well, bad news. I need it working."

"Are we heading out?" Anush asked.

I nodded.

She pulled her face mask down and took a sip from a canteen. "That was fast."

"How's the turret?" I grabbed the canteen and took a sniff, surprisingly it was water.

I took a drink anyway.

"We got the lock off." She slapped Suren on the back. "The hack job that loadmaster did was no match for him."

"Good, well keep working on that. I really don't want to have to try to remember how to shoot a rifle again."

"I'll keep trying boss." Suren smiled, taking up the hammer again.

At the front of the tank, Davit had the driver's vision lens removed from the hatch. The lens was shattered, held together only by a layer of ballistic lamination. I sighed and rubbed my face.

"And why hasn't this been fixed yet?" Davit looked at me, clearly annoyed.

"I can't exactly fix this by hitting it with a hammer." He

frowned. "I went to the mechanic's and they said they didn't have any replacements in stock. Look, I have no idea what they are doing back there but if I was planning the invasion of an entire Goddess-damned planet I would maybe think about keeping some extra parts laying around. What do I know? I only drive the damn thing!"

I ignored his little outburst. "Were they our mechanics or army mechanics?"

It was good when troopers still complained to you. It means they think you'll listen to their problems. It was when they didn't complain to you anymore you had something to worry about.

"Who do you think?" He deflated and kicked the broken lens off of the tank. "Those regular army twats wouldn't even look at my paperwork. Just shot me down as soon as they saw me."

I heard a voice behind me. "Those what?"

I turned and saw a short, stocky man in a bodysuit cloaked in an army-issued grey great coat. His face mask was pulled up as well as his hood, but on top of that, he wore a grey peaked cap, crushed down in the style of army tank commanders. Over the heart of his jacket, I saw the symbol of the Arshuni family.

"Sir!" Davit shot to his feet, quickly saluting.

The man chuckled. "I'm only kidding."

From behind his back, he produced a small box and set it on the front of the tank. "I heard about your problem. I know how the Army can be when it comes too..."

He thought for a moment. "...Inter service relations."

Davit opened the box up and revealed a new lens.

"Thank you, sir." Davit smiled gratefully and quickly went back to work installing it.

"You must be Andranik," the man said.

I raised an eyebrow. "You've heard of me?"

In my experience that is normally not a good thing.

"Of course I have, I volunteered to work with your troop.

Heard you all were short some tanks." He held a hand out. "I am Hayk Arshuni's brother, Arthur."

I took his hand in mine and he gave it a firm shake.

"Wait," I said, a sudden realization dawning on me. "You're the commander of the *Wrath of Terra?*"

"Not often you run into family in such a place as this." He was looking over the *Daredevil.*

The generations old tank had been through so many battles in its lifetime I could never hope to know about them all. Past commanders had etched their names into the turret wall, behind the commander's seat and it was a list that went on into the hundreds.

He ran his hand over one of the thousands of small divots that had been gouged out of its armor. The deepest would eventually be filled with a kind of composite resin the mechanics brewed up, but this was the newest, left by the rocket that had taken out Davit's lens.

"I don't think I have ever seen one of these outside of a museum. How in Terra do you keep it running?" He marveled over the hodge-podge of different armor plates that had been bolted into place over the years.

The track was of different makes and models and the road-wheels were all different colors. Almost nothing of the original *Solaris* tank was left.

"Our mechanics can pull off some miracles," Davit said, rapping his knuckles on his driver's hatch.

It was a lump of roughly welded steel that had replaced the original hatch years before I had been assigned to the tank.

"Truly amazing," Arthur marveled.

Nayiri, who had remained quiet thus far, sizing up the Army officer, cleared her throat. Arthur turned and saluted her.

She seemed surprised at the sign of respect and slowly

returned the gesture. "Apologies, Captain Gnuni, I meant no disrespect."

"None taken, Lieutenant." She glanced at me. "Is your old jalopy ready to go?"

"Hey!" I called up toward the constant sound of banging. "Did you fix it yet?"

"Uh." Anush leaned over the turret. "I think so."

She gave me a shrug that did not fill me with confidence.

I sighed. "It seems like it is as ready as it is going to be."

"Good. Let's get out of here before the colonel thinks of more brilliant plans. Mount up, we leave in five."

CHAPTER
SIXTEEN

IT WAS a relief to leave our small camp. Not the least bit just so I could find myself back in the warm embrace of *Daredevil's* heated confines. When we were not on combat footing, we had been given strict orders not to waste fuel. It turned out one of the things considered wasteful was running our engine so our heater would work. Of course, this rule didn't apply to the various command vehicles which we all heard running around the clock. It seemed the definition of waste came with a sliding scale depending on rank.

Once inside the turret and the hatches closed, we were able to peel off our bodysuits for the first time since we had landed. It was simply too cold to disrobe for any reason other than quickly using the bathroom. Due to that, a layer of filth had built up as we loitered around camp and I was beginning to feel disgusting. As Davit pulled the *Daredevil* in line behind the *Wrath of Terra*, in the turret we pulled out bodysuits down to our boots and scrubbed ourselves down with a towel. I dumped the contents of a canteen onto my bare chest and let its contents drip onto the floor. The bodysuit had kept us all from freezing to death but had also acted as a body odor incubation device and it felt like I had pulled off a particularly large scab as the biosensors were pulled from my skin.

"Just like the Corps to give us an actual functioning piece of technology and it makes you smell like a bag of piss." Anush had one leg up on the breach and was doing her best to dry off. "Hey, Ando, did you get a look at any of that guy's crew? Any lookers?"

"Are you asking me if I think any of the *Wrath*'s crew are attractive?"

"Well, yeah. I'm not going to fuck any of you, am I?" She recoiled at that thought.

I laughed whipping my towel at her, she jumped back, swatting at me playfully.

"Sorry, I didn't know I was in the presence of such a catch." I struggled to try to pull my bodysuit back up. "I didn't see any, but no screwing Lieutenant Arshuni, he's family and that would just be weird."

"He's family?" she cackled. "Well, now I'm definitely going to worm my way into his sleeping bag."

"It must be nice to have family out here." Suren fought with the zipper of his bodysuit. "I wish my brother was here."

"I've never met him before. I wouldn't even say we are really family, his brother married my sister. I'm not even sure what you call that."

"So, you're not even blood-related, eh?" Anush raised an eyebrow at me, I wasn't sure if she was trying to get a rise out of me anymore or if she truly meant to bed him.

I sighed. "Just not in the tank, all right."

Thankfully, my heads-up display blipped giving me a merciful distraction from Anush. I climbed back into my chair and slid my headset on, the network connection clipping into place at the base of my skull. She had sent me an image of the ridgeline we were meant to hunker down behind, which was just ahead.

"*Armor detachment,*" she broadcasted. "*Proceed forward to the designated position. The scout detachment and I will push forward to complete our mission while the weather is still clear."*

"Roger," Arthur answered. *"Don't be a stranger. You run into anything you come right back to us."*

"Don't tell me how to do my job, Lieutenant," she scolded.

She was putting on for appearances now, I was sure of it. She thought she had to play the role of the hard-ass commanding officer with an outsider around. I got the feeling that Arthur didn't care about the service rivalry enough for it to matter.

"Of course not, Ma'am," he said. *"Wouldn't dream of it, Ma'am."*

I sensed an edge of sarcasm in his voice and I knew Nayiri enough to know it had to drive her nuts. Rather than give him any more ammo for passive aggressiveness, her carriers stormed off, throwing up a cloud of icy snow as they went.

Wrath took a turn, beginning to climb up the most forgiving side of the ridgeline. Its tracks bared down on the ice, its engine directing its jet nozzles downward, and the massive tank effortlessly began to climb.

The *Daredevil* didn't have it so easy. Davit cranked the poor girl's engines as hard as he could. Her tired old engine screamed and cried and struggled to make it up the same slope.

"You all okay back there?" Arthur snickered.

The *Wrath* had easily pulled ahead of us and was out of sight, at the top of the ridge.

"Don't count the old girl out," I countered, unconvinced.

"Uh, Davit." I switched to internal comms. "Are we going to make it?"

"She can sense your doubt," he said, the engine dropping into another gear and the tank rocked with a loud clank.

I decided I wasn't going to get into it with him about the idea that my thoughts could influence the functioning of the *Daredevil's* engine. I was starting to get worried that left alone to his own devices in his driver's compartment his deep devotion to the church had somehow begun to turn into a cult based around our tank. Anush's concerned backward glance at me told me she was starting to think the same thing.

"Right. Just get us up the hill."

After a few more minutes of struggling, we finally crested the incline, finding the *Wrath* parked comfortably behind the ridge. We pulled in alongside them, our engine mercifully winding down before it caught on fire or Davit accused me of making it any angrier. I sighed and slouched in my chair.

In front of us was more frozen nothingness. Outside of the ridgeline, we were parked on, everything looked like a snowy moonscape. Barda looked like something out of an adventure comic book. An untouched wasteland waiting to be tamed by human hands. Somehow that idea was more comforting than the fact that tens or hundreds of thousands of soldiers were waiting out in the distance.

Soon, even my view of the wasteland was limited as a blizzard set in. It started as a light powder and soon turned into a blinding sheet of white that covered everything. I switched my periscope to night vision and saw nothing but a static, sickly green color. I settled into my fate of staring at a featureless grey thermal sight as the snow began to pile up on the turret.

"You all know the drill," I told them, leaning over to the small ledge next to the blast doors.

I took a small water heater and clicked it on. The battered old thing required a few attempts before it hummed with power. I set a small tin on top of it, adding water from a canteen and some instant coffee.

"I'll take the first shift, Suren you're up with me. Davit and Anush get some sleep."

"Don't have to tell me twice." Anush leaned forward on her gunner's controls, folding her arms up to act as a pillow.

"Is there enough coffee for me too, boss?" asked Suren hopefully.

"Of course, get your cup." Suren fumbled around in a bag that hung from his side of the turret, finding a small tin cup and holding it out to me greedily.

I held up a finger. "Hold on, it's not done yet."

The brown, powdery mess rippled across the top of the water. The water slowly began to boil, forming amber bubbles that quickly began to rise to the top of the tin. I picked it up with a gloved hand, tamped it down, and let the mixture boil up one more time. The smell filled the turret and was thankfully strong enough to cover up the accumulated stench of its occupants.

I poured a measure into Suren's tin and he licked his lips with anticipation.

"Pass me one of those rations bars, would you?" I told him.

He searched around in a brown box labeled "FSSR menu number ten," found one, and handed it to me. Each menu box had several different variations of the FSSR ration bar. They were named things like beef stew or chili macaroni but managed to all taste exactly the same. After a few years of eating them, the slight differences between them stopped mattering.

"Can you teach me how to make coffee one day boss?" Suren took a sip and smacked his lips. "It's so good!"

"Do they not have coffee where you're from? Mars, right?" He nodded, taking another drink. "Did I ever tell you I went to Tigranes the Great prep?"

"Oh." His eyes went wide. "That's in Olympus, right? I've never been there. What's it like?"

"I used to think of it as the best time of my life." I tapped a small container of cardamom into my coffee and stirred it with a foldable spoon. "But in retrospect, it was about as annoying as you would imagine a school for nobles would be."

"People always told me it was a school for all the smart kids. I could never get in."

"Lot of good it did me, eh?" I drank from my tin and the bitter mixture burned my mouth.

I had no idea what Suren saw in the instant coffee I made, it was terrible. "We're in the same tank, aren't we?"

I dumped more cardamom into my drink to make it more palatable. Meanwhile, Suren had already finished his.

"How have you never been to Olympus before?"

"I'm a tunnel rat," he said as if that required no more explanation.

"A what?"

"I'm from the mines." He held out his tin and I filled it again. "I was born there, just like my parents were and theirs before them. At least that's what they told me. The surface folks call us tunnel rats because we live down there and we never come up. I don't think they mean it as a nice nickname."

"You *live* in the mines?"

I knew mining was a rough trade to find yourself in and it wasn't for the faint of heart. Long hours, hard work, and a terrifyingly high chance to get maimed or killed while doing it. The miners of Sassoun were a grim bunch, but at least they didn't have to actually live in the mines themselves.

"Of course. The mine bosses built little apartments and stores down there so we don't ever have to leave. Wasn't that nice of them?" I said, frowning.

I wasn't sure if Suren was blessed or cursed that he had no idea his people were being ruthlessly exploited.

"Did you like mining then?"

"Oh, it was great!" He suddenly became more excited than I had seen him since the time the regiment adopted a puppy back on Gandak. "The work was great exercise and at the end of the day, the boss gave us a big meal. Not to mention I worked with my family all day. Who wouldn't love that?"

I screwed my face up. It was like reading an employment ad from Sassoun but instead of the ad being full of lies concocted by some PR contractor hired by a Boguni firm to rope in migrant workers, an actual miner was saying it.

I pinched the bridge of my nose. Somehow in all the time I had known him we had never talked about where the hell he had come from. For corpsmen, talking about their previous life was something of a taboo topic most of the time. Suren was hardly the talkative type and normally just followed around Anush like a sad dog. They had pretty much become siblings but it was becoming clear he was virtually a stranger to me.

"How in the hell did you end up in the corps, Suren?" I laughed. "Anush has her gambling problem, Davit was a smuggler, everyone under the Goddess knows what I did. But you? I don't see you as much of an outlaw."

"An outlaw?" He shook his head. "Not me, no sir. I had a son. Miner's wages don't go very far when you have a little one to care for, so I walked over to the recruiter and enlisted."

"You have a kid?" I spat coffee and it dripped onto my uniform.

He grinned proudly. "Suren Jr."

"Unbelievable. How did I never know this before?"

"You never asked, boss."

"*Daredevil—*" A static distorted voice rippled across my brain. "*Wrath—*"

It was so badly mangled by disturbance I could hardly understand it. "*Priority traffic! Someone answer damnit!*"

It was Nayiri.

"*This is Daredevil.*" I answered "*Your traffic is coming in broken. It must be the snowstorm.*"

"*Scout detachment has made positive contact with the enemy. We mapped their positions but the bastards saw us as we tried to get away. I think we have at least a troop of enemy armor on our heels. We are coming in fast. Prepare to displace back to camp as fast as you can."*

"This is Wrath," Arthur cut in.

He was making notes on the network map and his lines and marks were slowly etching their way in front of my eyes. *"We might be able to take these traitors. They don't know we are parked up here."*

He circled our position on the map. *"They think they have you on the run back to our lines. Let them and take this path here."*

He drew a line that passed directly in front of our ridgeline. *"We'll have the high ground and the element of surprise."*

She didn't answer immediately and the silence stretched on as she undoubtedly looked for a reason not to agree with him.

"I think he's right," I chimed in.

"All right, fine," she relented. *"Get ready and don't get us killed."*

I kicked Anush's seat and she startled awake.

"Battle stations!" I said. "We have enemy armor incoming. Suren load a sabot round. Davit get read to get the hell out of here if this goes sideways."

Suren opened the blast doors and heaved a sharp-tipped sabot round into the beach, slamming it closed and taking up his position against the far wall, one hand on the arming lever.

"I can't see shit out there," Anush cursed.

"Even with all this snow, we should see something on the thermals when they get close." I had no idea if that was true, but it sounded like it should be.

"Hey, Ando. You all okay over there?" Arthur asked. *"Have you ever done this before?"*

I laughed sarcastically. My combat experience, if you could call it that, boiled down to two or three minutes of blowing away some backward aliens who were armed with spears.

"We all saw combat for the first time on Gandak. Nothing like this."

"Wait, you mean when you lit up those Krag? I didn't even think they had guns." I bit my lip.

Word of our heroic exploits had spread, apparently.

"Whatever, that doesn't matter at this point. Look, this garrison was regular army, which means they are going to have Terra models. They might be a few years out of date, but they are going to be a fair bit better than that Solaris of yours. We're going to have the drop on them, but if you don't know how to kill these things it isn't going to take long for them to figure out where we are and return the favor."

My heads-up display pinged. I opened the message he sent and saw it was the full schematics of a *Terra* model main battle tank. A giant red arrow pointed to the area that joined the hull and turret together. Their joining created an incredibly small gap and weak point in the armor. I forwarded the message to Anush.

"It's small," he admitted. *"But if you can put a sabot into there, they aren't driving away. No matter what happens, don't even think about running."*

Did he take us for cowards? My face got hot and I punched a fist on my armrest.

"The corps doesn't retreat," I spat.

"I didn't mean it like that." I could hear him laughing. *"I meant it wouldn't matter, you couldn't escape anything in that slow piece of shit."*

We'd show him. I kicked the back of Anush's chair and she jumped.

"Would you stop doing that!" she snapped at me without looking back.

The turret kept humming as she traversed it back and forth looking for targets.

"Look over that schematic," I fumed, looking into my own periscope.

I still couldn't see anything other than a snowy static. "That uptight prick Arthur called the *Daredevil* a piece of shit. We're going to prove him wrong."

"Aye, sir." Anush chuckled. "But isn't there some irony in one noble calling another noble an uptight prick?"

"Shit talk me when you prove you're better than his gunner."

"Deal."

The terrified voice of Nayiri returned to my head. *"Wrath, Daredevil we are coming in hot! Get ready!"*

Before I could respond my thermal sights flared to life and I saw the fireball of an explosion in the distance. The squat boxy shape of Nayiri's carriers could be seen, hazy and distorted through the blizzard, faintly outlined in blue, telling me they were friendly vehicles.

"Visual contact on the scout detachment," Anush said. "There should be four carriers, I only see two."

"Same." I zoomed my optics in. "Let me check."

"Scout command, I only see two carriers, can you confirm?"

"They're gone!" she shouted. *"This is all we have!"*

I took a deep breath.

"Two is all they have left." I heard her swallow hard.

I leaned forward and patted her on the shoulder. "Don't think about it, it's not important. Head in the game, Anush."

"Got it, sir."

Out of the static haze emerged the burning red outlines of the *Terra* model tanks. First one, then two, then three, then four. An entire platoon. Then more appeared. Five, six, seven, and finally eight tanks rumbled out of the blizzard. They were all racing after Nayiri's carriers who were zigging and zagging back and forth trying desperately to keep away from them. Cannon shells exploded between them and tracers from their heavy-caliber machine guns stitched through the air.

"Uh." I heard the trembling voice of Arthur. *"It's a whole other platoon!"*

"Yo, boss are you seeing this shit!" Anush exclaimed.

"Yeah! I see it!" I turned to Suren. "Lap load, Sabot!"

Lap loading was so dangerous it was stupid and according to regulation, strictly forbidden. It required a loader to hold one shell in their free hand or balance it on their lap, while the cannon went off. If the empty shell from the cannon bounced back and so much as touched the other one he was carrying, the heat would cause it to explode, killing everyone in the tank. It was a cost-benefit analysis. It would cut seconds off of Suren's loading time and more cannon shells downrange meant a better chance of us surviving. If he screwed up and a shell touched off, we would be dead either way.

"Steady, Arthur," I said in the calmest voice I could muster. *"It's too late to run. Not like that would matter, right?"*

He laughed nervously.

"Yeah. That's right." His voice seemed to even out, the panic melting away. *"Hold your fire until they are close to us."*

"Roger. We'll need every advantage we can get. The first shot is yours, Wrath."

"Oh, so generous of you."

"No need to be stingy," I offered. *"There is plenty to go around."*

My optics flared with a brilliant explosion. One of the carriers detonated, cartwheeling end over end, spraying burning fuel. When it came to rest it blew up again, its ammunition cooking off.

The last carrier, trailing smoke from several near misses, its armor dented and pockmarked, tore by us going as fast as it could. The tanks chased after it, so distracted by the lone carrier they didn't see us looming in the distance.

"Target identified," Anush called, red numbers telling me how far away the target was jumped up in my eyes as she locked onto one of the enemy tanks with the laser rangefinder.

"Suren, arm the gun. Anush hold your fire until *Wrath* fires." Suren, balancing a shell in the crook of his arm, leaned forward and lifted the lever up.

I saw Anush thumb up the trigger safety of the cannon, her finger hovering just above the red button that would set it off.

To our left, the *Wrath's* gun boomed and the leading tank in the enemy column erupted into a ball of flames. Its turret flew through the air, cannon snapping off like the twig of a tree in a storm. I marveled at the burning, smoking, hulk as it tumbled back down until our own cannon fired.

The *Daredevil* rocked on its back sprocket. The shell slammed into the second tank in the column and bounced off, hitting just a few inches too high, its angled armor sending the sabot ricocheting into the sky. It made a strange, otherworldly clanging noise and it went.

"You were high!" I yelled, watching the rebel tanks halt in their tracks, looking for their attackers.

Wrath fired again, this time smacking the front of one of their turrets. Smoke rose from their target but it didn't die. Suren flipped the lap-loaded shell into the crooks of his arm and slammed it home. The breach closed and he grabbed another.

"Same target! Fire!"

"On the way!" Anush squeezed the triggers and the cannon belched fire again.

The shot crashed into the gun mantle of her target. The cannon dropped, smoke rising from its barrel. Then, the hatches of the turret blew off, fire and smoke spouting out of them.

"I think that's their ammo cooking off!" I cheered.

The shriek of an incoming shell snapped me out of my momentary glee. I heard something break overhead.

"*Warning!*" chimed Bitching Betty. "*Commander's gun platform inoperative.*" "Again?" I moaned. "Anush, hit the fucker who has a bead on us the next one won't miss!"

Her sight quickly spun to the next tank. Its barrel glowed red hot in my thermals and it was looking right at us.

"On the way!" The second she called out her fire command the rebel tank fired as well.

The tank shook violently and I saw stars. The sound of what seemed like metal being ripped apart assaulted my ears. Warning lights clouded my vision on my heads-up display as the *Daredevil*'s computers tried calculating all of the damage we had just received.

"Davit, update!"

"Looks like it bounced off," he responded.

I assumed whatever hit us, hit the turret somewhere. That would explain why my head felt like it had been crushed with a sledgehammer while Davit seemed as calm as he always was.

"According to Betty, everything is still operational." I tried to focus my vision enough to register things through the periscope and saw the tank that had hit us had gone up in flames.

Another shell exploded against the ridgeline in front of us showering the *Daredevil* with ice and snow that sounded like small arms fire.

The *Wrath* fired again, shredding the tracks of a rebel tank that was trying to reverse and put some distance in between us. The track fell apart as they went, leaving them helpless and spinning uselessly on the ice.

"Target the crippled one!" I ordered.

"On it!" answered.

The cannon bucked again, sending another sabot flying through the air. I watched it slam into the area just below the turret and punch through the armor like it wasn't even there, fire and smoke spurted out of the wound. A few seconds later, smoke began to roll out of the cannon and their blast doors failed, blowing their hatches open and venting fire into the sky.

The surviving and still functioning rebel tanks began to retreat. Several crewmen abandoned a wounded tank and began running after their comrades. A burst of machine gun fire from *Wrath* put them down before they got very far.

"Don't let them get away," I told Anush. "Keep hitting them."

"Roger." She locked onto the closest one.

It had already been hit at least once and its engine was coughing out far too much smoke. The cannon recoiled again. The sabot cut through the air and punched through the stricken tank's driver's compartment, throwing its hatch off in a violent pulse of flame. The driver had to have been killed instantly. The *Wrath* finished it off, its shot crashing through its turret ring and blowing it apart.

"*We have them on the back foot!*" hooted Arthur. "*We should go after them!*"

"*No!*" Nayiri scolded. "*That is not our mission, Lieutenant. We need to break contact while we can and get back to the camp. There is a lot more where those tanks came from and now, they know where we are. Your little trick won't work twice.*"

As much as I wanted to charge forward and kill the last two rebel tanks, she was right. We got lucky and playing that same card twice would end very badly for us.

"*Put out some thermal clouds and let's get the hell out of here.*"

"Suren, load thermal disruption." He didn't seem to hear me so I said it again, this time much louder, yelling at him.

The loader sighed and awkwardly put the shell he was holding back into the blast doors. He then grabbed a new one before loading it into the breach and arming it. Anush fired and a huge cloud of thermal smoke detonated in the air in front of us. It glowed white-hot and would obscure our thermal signature should anyone come looking for us while we were withdrawing.

"*Fine,*" Arthur conceded.

He fired a disruption shell as well and we began our slow withdrawal from the ridgeline the once empty expanse that lay in front of us having been turned into a graveyard and scrapheap in a matter of minutes.

CHAPTER
SEVENTEEN

"GOOD GODDESS," whistled a mechanic.

He was standing on the front slope of the *Daredevil* looking at the damage done to the loader's side of the turret. The glancing blow from the rebel tank shell had gouged a deep, ragged streak going down the length of it.

"How did getting hit with that feel?"

I frowned. "How do you think?"

Suren, who was closer to the impact was looking off into the distance with a blank look on his face. He hadn't been able to hear virtually anything since. If it hurt as much as it did where I was, it must have felt like he was going to die when the rebel sabot smashed into the armor only a few feet from his head. The mechanic looked at Suren with a look of concern on his face.

"Is your loader okay?"

"Yeah, he's always kind of like that. So, can you fix it?"

"Well." The mechanic took another look up and down the *Daredevil.* "We don't have any spare parts for the commander's gun platform, so that one is a loss. I can put in an order for it, but by the time it goes through the damn war will probably be over. Your armor was compromised there, though."

He pointed to the wound that ran the length of the turret. "That is way more important and luckily for you, we can fix it. Another hit to the side like this and even a bargain bin rocket would've punched through it like your old girl was made of cardboard."

I nodded. "Thanks."

My real thanks needed to go to Arthur. If he wasn't attached to our troop the chance an army mechanic would have given one single fuck about the armor on our tank was near zero. Unfortunately, even his connections wouldn't get me a new weapon's platform. I had a feeling I was going to end up using my carbine again before all of this was over.

Anush was busy passing up the empty shells that had piled up on the turret floor. Suren grabbed them from her and he tossed them off of the tank. Davit was walking around the outside checking the track and roadwheels for any damage. He occasionally stopped to pump more grease into the track system to make sure its tension was correct.

That is when I saw Nayiri. She was sitting on the back ramp of her carrier, the only surviving carrier, staring off into the distance, a small graveyard of cigarette butts had formed between her feet. Somehow, I had almost forgotten. Amongst the tank crews the mission had been something of a miraculous success. For the mech boys, it had been a massacre.

"Hey, Anush!" She peeked up from the turret. "Make sure ammo and fuel gets replaced."

I looked at Suren one more time, his eyes were cloudy and distant. "And take him to see the medic, would you?"

"Aye, sir."

I walked over to Nayiri and sat down on the ramp next to her.

"I told the colonel about what happened," she said unprompted. "I walked into his office and told that bastard I had lost nearly all of my troopers. Told him right to his face. I told him that I had found the rebel lines and gotten over confident. I ignored warnings that they might see us. I got too close..."

Her voice dropped to nearly that of a whisper. "You know what he did?"

She didn't wait for me to answer. She reached into her pocket and tossed a small medal onto the ramp in front of her.

"He gave me a fucking award." She laughed derisively. "I almost killed everyone under my command, and the only thing he cared about was the fact that I found the rebel lines. We could have all died for all he cared."

"I think when you get promoted to a staff position, they scoop out what remains of your humanity and replace it with spreadsheets and material inventories," I said, offering her another cigarette.

"He just ignored the deaths of so many of his troopers. Did they even matter to him?" she asked. "I knew every single one of them. They had families and friends. They had memories, hopes, and dreams. Now? They are a stain on some burning piece of metal out there on the plains. Ando, I did that. I killed them all because I'm a terrible commander."

I put a hand on her shoulder. I wasn't sure what I was supposed to do in a situation like this. It was normally her talking me down from an emotional cliff, not the other way around.

A voice came from behind us. "Ma'am."

Arthur was walking toward us, his hands clasped behind his back. "Is this a bad time?"

Nayiri quickly wiped away her tears with a sleeve and sniffed hard.

"No, what can I do for you, Lieutenant Arshuni?"

"I came to offer you my condolences about the loss of your men."

"Thank you," she said, her voice cold but slowly warming. "You've seen combat before this, have you ever lost anyone?"

"Yes." He cast his eyes downward. "I lost my first crew. A particularly nefarious kind of land mine punched right through my tank. I was the only survivor."

He pulled up the sleeve of his jacket and bodysuit to reveal a prosthetic arm, the metallic hand covered in a glove. "I left a piece of me behind."

"I had no idea, Arthur. I'm sorry," I said.

"With all of the battlefields and all of the wars of the Empire, I would hardly expect you to know about it." He sat down alongside us. "It was two years, six months, and... thirteen days ago. Hardly a day doesn't go by where I don't remember them. You're probably telling yourself you're a bad commander or you made a mistake. That you could have done something better. Even the best commanders will eventually bury their soldiers. It is just a fact of this horrid business we find ourselves in. What separates you from a bad commander is that this hurts. The second you stop feeling that knife if your heart every time one of your men goes into harm's way, is the second you become one of them."

He pointed in the direction of the command area. "And you all are in the Frontier Corps, if you don't care about your men, literally nobody will."

Nayiri stifled a laugh, sniffing back her tears.

"How do you deal with it? How do you go about your day always feeling like this?" Arthur reached into his great coat, producing a brown bottle.

"I find whiskey helps, personally." He handed it to her and she took a sip.

She passed me the bottle and I imbibed. After a few moments of silence, she took a deep breath.

"I'm glad neither of you believe that I'm a bad commander, otherwise it would make this next part a lot harder." My SEED blipped with a message from her.

When I opened it, a large map popped up in front of my

eyes. It was the result of her scouting mission. A several-mile-long rebel defensive line punctuated with hundreds of unit designations that must have totaled tens of thousands of soldiers.

"Because we are going back in."

"I think we gave these guys too much credit." Arthur took another drink. "Lining themselves out in the open like that just means the Navy will churn them into paste from orbit. It's like a fire controlman's wet dream."

"I thought that too." Nayiri sighed and sent us another message.

It was some in-depth organizational chart of the Imperial navy that I had no intention of reading. "A sectional task force doesn't bring any orbital bombardment craft with it."

She must have seen the dumb look on my face because she said "We are *in* a sectional task force. The type of thing slapped together with whatever the task force command can find in a specific sector to handle problems that might pop up in that sector. In his infinite wisdom, the field marshal only brought surface-level bombers to the task force. That means no matter what they and the artillery do, we are going to have to go in to finish the job."

"That explains why the regulars are fighting side by side with the corps, no offense," Arthur said.

"The feeling is mutual, I assure you." She glared at me. "I have a feeling Tigranes could have requested assets from other sectors but the rebellion wasn't deemed important enough to warrant it. Or he thought whatever was happening on the surface of Barda required an immediate response. Which, from what we've seen, doesn't make a lot of sense to me."

"So, we don't have the most powerful weapon that the Imperial Military has, outside of just glassing the entire planet with a neutrino bomb. Does Tigranes want us to just charge into the line without any kind of fire support? What do we have?" I took another drink from Arthur's bottle.

If he noticed me draining his liquor he didn't let on. The ground suddenly shook and a deafening thunderclap assaulted my senses. Then another and another. Soon, a steady drumbeat of crashes sounded throughout the camp area.

She nodded at the sky. "Artillery."

Dozens of blasts ripped through the air followed by the high-pitched shrieking of rockets and missiles that sounded like distorted, dying organ music. "Lots of artillery."

THE DRUMMING OF artillery fire continued as I made my way back to the *Daredevil*. Troopers and soldiers were swarming over their vehicles doing last second checks, or failing that, cleaning their rifles one more time. In the rush of activity and din of distant combat, nobody seemed to be noticing how cold it was.

The *Daredevil* and *Wrath of Terra* were parked alongside one another. The giant divot in the *Daredevil's* turret had been repaired with the quality that could be expected from a mechanic who only halfway cared about their job. A thick plate had been welded over the battle scar. Even the welds looked lazy. The plate was a dull tan, adding yet another color to the veritable rainbow of military-related colors the *Daredevil* was slowly turning into.

In between the tanks, the two crews were facing one another. Suren and Davit were seated on the front slope of our tank, their legs kicking in the air as Anush seemed to be in an argument with a member of their crew. The rest of the *Wrath's* crew looked to be staying out of the verbing sparring as well.

Arthur and I approached and I was surprised to hear that there was no real argument. Not in the traditional sense and certainly not in the way Anush generally had that led to someone getting knifed or Suren caving in another man's face. Instead, Anush, a smile on her face and her arms folded across her chest was seeming to be having a great time.

"That tank of yours is a hundred years newer than mine and I still outshot you. Does that hurt your feelings? Knowing you got outdone by a corpsman riding a rusted shit bucket?" she gloated.

"You didn't beat me," countered the soldier.

Sergeant's chevrons on his sleeve told me he was probably the *Wrath*'s gunner.

He looked to be the same age as Anush but had the build of a Terran. "We both killed two tanks, and we split the fifth. That means we tied!"

"Tied my ass," Anush said. "You blew its tracks off, last time I checked that hardly counts as shit. I put a sabot in its face and killed it. That kill is all mine. You can have the assist though if you want it."

"Whoa, whoa," I said, my hands up. "What's going on here?"

The crew of the *Wrath* quickly snapped to attention and saluted Arthur and me. My crew didn't budge.

"Oh nothing, I'm just rubbing it in these regular's faces that they lost to us is all," Anush was relishing in this, I could tell.

"That's all well and good. But I thought I heard you call *Daredevil* a rusted shit bucket. Never insult our big, fat baby ever again." I ordered, only half-seriously.

I knew how old my *Solaris* model was and I didn't care. *Daredevil* was my tank and as long as she was, it was the best tank in the entire Imperial military.

"And besides." Arthur slapped me on the back playfully. "Piotr is right. We tied."

"Oh, fat fucking chance," I shot back. "I got five hundred bits that the next time we ride out, we beat your ass again."

"I'll triple that," Davit said.

"You're on," Arthur agreed. Piotr, the *Wrath*'s gunner held a hand out to Anush and she gripped it, wincing with effort as she tried her hardest to crush his hand in hers.

"Don't bet more than you have, Arshuni," I joked. "I'll take that fancy metal arm in payment if I have to."

"Shit." Arthur pulled himself up onto his tank. "It's still worth more than that museum piece you call a tank."

I was about to retort, probably with something derogatory about his mother, when I was overcome by a blinding pain.

It started at the base of my skull and hit like someone was wailing on me with a baseball bat. I collapsed to the ground, curling into a ball as the pain morphed into a searing, horrible, hot pain. From where it started the fire crept across my head, finally burning its way into my eyes. My implants flashed and flickered before going out entirely.

My nerves twitched and my muscles retracted against my will. As I writhed around on the ground an image popped floated in front of my eyes. It was an old man, hunched with age and propped up with a cane. He wore the spotless white vestments of the church. His hands were held out on either side of him like he was giving a sermon. Like he was welcoming me.

"*Children of the Goddess.*" His voice sounded distorted, like it was being piped through a set of speakers whose wires have shorted. "*Why do you take up arms against us? We are not your enemies. It was not the Holy See of Barda that trapped you in a caste system, struggling to get by. Selling your souls and your bodies for a pittance. It was not the Holy See of Barda that made the profession of arms the only way for you to escape your sinful past. The uniforms you wear and the corrupt nobles you obey were not ordained by the Goddess. Instead, the Holy See of Terra has empowered these heretics through a culture of decadence, depravity, and degeneration that grew so powerful that the word of the Goddess could no longer be heard above the cumulative volume of their sin. This sin, children, this sin must be washed away and the light of the Goddess must shine through the Empire once more.*"

His hologram struggled to stay in focus, constantly blurring in front of my face like it was fighting just to remain lodged in my brain. "*Oh, children of the Goddess, I know you are full of fear right now. But please, fear not. Your sins are not your own doing and you have been led astray by these charlatans wearing crowns and robes. The Goddess tells us any sin can be absolved if you ask for forgiveness. Please, children, I beg of you, lay your weapons down and come to me so I can receive your confessions. All will be forgiven!*"

The holograms flickered and faded, his voice growing more distant by the second.

He managed to say, "*Those that reject the Goddess will be burned by the light of her purity and justice,*" then he vanished entirely.

My implants rebooted and the pain receded until it was gone. I, and everyone around me, slowly pushed ourselves up from the ground, terror and confusion plastered across our faces.

CHAPTER
NINETEEN

THE SECURITY SERVICES task force representative called all officers to her vehicle in the aftermath of the surprise sermon we had received through our implants. She told us all that the rebel's Neural Warfare detachment had hijacked our SEEDs and ocular implants to transmit a prerecorded message by Grigori to everyone on Barda. They had even heard rumors that the signal was so strong it reached naval personnel in orbit. The neural warfare detachment operatives closed the link as soon as they could, and we were promised that it would never happen again.

However, the damage had been done. The impact of Grigori's transmission was felt immediately across the entire task force.

Every Frontier Corps and Army unit was hit by desertions. Whether it be the devoutly religious or those who saw an out from their long-term enlistment contracts, hundreds of people fled the camp in the middle of the night. Two of Nayiri's scouts vanished with a logistics truck and all of their weapons.

Sitting in my commander's seat, unable to sleep and watching the frozen expanse in front of me, I was only worried about Davit. Suren wouldn't abandon his kid, and the Goddess knows what the security services would do to the family of a traitor. I had a feeling even Suren understood that. Anush had no reason to stay and wasn't particularly religious but I couldn't see her running off.

Davit never missed a church service and followed the tenants of the Book of the Goddess more thoroughly than any actual member of the clergy I had ever met. That is, of course, if you don't count the gambling and whoring. Compared to old Levon back home, Davit was practically a saint.

"You're awake, aren't you?" Davit asked from his driver's position.

Due to the number of desertions, the colonel had ordered more of us to stand to watch at night. As the artillery still drummed behind us, we were to watch the wasteland for anyone who might try to take off. We all rotated through for several hours at a time so the others could sleep. It was Davit's shift, but I didn't want to take my eye off of him. Part of me was worried I wouldn't be able to replace him. The bigger part of me was worried about what the colonel would do to me if one of my troopers did a runner.

"What gave it away?"

"I just had a feeling," he said. "Do you really think I'm going to run off into the night?"

"Or just fire up the tank and drive all of us over there. I'd be lying to you if I said the thought didn't cross my mind," I admitted.

"You think me disloyal?" It sounded like I had hurt his feelings.

I sighed. "It's not that, Davit."

"Then what? The church?" He laughed. "I know you're not religious, most of the nobles aren't, even though the church seems to dote on you all more than anyone else. For you, the church was just a body to forward your political power."

I wanted to object to that, but then I remembered the rumors about the vast quantities of bribes my father had paid Levon. The lower classes were much more pliable to change that actively went against their own self-interest if they believed whatever the duke was doing had the blessings of the church, or more likely, the blessing of a local clergyman they trusted who also happened to be very corrupt.

"I don't care about the church, or the All Catholicos, sir. That isn't what faith is. Men are fallible. Their institutions are as fallible as they are, the Goddess tells us this. The Goddess is above men, above our earthly problems and concerns. She cannot be corrupted by a church run by perverts and gangsters. That is what I have faith in. This, Grigori..."

His voice dripped with venom. "Is no different from all of the others. A disgusting heretic using the church as a pathway to political gain."

I shifted uncomfortably in my seat, suddenly feeling guilty that I ever doubted him. "Are you religious, sir?"

"Me? I was baptized, sure. And I went to all of the ceremonies and rituals you probably expect nobles to go to. But I wouldn't say I'm a believer."

"Thankfully, sir, it doesn't matter if you believe in the Goddess or not. She believes in you and as long as the sun continues to burn her light will bless all of humanity."

"And the rebels?" I asked. "Does she bless them?"

"Of course," he answered without hesitation. "She blesses the sinners and the saints equally, sir."

"So, don't you feel bad about killing them then?"

"I haven't killed anyone, sir. The Goddess says that killing one man is just like killing all men. Me? I just drive the tank. That is a burden for you to handle, though I will hear your confession if you want me to, sir."

"No, I don't think that'll be needed, Davit. Thank you. Now that I know you're not going to running off on me, I'm going to get some sleep."

"You do that, sir."

As my eyes began to close, I heard the faint sound of distant machine gun fire. A short, quick burst that sounded like it came from somewhere on the western side of the line. Neither Suren nor Anush stirred, fast asleep.

"All watch stations, this is Reaper Six-Seven." It was the call sign of one of the regular army infantry companies. *"That was us, we caught another one of those green jacketed traitors making a run for it."*

"Good job!" called another unit. *"We should do that with the rest of them, just to be safe."*

"Ha ha!" laughed a third voice. *"Do the whole Empire a favor."*

"On second thought," Davit said. "Making a run for it might be worth it if it means I get to take a couple of shots at these regulars."

CHAPTER
TWENTY

AS THE SUN broke above the horizon we found no relief. Whether the sun was up or down, the temperature never raised above freezing. It was made worse by the fact that once again the colonel had called us out of the warmth of our tanks and carriers and into another meeting outside of the command vehicles. I would complain, but the infantry commanders standing alongside me had nothing to take shelter in. They had been left in the cold to swaddle themselves in anything they could find, hiding from the constant wind and blizzards inside a hole that they had managed to chip out of the frozen ground.

"Ladies and gentlemen, the time of victory is near!" Colonel Boguni cheered, a holo-map floating behind him. "Field Marshal Tigranes has informed us that at noon today our attack against their line will begin."

He turned to his holo-map, which began displaying our units being directly by big blue arrows toward sections of the rebel line. Virtually all of the Frontier Corps units were in the front, with the regulars behind us. Again.

"The field marshal has blessed the Corps by allowing us to become the tip of the spear!"

After the colonel finished saying that I noticed his personal vehicle wasn't part of the attack. Its small blue square remained back at base camp.

"We will burst through the traitor's lines, while the regular forces exploit that opening, charge through and envelop the enemy."

"Ya know." Arthur leaned in close to me, whispering. "In history, there was something called a *Forlorn Hope*. A bunch of officers ran headlong into the strongpoint of the enemy in order to create an opening for the people behind them, either for glory or promotion. This could be your way to finally make captain, or maybe even to transfer to the regulars."

"This *Forlorn Hope*. What exactly was their survival rate?"

He stifled a laugh with his hand. "Oh, damn near zero."

Nayiri interrupted his laughter. "Arthur."

I expected her to chide him for talking during the meeting but then I noticed she used his first name. Maybe she was beginning to warm up to him, or not hate him for being a regular at the very least.

"What's your take on this?"

"This plan?" He pursed his lips. "The field marshal is using the Corps as a sacrifice to make the regular commanders happy. A lot of them have been pissy about having to work with you guys ever since we landed. Now, you'll take the brunt of the fighting and they will reap the rewards."

"We're a meat shield." She frowned. "And I thought the field marshal used to be one of us."

"He was," Arthur pointed out. "But he is still a prince. Politics and old service loyalties don't mix."

"So much for the Corps being our home world," I said. "I guess that stipulation comes with an asterisk if you happen to be in the Tigranes family."

"Ando, everything comes with an asterisk if you're in the Tigranes family," Arthur corrected.

"At eleven thirty our artillery bombardment will be called off. We step out not five minutes later."

"Sir, will we have any air cover from the fleet?" asked one of the infantry commanders. "And what about the surface bombers? I haven't seen any of them yet."

"No." The colonel shook his head. "Something to do with atmospherics, the fire controlmen could explain it better. The amount of ice in the clouds plays hell with their engines I've been told. But, have no worries, I've been assured the previous bombing runs along with our artillery have shattered their line. Some say that there is virtually nothing left for us to attack!"

Boguni let out a hearty laugh and one or two officers followed suit, clearly faking it. The silence over the group of commanders did not fill me with confidence. It didn't seem like anyone was buying anything the colonel said other than the colonel himself.

At the next vehicle over the regular army commanders were being briefed. Rather than the dour attitude we were showing they were nothing but smiles and laughter. One of them was passing a bottle around, toasting with the others without a care in the world. Already drinking to the victory we hadn't achieved yet. I noticed Arthur watching the scene with me.

I nudged him. "You wish you were back with them?"

"Every corpsman I've talked to looks at me like they hate my guts, like talking to me is toxic or something," he said. "But, at least nobody over here is trying to arrange marriages, business deals, or settle old political scores from wherever they came from. Every single one of them is a prissy drama queen with one foot out of the door. Half of the time if you listened to their conversations, you would forget they were even in the military at all."

"Must be nice to be an Arshuni," I joked. "Never have to worry about anything."

"Technically, you're one of us now," he pointed out.

I pointed to the green field jacket I was wearing. "A lot of good it has done me."

"You know, I might be able to do something about that. After all this is over, I mean. The emperor and Vaz are very close. It wouldn't be very hard to get your transfer paperwork signed if I pushed him for it."

"Could you imagine me in the regulars?" I said dismissively. "I don't think someone who did what I did gets a transfer."

"You'll find criminal justice in the Empire is quite flexible depending on who you know, Ando. And besides, everyone hates the Boguni family."

"Does everyone understand what is expected of them?" the colonel asked.

He had been talking about some other details about the upcoming attack but I hadn't been paying attention. Nobody had any questions this time, it seemed everyone understood that no matter what they asked, nothing was going to change. The field marshal had ordered us to attack the enemy, and that was going to happen whether we had objections to the plan or not. The colonel wasn't there to adapt those plans to our concerns, he was just to pass along the message. Even that was a job he seemed hardly capable of. He was going to make general in no time.

"Then I will leave you to your last-minute preparations. Good luck, ladies and gentlemen. May the Goddess bless and keep you."

TWENTY-ONE

THE CAMP EMPTIED out rapidly as the Frontier Corps' vehicles loaded up and departed as yet another blizzard cloaked the empty wasteland. Suren sat on his loader's seat, feet kicked up on a pile of small arms ammunition that had been stored under the cannon's breach, fast asleep. Anush stared into the gunsights, slowly moving the turret around.

"I can't see shit in this," she moaned.

Even through our thermals everything in the distance was obscured. Our entire world was limited it what was in our immediate vicinity. Gazing through my commander's sight I saw the thousands of heat signatures around me. The burning heat from tank, carrier, and truck engines glowed brightly in the haze of the blinding storm. I could even make out the heads of the infantrymen seated in the backs of the uncovered trucks as they surged forward to our starting positions.

White-hot streaks cut through the air above our heads in a long arc, coming down somewhere beyond my vision. I glanced down at my watch and saw that we were witnessing the last five minutes of the bombardment.

I looked at my watch again. "All right, Davit."

It felt like the seconds had begun to slow as we got closer to go time. "Make sure you keep an eye on your left and right when we move into attack formation. I don't want to be the one caught at the head of the advance. We'll catch a *Pilum* straight to the face and that'll be the end of us."

"Yes, sir."

"Suren." He didn't budge, still fast asleep.

I climbed down from my seat, leaned over, and kicked him in the leg. He jumped awake, eyes wide.

"Are we under attack?" he blurted out, still half asleep.

"Not yet." I pointed to the blast doors. "Load a sabot and have another one ready. I have a feeling we are going to need it."

I noticed he was trying to read my lips, but still hadn't managed to understand. "Hey, Anush, what did the medic say about Suren by the way?"

"Oh yeah, I was meaning to tell you that. The medic said both of his eardrums got blown out when we took that glancing hit. They ordered some implants to be put in but they were waiting on a shipment of medical supplies from the fleet."

"So, he's deaf." I looked at the man who was grinning stupidly at us and trying to follow what we were saying by watching our mouths.

"Pretty much. He is trying to learn how to read lips, but he really sucks at it." She reached over to her bag and fished out some pieces of paper. "I was thinking about how this would work."

She held up the papers. Each had the name of a type of tank shell scrawled upon it in bad handwriting.

"Just hold up whichever one you want him to load."

"This is ridiculous. Wait, I thought he couldn't read." I dropped my face into my hands.

"I'm not entirely sure about that either, so I thought ahead." She flipped the papers over and showed a badly drawn sketch of each shell on the back. "Flash cards!"

She smiled. I sighed, grabbed her papers, showed the paper with the drawing of a sabot on it, and pointed at the breach. He nodded and went to work.

"Great." I closed my eyes. "Just great."

"*One minute.*" Nayiri's voice popped into my head. "*Stay together, no heroic shit out there.*"

"*Wouldn't think of it,*" answered Arthur.

"*Understood. How do you feel about explicitly unheroic shit,*" I asked, trying to lighten the mood.

"*I will accept nothing less or more than average soldiering. I know that will require more work than you're used to, Ando,*" she fired back.

I couldn't help but think the humor was born from nervousness.

"*Yeah, yeah.*" I smiled. "*Arthur better pay up when Anush makes his gunner look like shit.*"

"*Big words!*" Arthur challenged. "*Let's see if she can back those up for you.*"

I was about to say something when the sky lit up. The thermal sights became so bright I had to duck away from them, blinking away the stars.

"*Priority traffic, priority traffic,*" Nayiri's voice returned, now deadly serious. "*Looks like they finally let loose with their own artillery. Spread-out, hold attack formations, we are going in.*"

The ground shook under the *Daredevil* as an enemy missile slammed into the frozen ground belching fire and ice into the air right in front of us. The tank dipped into the crater it left behind as another exploded behind us.

"*Hey, Nayiri this fire is right on us!*" I yelled.

"*They probably have targeting drones overhead!*" Arthur shouted over something I couldn't hear while another missile crashed into the ground next to the *Wrath*. "*Wooo boy these are getting close.*"

"*Understood,*" Nayiri said. "*We can't do anything about the drones but we are forwarding their missile battery's location to our artillery. Just keep pushing."*

"Roger." Before I was able to transmit my message, an army carrier off to my right exploded in a bright fireball that began to spread as burning fuel was thrown from its shattered hull.

The burning shapes of men were catapulted away from the wreckage by the blast.

"Uh," Anush said. "Didn't the colonel say something about their line having been smashed by artillery?"

"Yeah." I winced as another incoming missile detonated behind us. "Why?"

"Switch to my gunner's sights," she said.

I clicked the button on my controls that allowed me to see what she was seeing. In the expanse in front of us, cutting through the blizzard and rising smoke of burning men and material, was a wall of pulsating red. Tens of thousands of rebel troops were dug in and facing us.

"Are you seeing this, Wrath?" I asked.

But he didn't have time to answer. The *Wrath* was rocked by an explosion, a plume of smoke and fire rising from their front slope. Another incoming shell flew passed our tank so fast that I had barely enough time to register it. Somewhere to my right, another shot found purchase, and an army *Terra* model caught fire.

"Status update!" Nayiri demanded.

"We're good," came the slightly groggy voice of Arthur.

It was the sound someone makes after having their bell rung and their brain was having a hard time keeping up with what they were trying to say.

"What are you waiting for?" I snapped at Anush. "Pick a target and start shooting!"

"I'd love to!" she fired back. "But we aren't in fucking range yet. Look at those thermal signatures, those are all *Terra* models, just like the ones we fought the other day. They have hundreds of meters of range on us even if we weren't hauling ass through a Goddess-damned blizzard!"

As if to punctuate her words a shell slammed into the ground in front of us, skipping off of the ground and exploding under the hull. The tank shook with the impact, but everything seemed to be fine.

"Davit, serpentine. Let's not make this easier for them than it already is."

"Yes, sir."

The tank began slowly gliding in a zig-zag pattern. It wasn't much of a defense against a tank that was better than us in every way, but it was something. The tank shook again, this time from a glancing hit to our front right. A headlight was torn off and thrown into the snow along with a mud flap that covered the front of our tracks.

"Fuck it," Anush said, wincing. "At this rate, we are going to die before we even get close enough."

She picked a target in the distance and brought the gun above it by a full meter. "On the way!"

The cannon bucked and spat out an empty shell. The smell of burnt propellent curled into my nose as I watched the sabot come crashing down onto the turret of her target, angry fire venting out of every hatch.

"Holy shit, that worked!" I cheered. "Hit 'em again!"

She slapped her control panel. "Tell that Piotr that's one for me."

Suren quickly reloaded the cannon and Anush fired again. This time she wasn't so lucky and the shell went high, flying harmlessly off into the distance.

"*Warning!*" Blared Bitching Betty. "*Deploying countermeasures!*"

The *Daredevil*'s automatic defense system jumped to life and an incoming rocket exploded in midair.

"Deploying countermeasures!" she said, again and again, then another rocket was blown up in a flash.

Anush grimaced, firing the cannon once again. "Getting kind of hairy!"

This time her shot bounced off the side of an enemy turret, cartwheeling away and exploding amongst the rebel infantry. *Daredevil* shook once more, this time more violently, and warning lights flickered in my eyes.

"Armor penetration," Betty complained.

My heart jumped into my throat.

"Son of a bitch, status update!" I demanded.

I heard Davit, coughing so hard it made him hard to understand.

"Fucking *Plium!*" he hacked. "Hit us somewhere in the front."

"Are you okay?"

"Yeah. Must have set some of the wires on fire or something, it smells like burning plastic in here."

He wheezed, I could hear the fan system kicking on in the background, venting out the smoke that was filling his driver's compartment. "And I think we have a hydraulic leak."

"I don't have a leak warning light, what makes you think that?"

"Because I'm sitting in a puddle of damn hydraulic fluid, sir," he spat. "The *Pilum* must have burst the line. Every time Anush traverses the turret it sprays more of the shit onto my feet." Anush cackled to herself as she moved the turret to her new target and fired off another shell.

"Sorry," she said, clearly not meaning it.

Something else hit *Daredevil* and smoke pulsed around the cracks of our turret hatches. It smelled like something was burning rather than being hit with an incendiary round. The only thing we had in the storage racks were our boxes of rations. The bastards had blown our food away.

I sighed, reached over and flicked on the pressurization system, venting the smoke back out.

"We're in effective range now!" she hooted. "Time to party!"

The cannon boomed and a rebel carrier exploded in a brilliant ball of flames. Thick gouts of burning fuel rained down onto their defenses and the rebel infantry ran for their lives. Their burning bodies lit up like candles in the thermal sights.

Our mood was dampened slightly as another *Pilum* flew by and cut through an army carrier. The force of the anti-tank missile blew straight through the stricken carrier, fire blew out of its troop compartment sending an atomized cloud of burning metal and flesh into the sky. Our tanks and carriers surged forward toward the rebel lines, cannons, chain guns, and machine guns chattering and blowing chunks out of their defenses. Pillboxes exploded, touching off ammo stores. Lengths of trenches collapsed, burying men alive. Air busting fragmentation shells churned groups of rebels into expanding clouds of gore that polluted the white snow around them.

A kind of exhilaration I had never felt began to build within of me. My pulse throbbed in my temples and my heart raced and my mouth went dry. I began to shake as I watched the enemy line be reduced to a back-alley butcher shop. Everywhere I looked in front of us was filled with the dead and dying. Surrounded by incalculable amounts of human misery and swaddled in undiluted killing and dying, the morality of combat melted away. It was replaced by a sense of overwhelming excitement and pleasure. Any moment they would break.

The rebels would run and try to save their own lives as they realized their hopes and dreams had been crushed by thousands of tons of Imperial armor. They would see the overwhelming force that the Empire had brought to subjugate them and see that all of their efforts were pointless. Hopeless. A grin began to spread across my face, backlit by the fires glowing on the other side of my thermal sight. Victory was about to be firmly in my hands.

A real victory. No matter what Colonel Boguni did, he would never be able to take this away from me. He would never be able to simply give credit to someone else. Even though the glory would go to the regular army, my role couldn't be ignored! With Arthur's help, I would finally be out of this green rag of a uniform and be where I always should have been! Anahit would have to forgive me when I showed back up at home wearing Imperial blue.

I saw a flash so bright my implants failure to register it fully. A blur, then a blink of light. A swirling mass of red light gathered in the distance, hovering in the sky like a miniature sun. Crackling and furious, the mass grew larger before it flashed once again. A beam of light cut through the blizzard and cleaved through our advancing line. Anything it touched vanished. Its flash melted tanks and carriers into heaps of slag and vaporized the soldiers and troopers inside.

"What in the name of the Goddess is that!" Davit screamed.

My eyes went wide as the energy weapon lashed out once again, slicing through the vehicles in front of us. I watched a platoon of *Terra* models disappear in front of my eyes, leaving nothing behind by a black scar on the frozen tundra. The network came to life with shouts of confused terror. People screamed and yelled as they ordered their vehicle to stop, reverse, and run away from the thing that was attacking them. I heard the panicked fizzle from their SEEDs as their dying brains sent out confused messages.

A wave of panic crashed over me. My eyes locked onto the pulsating mass of energy as it gathered ahead of us once again. I couldn't see where it was coming from, dozens of meters above the ground, high above the enemy lines, but my thermals registered nothing. I felt trapped in its eerie glow like a hunted animal caught in the gaze of a predator.

"Holy mother of the sun," Anush gasped.

"Sir!" she exclaimed. "Sir!"

She finally pulled me out of my own mind. I tore myself away from the nightmare in front of me as it fired again. Dozens of SEEDs went dead in seconds.

"Turn off your thermals."

I did as she said. My eyes could finally see what was in front of me, but my mind could not comprehend what it was.

Something like a tank stood in front of us, as tall as a skyscraper. It was almost humanoid in form, with weapons platforms jutting out on either side of its snow-white armored torso in place of where arms would be. A cannon with a twisted, warped-looking barrel protruded from the top of it, and heavy cables and support structures from the monster's chest kept it steady. Dark energy the color of blood gathered around the tip of the cannon's barrel, its heat sending a cloud of steam rising into the air, melting the snow for hundreds of meters around it.

Everyone who still could, returned fire, doing everything they could to kill or suppress it. But every weapon that was fired at it had its munitions reduced to nothing but a small plume of smoke. None of it got through to the machine itself. That was when I saw something shimmering in the air around its immense frame. Was that a shield or some kind of defense system? Was that mysterious light what allowed it to hide its thermal signature? More importantly, what the hell was this monstrosity?

"*Priority traffic!*" came the blood curdling scream of Nayiri. "*All units break contact! Disengage immediately! Pull back to camp!*"

"Sir, what the hell is that thing?" Davit cried.

"I don't know Davit, just get us the fuck out of here!" I ordered.

The tank shook as he mashed on the breaks, throwing the tank into reverse, and forcing the engine to put out as much power as it possibly could.

"What should I do?" Anush asked, panicking.

"Shoot!"

The cannon recoiled and the sabot was thrown toward its target. One of the most powerful anti-tank weapons ever designed by man, flying at nearly four thousand miles per hour, hit the shimmering light that danced around the machine. It was swallowed whole by the strange shield, leaving not even a scratch on the monster's armor.

"It's not doing shit!" Anush yelled back at me. "What do we do?"

"I don't know! I don't know!" I pressed my face harder into the periscope as if it would reveal a weakness in the thing. "Just keep shooting it!"

At the sight of us retreating, the rebel line came to life. They pushed out of what remained of their defenses and came charging right at us. I quickly scrawled onto a loose piece of paper a cartoonish cloud of smoke and showed it to Suren.

He nodded. "Put some smoke out!"

The cannon bucked and a cloud of white smoke exploded in the air in front of us, slowly drifting down to the ground. Missiles, rockets, and tank shells crashed all around us. The rattle of small arms fire bouncing off of our armor sounded as if we were caught in the middle of a hailstorm.

Another flash of the monster's beam weapon silenced several of the panicking voices I heard shouting at one another over the network. Vehicles crashed into one another, each just trying to get away from the rebels as fast as they could. All order was disregarded. This stopped being a withdrawal and had turned into a route.

"*I'm hit!*" screamed Nayiri. "*Something hit our engine, we have no power!*"

"*Send me your location,*" I told her.

"*No!*" she shouted. "*Get out of here!*"

"*Fuck you, send me your location damnit!*"

Nayiri was my only friend in the world and I was going to be Goddess-damned if I left her behind. She refused to tell me, I knew she would. I quickly tabbed over in my SEED heads up display until I found the carrier with her listed as its commander and forwarded its position to Davit.

"Davit, go toward that location, now!"

"Sir, we were ordered to retreat!"

"The captain took a hit and needs our help. Go now!" The tank rocked violently as he stepped on the brakes and turned it toward her location. *"Hang on tight I'm coming. Wrath are you with me?"*

"You know it, buddy," Arthur responded.

Our tanks became like two fish trying to swim upriver in the sea of fleeing vehicles. They paid us no heed as they crashed and bounced off of us as we went. No real damage was done to the other tanks or carriers but the regular trucks were left with mangled and twisted metal for their efforts. I worried for a moment until I saw that they wore army grey.

Nayiri's carrier was ahead of us stranded and on its own. Another carrier was flipped over and burning next to it with the ruined remains of dozens of vehicles just a short ways off. More victims of that thing's beam weapon. Smoke and fire poured out of the carrier's back deck, licking out of a jagged wound. Whatever had hit them would have killed them all on the spot if the person who fired it had better aim.

The track on the right side of the carrier had been broken by the blast and it laid in pieces all around her. Troopers were on the ground next to it. Some were trying to repair the track while others were firing at the oncoming enemy. One of them lay in a twisted heap, a bullet having blown out the back of their head.

"Pull up in front of her. Those idiots aren't going to be able to fix the track in time. We're going to need to tow her out." As the words left my mouth, I watched another one of her troopers crumple to the ground dead.

"Nayiri get those people back into the carrier before they all get killed, we'll get you hooked up."

"You shouldn't fucking be here!" she hissed.

"Shut up and let us save you," replied Arthur, annoyed.

Our tanks pulled in front of her burning carrier, acting as a shield and we were greeted as such. A fusillade of fire crashed into us. Every size of gun available to the rebels assaulted us as our countermeasure system fired over and over again.

"Get out there, Suren!" I ordered before realizing the flaw in my plan.

If he was deaf, he wouldn't be able to use the radio. Hell, he probably had no idea what was going on or if we were even retreating.

"Anush." I kicked the back of her chair. "You're in charge, I'll be right back."

I leaned over to Suren and smacked him on the shoulder, pointing up to his hatch and mouthing in big, slow words "cover me." He nodded and jumped up to his position.

"What the hell are you doing?" Anush asked.

I reached up and unlocked my hatch, grabbing my carbine as I climbed out.

"Something very stupid."

The bitter, cold wind battered my senses, burning my exposed skin and rapidly chilling me through the regulated bodysuit. Bullets sparked off of the top of the tank as Suren began hammering rounds into the distance. Soon, Anush joined in hosing thousands of bullets out of her coaxial machine gun. The cannon of *Wrath* fired, sending a shell screaming into the distance.

As I jumped down from the turret to the back deck, the countermeasure system fired, blowing up an incoming missile only a few dozen feet away from my head. The force of the blast slammed me into the metal grates of the deck and I could feel the warmth of the turbine engine humming under me. I scrambled across the deck and tossed myself over the edge, landing in a pile on the cold ground. I reached up to the tow hook that protruded from the rear of the tank, grabbed it, and began to sprint toward the carrier, the tow cable unspooling behind me.

The air around my head came alive with the snaps and pops of near misses. One of Nayiri's troopers rushed out from behind cover to meet me halfway but was jerked awkwardly off to the side, blood spraying from a grotesque neck wound. I took a deep breath, resigned myself to running the rest of the way to the down carrier, and forced my legs into action.

The ground in front of me rippled with fire as the attackers attempted to lead me with countless guns as I ran. They were either terrible shots or I was luckier than any man had any right being as I zigged and zagged toward Nayiri. I finally got to the front of her carrier, slapping the hook onto its tow hitch. Scrambling up the side of the carrier, I hurled myself into an open hatch, landing with a thud on the inside amongst a crowd of troopers.

"Davit, drive!" I keyed my radio and screamed.

The *Daredevil* lurched back to life, pulling the tow cable taut and slowly we were once again on our way.

"*You alive in there?*" Arthur asked.

I slowly righted myself into one of the infantry seats in the back. I noticed there were only half as many troopers in the carrier as there should have been. Their bodies must have been left behind in the snow as we ran.

"*Barely,*" I huffed.

"Nayiri!" I called out. "Are you okay?"

She lowered herself down from her commander's position and stepped into the infantry compartment.

"I told you to leave us and go," she fumed. "You could have gotten the entire platoon killed."

"But I didn't, did I?"

One of the troopers offered me water and I took it. My face had become wind burned from the blasting storm and just pulling my facemask down stung my raw skin.

"If it makes you feel any better sir," said one of the troopers sitting next to me. "We're glad you disobeyed her orders."

The compartment filled with nervous laughter before we all fell back into an eerie silence. Our eyes jumped nervously at each sound as the next one could be the one that punctured the carrier's thin armor. Slowly, the sounds of gunfire relented as we got further and further from the front line and away from the rebel advance.

AS WE GOT BACK into the area that made up our camp, all hands were on deck as we dug in to make our stand, the rebels on our heels. Tanks and carriers, even the ones that could hardly still function like Nayiri's, lined up to fight. Infantry disgorged from their vehicles to hack small fighting positions into the frozen tundra with their shovels from which they were to make their last stands.

I left Nayiri's shaken crew behind to retake my position at the command of the *Daredevil.* As I sat down Anush sighed, opened a small door that separated us from Davit, and handed him several bits.

"Did you two put bets on me dying again?"

Anush leaned back in her chair. "Maybe."

"And you bet on me dying?"

I pressed my face to the commander's periscope and saw only the empty expanse of Barda in front of us. The rebels were sure taking their time.

She shrugged. "I figured it was a safe bet."

I switched between my regular vision and thermals, but still, the rebels didn't appear on the horizon. "Sir, what do you think that thing was out there?"

"I have no idea, Anush." I sighed. "But the real question is if you have something like that and have us on the run, why not close in and finish the job? What are they waiting for?"

"You don't think we can hold it off?" Davit asked.

"Are you kidding me?" Anush dismissed. "Whatever that damn thing is, our cannon couldn't touch it. I hit it dead on with a sabot and not even a scratch! And did you see what it did to our tanks? Those *Terra* models looked like toys someone put in the damn microwave."

"Enough," I snapped.

The last thing I needed was the crew devolving into a fatalistic nosedive until they couldn't do their jobs. Anush wasn't wrong, though. I watched that strange energy field absorb all kinds of fire. It was like we were firing cap guns at it. I had never read anything about any weapon of war that could do such a thing. Other than the clatter of Suren hurling the empty shells out of his hatch, a deathly silence fell over the tank. I expected the rebels to show up any second, that giant tank monster close behind to finish us off. After several hours of waiting, it was decided they probably weren't going to attack.

The camp, once mostly quiet as everyone huddled into their vehicles for warmth, had turned into a blur of activity. The wounded were offloaded and rushed over to the medical centers where the few able to be saved would be worked on. The pile of the dead quickly began to grow outside of it. The nature of armored combat meant that most of the wounded wouldn't make it. There wasn't much hope of walking away should something penetrate the walls of your tank or carrier.

Officers gathered in a loose circle outside of the command vehicles, there were significantly fewer of us than there was last time. My eyes were locked onto something out in the distance, but

I couldn't tell what it was. The only thing I could see was the weaponized skyscraper, burning its way through our forces, unchallenged. I heard the hiss of static of the dying brains of my peers on a loop in my head. Those of us who escaped death or injury were wide-eyed and exhausted, wearing uniforms stained with blood and smoke.

Boguni appeared, his uniform clean and looking refreshed. The look on his face was one of restrained displeasure, but it was hard to tell the difference from his normal mood.

"All right men, listen up," he said, looking down at his device, not even wanting to cast an eye at the haunted remains of his officer corps. "The field marshal sends his condolences, but he expects you to have your head in the game, is that understood?"

"Game?" stammered a captain.

She looked like she had aged ten years in the last two hours.

"Did you see that thing?" Nayiri asked, her voice unsteady. "Nothing we did could even hurt it. And that cannon…"

She trailed off, probably being haunted by the same memories as I was. They were still fresh, still visceral, like an open wound. Boguni turned toward his holo table, tapping it a few times until the blue outline of the thing we fought appeared. I could hear a gasp come from someone.

"The Ministry of State Security Services has authorized the field marshal to disclose a matter of the highest level of secrecy to you all. However, it doesn't leave this vehicle, your troopers are not to know. The emperor didn't want us to secure Barda because of its resources. Barda actually doesn't have a single mine and none of the people here are miners. Its only real resource is that it's a barren wasteland so far out in the middle of nowhere that nobody would ever come poking around. It turns out this made it perfect for the location of a development and testing facility for the Ministry of Munitions. Barda Prime is full of various weapons the emperor really doesn't want falling into the hands of a mad man calling himself the All Catholicos. That thing that you ran into is just one such thing they were working on, they call it an orbital strider."

"A testing facility," Nayiri whispered into my ear. "That's why we had never even heard of any 'Barda' even though it was in our sector. They were hiding it."

"They could have warned us that we were charging into a goddamn doomsday weapon factory," I whispered back. "What the hell were they thinking?"

"So, they built this thing." Arthur raised his hand, addressing the colonel. "That means they can tell us how to kill it, right?"

"No, Lieutenant," Boguni responded, a mild annoyance showing on his face from being interrupted. "This isn't an action movie. They don't build weapons with secret weak points, that would defeat the entire purpose, wouldn't it?"

Normally, this would inspire laughter in the group, but nobody felt much in the mood for laughing at the moment.

"However, the Orbital Strider is still in its beta stages of development. It is the only one in existence and still has some problematic kinks. For instance, it consumes a vast quantity of energy for operation, more so when they are firing off its particle beam cannon as much as they were. The ministry engineers told us that they almost certainly expended its entire battery and reserve, meaning it will take them an entire day to recharge back at the main facility. The particle weaponry is still in its beginning stages of development, meaning the batteries it uses to fire need to be completely removed in order for them to be charged, which takes some time. The developers haven't quite figured out a way to fix that little flaw, but it gives us something of an opening. Our only opening. In order for this to work, we cannot delay."

We glanced at one another. Nobody dared to ask what that meant, but we all had a good idea. I kept replaying the scene of the

Strider's beam cannon searing a tank into a babbling puddle in my mind.

"If it wasn't for this infernal machine, we would have cut through their line and stormed directly into Barda Prime. The field marshal believes that if we launch another attack before the Strider is recharged, we will be able to do just that and capture its facilities so it cannot be used against us again. Without that trick to play, the rebellion will surely fail. They think their little surprise has us beaten, they think they have us on the ropes, they will never see a counter punch coming their way!"

This was meant to be a rousing line, but nobody reacted. Even the colonel's most ardent sycophants had finally been silenced after watching their friends burn alive.

Boguni was clearly not pleased with our failure to cheer for his almost certainly rehearsed boxing analogy. He cleared his throat, clasped his hands behind his back, and turned to his holo table. The strider vanished and was replaced with a map. The rebel line flickered into view once again and big blue arrows showed our route of attack. The only friendly units taking part in this attack were labeled "FC" for Frontier Corps.

"You will drive into their line here. You're not to stop for anything. Consider the rebel line merely an obstacle this time around rather than the goal."

That was one hell of an obstacle I thought to myself.

"Instead, you are to penetrate and drive straight toward Barda Prime, here." He motioned to a small city structure on the map. "Once in the settlement, you're only goal is the Ministry of Munitions facility. Armor, you secure the outside, infantry and scouts will breach the facility itself and eliminate any resistance that you find inside. If that fails, the field marshal has given you explicit orders to destroy the entire facility, nothing escapes from that place, not even you, should the need arise. The rebels cannot be allowed to control the facility or its contents. Is that understood?"

"Sir," Nayiri spoke up. "If this mission is so important, why are there no regular army soldiers helping us?"

"In the event that our mission fails, the Army will secure the Empire's foothold on Barda to insure this rebellion doesn't spread."

"Sounds like to me the Army decided this was a suicide mission and left it to the corps." Arthur pointed out.

He was almost certainly correct and we all knew it. There was nothing Boguni could do to harm Arthur's career. Colonel or not, he was still a corps officer to his staff officer peers and his opinion would be disregarded immediately if he told them this army lieutenant was doing something he considered disrespectful. Not to mention nobody wanted to be the one to sign their name on the demotion paperwork of an Arshuni family member.

"Does that mean you will not be joining the attack, lieutenant?" Boguni said.

The grin tugging on his face meant he probably thought Arthur would use his position to get himself out of harm's way. He probably assumed that because that is what he would have done if he was in Arthur's shoes. Hell, it was what Boguni was doing if he was himself.

"Of course not, sir. Missing out on such an important mission would bring me and my family great dishonor. Any soldier and corpsman should answer the call of the emperor and Goddess at a moment's notice, regardless of rank or position."

It was Arthur's turn to smile. He knew Boguni, once again, would remain in the rear while we attacked.

Boguni screwed his face up, knowing he had been caught. "Colonel, will you have the privilege of leading us in such a glorious venture?"

The colonel's eyes went wide and they jumped around in his skull as he tried to think of an excuse. He couldn't simply say he wasn't going to jump in his tank and lead us because he didn't want to die, even though that is what we all understood. The man was a coward. Born of a cowardly family and elevated to his position based on years of faithful service, millions of miles away from any real danger. Knowing him, he had done some kind of backroom deal to make sure he got stashed on Gandak rather than being sent off to one of the countless campaigns the Corps was involved in all throughout Imperial space.

"Of course," he finally said, swallowing deeply. "I am simply waiting on my vehicle to be returned to me from the mechanics. It should be any moment."

I appreciated the empty commitment followed by giving himself an easy out should his nerve fail him. It was always interesting to see a lifelong worm in action, once again squirming his way out of something that would put him in danger.

"We all know how those mechanics are, eh?" I added.

Nayiri didn't find my comments funny and elbowed me in the ribs.

"Sir, we were at the front of the last attack. That Strider chewed us up something bad. Is there any chance of reinforcements before we attack again?" she asked.

"There is no time, Captain. We must act now before that strider is charged and back on the battlefield. I dare say we would not survive another encounter with it."

I noticed he was using "we" an awful lot for an event he wasn't present for, but he was right. Another run-in with the Ministry of Munitions' doomsday weapon would leave us all melted into the snow in a rather short amount of time.

Nayiri sighed, pitching the bridge of her nose. We would have to attack them with what we had, and she had to know that wasn't much. Even her own carrier had been rendered useless. The regiment had been reduced to tatters in a matter of minutes. She must have been thinking about how she was going to pull this off and coming up empty.

"How much of a bombardment can we expect to preempt this assault, sir? If the last one was six hours long, I assume we are going to need a much larger one if we are to actually break through. Not to mention surface bombers to cover our attack, it would keep some of their armor off of our back and—"

He cut her off. "No, Captain, there will be no support."

She gasped. "What?"

Not even Arthur could keep his cool now.

"You've got to be kidding me. This is a fucking death march!" he spat.

"Mind your tone, Lieutenant. Our goal is to surprise them and push straight toward Barda Prime. If we preempt our attack with artillery and fill the air with bombers, they will know we are coming! They could deploy the Strider, even half a charge is more than enough to ruin our plans."

"You can't surprise someone when you're charging over open ground you damn moron! If you had been with us in the last attack maybe you would have known that!" Arthur stepped toward Boguni, fists balled up in rage and ready to attack.

As much as I wanted to see the colonel get laid out, I pulled Arthur back. I didn't want to give the colonel the satisfaction.

"Lieutenant!" Boguni barked. "I've dealt with your mouth for quite long enough. I should have you charged with insubordination! Let your friend Haduni tell you what happens to puffed-up little pieces of shit who get on my bad side!"

And with that, I let go of Arthur. It dawned on me that any future charges he might lay against us didn't really matter if he was ordering us to our deaths. We wouldn't be around to deal with the aftermath.

The flat, meat-packing sound, of Arthur's knuckles against the colonel's jaw, was satisfying. He stumbled backward before falling onto his back, a small rivulet of blood came from his newly torn lips.

"I have wanted to do that ever since I met him." Arthur sighed, shaking out his stinging hand.

"You have no idea," I added.

Nayiri stood frozen, staring down at the fallen form of the colonel. Other officers stayed where they were, exchanging hushed whispers with one another. Nobody stood to defend the colonel or even to detain Arthur, who had committed a serious crime in front of dozens of witnesses.

"I'll call the gendarmes!" the colonel stammered, scrambling up to his feet.

"Give it a rest, they are all still up in orbit." Arthur approached the colonel and poked him in the chest with an outstretched finger.

Boguni flinched as if he was about to be attacked again. "Now you can go home after all of this and tell your idiot family that you saw combat with that little scar of yours."

He pointed to his split lip. "But rest assured I will be reporting your conduct here to my family on Mars. You can bet they will not want to dirty their hands working with such a dishonorable family as the Boguni any longer than they already have. Maybe the Duke of Sassoun will take a closer look as some of your business licenses while he is at it."

He nodded at me before turning and walking back toward the *Wrath of Terra*.

Nayiri finally spoke up. "Colonel, I will lead this attack against the enemy as ordered. But I have a feeling neither myself nor my men will survive long enough to ever see you again. It is my most sincere hope that you will die on this planet with us."

She gave him a halfhearted salute before marching off. For the first time since I had been assigned to his regiment, I was standing in front of Colonel Boguni and didn't have to worry about the consequences of my actions. I had no idea when but in the coming minutes, or hours I was all but certain that I was going to die.

Whatever punishment Boguni was thinking of, I wouldn't live to see.

I thought for a moment about the sidearm that hung from the holster on my hip. I had already killed so many members of the Boguni family, what was one more? There would be no doubt that he more than deserved such a fate. Telling him off was one thing, but I was sure if I put a round between his eyes in the middle of the camp, I wouldn't last long enough to even take part in the coming attack. The end result would be the same, but I couldn't do that to my crew. They were going to need me.

Instead, I leaned in close to him. I could smell the fear stink on his breath and the whites of his eyes looked like they would swallow his pupils as he attempted to come to grips with the fact that his station and rank had been collectively disregarded. He was the kind of officer that never learned how to be a leader and simply demanded the respect of his men based on his position. With that stripped away, he was nothing. Worse still, I think he was starting to realize that.

In books and movies, the protagonist always has a quippy one-liner to spit into the face of his long-time enemy in a situation like this. But then, as I loomed over him, watching him shake and bleed from his mouth, I couldn't think of anything. Seeing such a pitiful man watch his entire world get upended, even if only temporarily, made me almost feel sorry for him.

Almost.

My punch landed on the other side of his face and I felt several teeth loosen as I made contact. Boguni spun and landed awkwardly, moaning and writhing in pain on the snowy ground. The cold weather made the punch sting worse than normal and I shook my hand out. I delivered a kick to his ribs and felt something crunch.

"Anahit sends her regards."

TWENTY-THREE

SUREN SAT ON THE GROUND, legs splayed out in front of him. A medic was standing over him, a small syringe in his hand. The big loader was sniffing and dabbing tears from his eyes as the medic withdrew a long needle from his skull, the sight of which made me cringe. Despite the fact the Corps had been injecting things into my eyes and brain for years, I had never gotten over the human instinct to recoil at the sight of needles.

"Quit whining would you," the medic said.

Nobody ever claimed that army medics had good bedside manners. Suren's eyes followed the sound of the medic's voice and even though tears still streamed down his face, he broke into a grin.

"I can hear you!" Suren exclaimed, clearly relieved.

"Good, that means I didn't miss." The medic began packing away the implant kit into his bag. "These things can be tricky even when the person getting it isn't trying to fight you off like a toddler at the doctor's office, ya know."

"Sorry," Suren said, but didn't seem to mean it.

He got up, pushed by the medic and wrapped his arms around me. "I can hear again!"

He didn't know his own strength and I felt my back pop in his embrace.

"Good to have you back again, buddy," I said, coughing. "Anush, how is the tank?"

Anush was sitting on the turret, watching the medical show from afar with a mix of interest and revulsion on her face. The way she smacked her lips after taking a drink from a canteen told me that it didn't contain water.

"Ammo and fuel topped off," she said, taking another drink. "Davit is working on the hydraulic leak, but he thinks it's probably rightly fucked and needs some actual repairs."

"What's in the canteen?" I asked.

A guilty look spread across her face.

"I'm not in trouble, am I?"

"No, I just need a drink."

She tossed it down to me. I uncorked the top and sniffed it. I could have sworn it smelled vaguely like jet fuel, but I decided I didn't care and took a drink.

It turned out the concoction also tasted vaguely of jet fuel. "You're not in trouble, but I am disappointed in whatever the hell this is. I expect better from you."

She shrugged. "Piotr brews it over in their tank. I think we drank all the regular stuff already."

"Tell Piotr to stick to being a gunner because he's a shit distiller."

I tossed the canteen back to her and went to find Davit. The outside of the *Daredevil* was nearly unrecognizable. The paint had been sandblasted away by thousands of enemy bullets, reducing everything to a pockmarked and scarred gunmetal grey. Larger divots and been drilled into the armor where the countermeasure system failed to save us. I didn't even want to think about how many times we came close to dying and didn't even know it.

Davit's upper body was pitched over into his driver's compartment, his legs hooked around the front edge of the tank to keep him from falling in. The pneumatic hiss of a pump could be heard and at the end of a long tube leading out of the tank, a neon green shade of liquid spurted out onto the snow.

"Everything working?" I asked.

Davit pushed himself out of the compartment, his uniform was stained a sickly green color from the waist up.

"This leak isn't going to fix itself," he said. "I'm trying to pump all the excess out so I don't have to sit in it again, but I can't fix the damn thing without taking apart the entire compartment and..."

He squinted at me. "I have a feeling you're about to tell me we don't have time for that."

"Something like that, yeah." I nodded. "Will it work with a leak for the time being?"

Davit rolled his eyes and thought for a moment. "I suppose I could just keep a barrel of fluid down here with me and replace it as it leaks. But that would be the dumbest fix to a simple problem I've ever heard of."

He probably expected me to stop him from doing that, or tell him that he was right and *Daredevil* would need to be lifted back up the fleet for serious repairs. But I didn't.

He sighed. "So, we're going with the dumbest fix."

"That's my man." I smiled and gave the front slope of the tank a slap with the palm of my hand. "She's gotten us out of worse situations with less. It'll be fine."

It wouldn't be fine and I think we both knew that. Davit had his Goddess and had probably already made his peace with the idea of death. Even us without belief had accepted that death was the inevitable end of every corpsman's service obligation. We just lie to ourselves and think about happy endings to get us through the day.

"*Hey,*" popped in the voice of Nayiri. "*Meet me by my carrier.*"

I sighed and rubbed my eyes. I couldn't remember the last time

I had slept and was looking forward to sneaking in a few minutes before we went on what had all of the appearances of a suicide mission. Can't be too well-rested when you confront your own death, after all. I fished a ration pack out of a stray box and made my way toward Nayiri's burnt-out remains of a carrier.

Every corps unit was winding into high gear trying to get everything together for our coming attack. Ammo and fuel were being loaded into tanks, carriers, and trucks by long lines of corpsmen. Others attempted to repair what they could, cannibalizing the worst of the vehicles and using their parts to fix the ones that actually had a chance at running again. Still, others strapped extra armor plates from broken-down vehicles to give the others more of a fighting chance.

I found Nayiri seated on top of her broken-down carrier as her surviving troopers offloaded equipment and parts toward a new one. The replacement vehicle looked like it was in rough shape too, but at least it ran. Around her stood a collection of other corps officers, the same ones who had just sat through the colonel's meeting getting increasingly more despondent as it went on.

Nayiri had her device in her hand, showing a map of the enemy line. She had made countless drawings showing different units and routes of advance. Officers were taking notes of their own while others were raising their hands and asking questions. Arthur was seated on the ground, his device propped up on his knee when I tapped him on the shoulder.

"What's going on?"

"Meeting," he said, unhelpfully.

"About what? Voting on a mutiny or something?"

"If only. Nayiri decided it isn't technically disobeying an order if we come up with our own plan that still accomplishes the field marshal's goals in the end. Maybe we don't all die as we want, we take out that strider like he wants, win-win."

"Andranik, thank you for joining us," Nayiri said. "I'll forward you our notes so far."

"Ma'am." Arthur raised his hand. "Your ideas are all very good."

I recognized this tone of voice. It was the tone of a man who knew better, wanted to correct you, but didn't want to insult your intelligence while doing so. It was how Ana had always talked to me.

"But I'm worried they are all a little bit more complicated than our current forces could manage. I think the colonel might actually be right about one thing, the rebels probably think they have us beaten. After all. They unleashed that strider on us and watched us scurry back to camp like scared rats. They probably think they are about to watch our evacuation shuttles come down from orbit at any second."

"Don't let the colonel hear you say you think he's right," joked a captain in the crowd. "In my opinion, we should split our forces. Send one group to the right flank here." He drew on his device with a finger. "They could try to make an obvious attempt to bypass the line, drawing the enemy into contact. Once the enemy is engaged our true force swings around the left flank, hopefully bypassing them for real and they make a run for Barda Prime. The distraction force holds the enemy for as long as they can while the strike force takes the facility."

It was a much better plan than the one the colonel gave us. Then again, most ideas are better than charging headlong into a reinforced line that you know is stronger than you are. Splitting our forces seemed like a bad idea, but the distraction would probably work. The rebels all used to be regulars. Even if their minds were being warped by Grigori's insanity, the chance that they thought very little of the Corps was incredibly high.

"I like your idea," I said. "But what if we added something?"

Arthur motioned for me to continue. "Shoot."

"Arthur, before you joined us, what did you think of the Frontier Corps?"

He smiled nervously. "I think you and I both know I shouldn't answer that question in my present company."

"Exactly." I snapped my fingers. "Regulars think the Corps are full of criminals, dead enders, or idiots and all of us are just looking for the first chance to drop this green jacket and go running into the hills. The rebels, traitors though they are now, were still regulars once. They probably think the same thing. So, why don't we use that to our advantage?"

"How do we use that to our advantage exactly, Ando?" Nayiri quizzed. "Are we going to kill them with your low self-esteem?"

I decided to ignore that last part.

"I think splitting our forces is necessary but engaging the line in a straight-up fight is asking to get killed. Though it sounds like we might all die anyway, we need to live along enough for the plan to work. What if the detachment acting as a decoy pretends to surrender?"

"Then launch an attack up close and personal when they let their guard down?" Arthur laughed. "That's just plain rude."

"It's cold-blooded," Nayiri said and smiled. "But I like it."

"It sounds like surrendering force is going to see the most combat," mused a young captain named Karena. "What if we load the trucks and carriers that can still run with the infantry to skirt around and use the tanks as the surrendering force? They can do a lot of damage in a short amount of time and might even be able to break through and join us in Barda Prime."

"She has a point," Arthur agreed. "And our tanks are shit for a street fight if it comes to that."

"So, no air cover, no artillery, and all of our tanks pretending to surrender," an infantry lieutenant named Garo said, rubbing his hands together in an attempt to stay warm. "Are we sure this is better than the colonel's plan?"

"Nope." Nayiri shook her head. "But it's what we've got. Anyone have any questions?"

The crowd of officers remained silent, seemingly accepting our collective fate. I wasn't sure if my stupid idea was any better than the colonel's either. But if it wasn't, we would die all just the same. At least now, we would die following our own orders, rather than the colonel's. The only sound heard amongst the group was the flicking of lighters in moments of panicked nicotine urges.

"All right. We'll see you in an hour."

CHAPTER
TWENTY-FOUR

AFTER TELLING the crew of the plan and dealing with the constant momentary near mutinies that came with giving troopers bad news, we had gotten to work. We first decided that if we were going to act like we were surrendering to a rebel army led by a religious nut, we had to look the part. This would require a new paint job.

This, of course, would require paint. Informing the colonel of our new plan would have not been a good idea. Pretending to surrender as a military tactic would have never been approved and almost certainly would have been the thing that finally landed me in front of a firing squad. Without his approval, we couldn't requisition any paint from the supply clerks.

Unfortunately for the supply clerks, we were the Frontier Corps and there was never a shortage of talented thieves in our ranks. Anush was one of the most prolific thieves I had ever met to the point it was more than likely a compulsion than anything else. The only people she didn't steal from were those lucky enough to be in the same tank as her and even then, it depended on if she liked you or not. It took her two years to stop nicking my stuff and another year after that for me to trust that she wouldn't. Once unleashed on the supply clerk's stores, it didn't take her long to liberate several cans of paint as well as an entire crate of whiskey meant for the staff officers.

Paint in hand, that is where Davit's encyclopedic knowledge of the church's holy books finally came in handy. Suren, Anush, and I, armed with paint brushes and cans, daubed various mantras, slogans, and designs all over *Daredevil* as he called them out. It didn't take long for the poor tank to look like a child's school project done at the last minute. None of us would ever be accused of being artists, that much was sure.

Other crews did the same thing with varying levels of success. Some simply drew a large sun on the front slope of their tank while Arthur rechristened his tank *Wrath of the Goddess*. Regulars and staff officers watched on in confusion, having no idea what we were planning. They must have thought we had either lost our minds or were becoming strangely religious seemingly out of nowhere.

Davit had snatched up the dozens of sun pendants from his driver's compartment and handed them out to anyone who would take one and even some that wouldn't. After several attempts, he finally forced one of them on me. The sun looked like it had been stamped out of tin by hand with a lot of effort and care. It shined as brightly as something could when worked over with a rag and spit. A hole punched through the middle of it allowed an extra bootlace to be strung through and act as the necklace's chain.

After the painting festivities wound down, I climbed back into *Daredevil*, closing the hatch as I sat down in my commander's chair. Suren was fast asleep, his feet kicked up on the breach of the cannon, drool dribbling down the side of his face. Anush polished her gunner's sights with the sleeve of her filthy uniform jacket.

A silence fell over us as everyone tried to busy themselves with some activity to take their mind off what lay ahead of us. I could only clean my carbine so many times before the enormity of what we were about to try settled in and I couldn't reach for my cigarettes fast enough.

Anush broke the silence, leaning back in her chair and looking up at me. "You know what would take the edge off?"

I had forgotten about the case of whiskey she had stolen. She was as much of a drinker as I was and I should have assumed she had stashed some aboard the tank.

"I'm going to need more than an edge taken off right about now," I said.

She reached an arm under her gunner's controls and handed me a bottle full of amber liquid.

"You would allow me the first drink?" I quizzed. "Did you poison this?"

"This seems like high-class type stuff, I thought you might be able to tell me about it, being a noble and all."

"You want me to tell you about the whiskey you stole?"

"I'd rather fill my head with meaningless whiskey facts than confront my own impending doom, so humor me."

We both smiled. I looked down at the bottle she had handed me.

"Oh, it's from the Titanian distillers," I told her.

I popped the cork on and smelled the contents. Titan was known for producing vast quantities of alcohol and bottling it in dozens of different ways, each bottle more ornate than the last so they could charge more and more the fancier it looked. For commoners, buying the top-shelf Titan bottle was a way to show their wealth in a way that was accessible to them. Unfortunately, it all tasted like crap.

"That bad, eh?" She laughed, looking at my face. "I always thought Titan made the good stuff."

"You sweet summer child." I clicked my tongue at her. "Titan is what poor people drink at a club to try to convince a woman they're rich. It's all the same swill, just up charged to people without taste."

"Yeah, I fell for that one before," Anush said and groaned. "But all of your fancy rich people shit tastes bad. I had caviar before when I was working at the port. Stole it out of some boxes, but that's beside the point. Anyway, it tasted like salted garbage. You nobles love that crap though."

"I'm with you on that one." I laughed. "My dad though, he loved caviar."

I took a swig of the whiskey and winced at its flavor. It burned down my throat and only tasted slightly better than the fuel byproduct she had given me earlier.

"You know, I have something," I said.

Leaning over to my bag, I grabbed a small flask and popped the cap. The rich, bitter aroma of gini floated out of it. I had forgotten that several years before I had run into a trader from Sassoun and gave him more than one paycheck for the stuff.

She eyed the flask. "What's that?"

"You know how on Luna you pride yourself on your beer?"

I wasn't entirely sure why they did. I had drunk some when the Haduni family met with the local noble family regarding a trade deal. Nothing to write home about.

"Well, back on Sassoun, this is what we make." I handed it to her and she took it.

"You sure you want to share this with me?"

I smiled weakly. "I was saving it for something special. Preferably the end of my contract but I don't think I'm going to be around for that anymore."

"Yeah. I got further than I thought I would." She sighed. "Sucks we are going to die on this frigid hellhole, though."

"Prefer something tropical?" I joked. "To die somewhere with a view?"

"Hell yeah," she said, perking up. "A nice beach and as much beer as I can drink. Failing that I could go for one last lay."

"No luck with Arthur?"

"You told me not to try," she reminded me.

Then she admitted, "I tried, he's married. One of the faithful types."

"A noble who's faithful to their spouse?" I whistled. "Never thought I'd see the day. What about Piotr?"

"Gay." She sighed. "Him and Suren got along great though."

"Wait, Suren's gay?"

"Nah." She shook her head. "Not really, he just has sex with whomever he's attracted to. Martians are pretty fluid about that kind of thing."

"I went to school on Mars, how did I never pick up on that?"

"Because you probably went to school around a bunch of stuck-up pricks too busy arguing over which coat to wear to dinner to actually enjoy life. Or maybe you're just clueless. Most men are."

I was reminded that Tigranes the Great Prep had no fewer than three different formal dinner uniforms, but I decided not to bring that up. "What about you? Anyone waiting for you at home?"

I laughed at her question, though I shouldn't have. She hadn't responded to a single letter of mine in years, not a day went by where I didn't think about how Anahit was doing. I wondered maybe if I survived my contract, I would be able to go home and she would forgive me for what I did. I realize now, that would never happen. Maybe when ten years passes and I never returned, she could forgive me then.

"Just a sister who hates my guts." I sighed. "I was never one for romance."

"Don't they normally pair you guys up with someone else's kid for political alliances? Seems grim."

"Something like that." I pointed at the flask. "Are you going to drink that or not?"

She swatted my hand away playfully and took a drink. The gini left a purplish tinge on her lips. She paused for a moment in consideration, then nodded.

I snatched the flask back from her. "Not bad for some stationer shit."

"I'll take that as a compliment." I tipped the flask back and downed the rest of it.

I had never paid so much money for such little amount of gini before. I guess I never would again, either. I licked my lips, tasting the substance for the last time. Before I could stop myself, the corners of my eyes began to burn and tears cut down my cheeks. I tried to hide them but it was no use.

"It's all right," Anush said, not in a comforting way, but rather, in a knowing one.

It was like she had already gone through this phase of acceptance of what was going to happen next. I sniffed and dabbed my sleeve at my eyes trying to will them to stop, but they wouldn't. No matter what I told myself, or Anush, or Nayiri, or whoever. I didn't want to die. Not here. Not like this.

"How did you get over it?" I sobbed. "Anush, I'm fucking scared."

She looked up at me with watery eyes. "I am too."

At some point, our conversation had woken Suren. He was standing in front of the breach, one hand on my shoulder and another on Anush's. He was crying too but had a smile on his big face.

"I'm not," he said, his voice thick with emotion. "You're my family and I couldn't think of anyone else I would want to be next to me right now."

I put my hand over his.

"Thank you, Suren." I sniffed again. "You're my family too and I love every single one of you. I mean that."

"One big happy, fucked up family." Anush laughed, tears spilling out of her eyes.

"I always used to miss Sassoun," I cried. "I missed home but I was looking at it all wrong. Sassoun isn't home, it never really was."

I slapped the side of the turret. "This is home, right here. With all of you."

"The Corps is our home world." Suren recited one of the oaths of the Frontier Corps, before adding, "And *Daredevil* is our house."

We all broke into a strange mix of laughing and crying, pulling each other in closer as we did. I wasn't sure what it was that we were going through. A collective mourning for our own lives, maybe. A living wake for those that nobody else would miss. One final chance to say goodbye to one another, before it started.

"All stations, all stations," came the voice of Nayiri. *"Begin movement toward your predetermined areas and take up attack positions. May the Goddess bless and keep every single one of you."*

Her voice began to waver as she went on. *"Good luck and I will see you in Barda Prime."*

CHAPTER
TWENTY-FIVE

OUR TANKS CREPT out of the camp as the sun began to dip below the horizon. Our instincts told us we needed to spread out, get set in our battle formations, and prepare for the coming hell. Our plan, however, said we couldn't do any of that. We weren't driving into battle, we were supposed to look like we were surrendering, which meant we had to look as non-threatening as possible.

The ten vehicles drove through the snow and ice in a single file line, our main cannons raised up to the sky to show we meant no harm. Inside, we were prepared. My commander's gun was still down so I kept my carbine just inside of the hatch, a bandolier of magazines and grenades hung next to it. My tank was the leading element, which meant we were probably going to get up close and personal as we bought as much time as we could.

Once things popped off every second was going to count. We would only have enough time to fire once before the superior enemy tanks would be on us. To facilitate that, Suren had loaded a canister round into the breach. It was a heavy, nearly one-hundred-pound beast loaded with thousands of ball bearings that would cut a swath through the infantry that was almost certainly going to swarm all over us. However, it was only good for close range. In his arms, he held a sabot round for the tanks that would follow. The cannon was already armed and Anush had a white-knuckle grip on her controls, waiting for me to give the order.

For the first night in many, there was no blizzard and it was as clear as any night back on Gandak. In the distance, I could see the shapes of enemy fortifications. As I switched to thermal vision, I saw hundreds, maybe even thousands of small heat signatures running around, getting back to their battle stations as we approached.

"Are you ready for this?" asked Arthur across the network.

I swallowed hard. I wasn't ready at all.

"Yeah," I lied. *"But if they just shoot me out of my turret you better avenge me."*

"Got it, one avenging."

"All right guys, this is it." I turned back to my crew. "Be ready for anything. If I get shot, Anush you take over and make them pay."

She gave me a thumbs-up without looking away from her gunner's sight

"Like you even had to tell me that." I reached up and unlocked my turret, feeling the frigid air blow in and burn my face some more.

I pulled my mask and hood over to protect myself as much as I could as I climbed out. I reached back into my hatch and found our mechanism of surrender.

Anush had stolen a standard-issue white bedsheet from one of the command vehicles and fixed it to a broomstick with a length of twine. In the middle of everything, I found it quite amusing that thousands of tons of armor, some of the deadliest machines to ever be dropped onto a battlefield, were being given up via a bedsheet.

I took a deep breath and hoisted the ad hoc white flag high. As it flapped in the wind behind me, I closed my eyes expecting to feel the blast of someone's rifle, but it never came. The thermal signatures in the enemy positions scampered around more, vehicles began to pull up, and soon a very well-armed and probably not very happy, welcoming party was waiting for us.

"Our first round is going into the infantry, everyone else target their armor or we are dead faster than we can reload," I broadcasted across the network.

"Roger," answered a voice. *"I'll highlight and assign targets."*

I recognized the voice as a young commander named Taline. Within seconds, red outlines formed in my eyes overlaying the enemy tanks, each with a number on them corresponding to which one of us was supposed to engage it. I had no doubt the rebels were doing the same thing as we got closer to them.

I squinted through the wind and made out the shapes of several infantry soldiers and a carrier coming out to meet us.

"All right Davit, prepare to stop. Don't get too close. Remember, look pliant."

"I was born pliant."

"What does that even mean?" Anush cut in.

They were about to launch into one of their constant bickering sessions before I cut them off.

"Not now, damnit."

The tank slowly ground to a halt as the infantry in front of us cautiously moved forward. Eventually, what looked like a leader, clad in a bulky great coat, several scarfs, and a hat called up to me.

"Who are you?"

"Lieutenant Andranik Haduni, Sixteenth Cavalry Regiment."

"Are you Frontier Corps?"

"Most of us, yeah. But a regular tank joined us on our way out." I motioned to *Wrath*.

"You mean to surrender?"

"We wanted to surrender when His Holiness Grigori reached

out to us over our implants. But you know how they keep the gendarmes close at hand when there are corpsmen around."

"So, how did you get away then?"

I didn't expect them to ask so many questions.

"After that machine of yours did a number on us, it took so many of the cops out that there are hardly enough of them left to keep an eye on all of us anymore."

I noticed that as we were talking, other soldiers began advancing on either side of *Daredevil* moving toward the other tanks. "They're so busy planning their evacuation they didn't even notice us drive away."

The soldiers glanced around at one another and slowly their rifles, once held up at the ready, began to slacken. The one I was speaking to turned to talk to a few others around him, before stopping for a moment, I imagine transmitting something across the network.

"Evacuating? Are you sure about that?" he asked.

"They haven't started yet, but last I heard the field marshal was ordering the task force to pack it up as soon as possible. Something about it being safer to wait up in orbit for reinforcements to show up than try to keep a foothold against that orbital strider of yours."

"Sir, more soldiers are coming out of their dugouts to the right," Davit said.

Out of the corner of my eye, I saw them. Dozens of soldiers crawling over the parapets of their trench and inching closer to our flanks.

"*Guys, I think they are onto us,*" I said, losing count of the number of grey-suited soldiers.

I pulled up my map and saw Nayiri's attack element was already speeding toward Barda Prime, rapidly approaching the left flank of the rebel line.

The soldier I was speaking to climbed into the front slope of the tank, looking around at all of the artwork we had covered it in.

"One hell of a paint job you have here," he remarked.

His eyes were masked by bubble-eyed goggles that reminded me of a kind of insect, but even through those, I could feel him staring at me.

"It only reflects our devotion to the word of the Goddess," I responded nervously.

One of my hands began to move down, toward the sidearm hanging from my belt. As the man made his way up *Daredevil,* leaning against the turret and looking up at me, I wasn't sure my draw hand would be fast enough to beat the rifle he was still holding.

"Is this a *Solaris* model?" he asked. "They really give you Corps guys the worst crap, don't they?"

"Tell him 'it isn't the tools used to serve the Goddess that are important, but the intention of those using the tools'" Davit quickly cut in.

I think I remember old Levon saying the same thing once or twice. I repeated the line and the man laughed.

"I get it, you've read the books." He hoisted himself up onto the turret, bringing his rifle back up into both hands, his shoulders tensed and he slowly began to trace the barrel back up, toward me. "Quick question though, how did you know that it was called an orbital strider?"

My throat went thick. How fucking stupid of me! I couldn't believe I let that slip! A regular corpsman would have had no idea what that thing was called, more so for one considered so useless that nobody would notice them fleeing a camp in order to surrender.

"Sir!" Screamed a voice from the ground. "Enemy sighed on the left flank! They're making for Prime!"

The man on the turret whipped his head around to the soldier that had called out to him, beginning to bark orders, to respond to Nayiri's column.

Now was my chance. I ripped the sidearm from its holster, thumbing its hammer back in one fluid motion, and fired. The man on the turret was pitched backward, blood spurting from the wound in the center of his chest.

"Now!" I yelled.

The cannon roared, sending thousands of ball bearings tearing into the gathering of soldiers in front of us. In seconds the immediate area was churned into a butcher's shop floor. Ragged remains were blasted into the air and the enemy positions were coated in a fine mist of their former occupants.

"Guns free!" I ordered.

I dropped the side arm in front of me, reaching down and grabbing the carbine. By the time I flicked it from safe to fire, the soldiers that survived the blast of the canister round had begun firing back at us. Their armor began moving, trying to find a fighting position as soldiers ran between them.

The tanks behind us had fanned out, forming a line and pumping their own cannon rounds into the fray. Their sabots cut through the enemy tanks at such close range, killing them so quickly that many continued rolling backward, obeying the last commands given to them by their crew that had been vaporized by a penetrating shell only seconds before. I leaned over the turret, firing my carbine without taking the time to aim. Soldiers scattered, trying to run back to their defenses but were swept off of their feet by bursts of machine gun fire from somewhere behind me.

Anush fired again. Caught in the moment, she hardly aimed. The sabot round crashed into the ground, bounced up, and hit the rebel tank she was shooting at, before bouncing again. Having lost all ballistic properties, the cartwheeling round flew wildly through the air before slamming down on top of a rebel bunker with such force it detonated the ammunition stored within. It exploded in a bright fireball, raining burning debris down on the soldiers around it.

"Meant to do that," she noted, before firing again.

This time her shot found its target, puncturing the rebel tank's gun mantle and exploding their ammunition storage. Fire vented out of its wound as the machine died. From the defenses, stomping through the blasted remains of their comrades, came the anti-tank teams. They lugged their *Pilum* missile systems into crews of three, each one of them having the power to kill us in a matter of seconds.

"Put some damn canisters in those trenches! Davit, advance!" I ordered, dropping an empty magazine from my carbine and slamming in a fresh one.

The tank lurched forward, crushing the dead and wounded under our tracks. The rest of the tanks followed, staying on line as we turned to press the flank of the rebel defenses.

I shot down two of the anti-tank crewmen before Anush let fly another canister round. Several of the soldiers tried to turn and run as her gun slowly swiveled over to meet them. Staring down the cyclops' eye of the *Daredevil*, they had nowhere to go and only milliseconds left to live. They were gone in a flash.

Before we could celebrate the tank was hit by an explosion. The force tossed me from the hatch and I landed in a pile on the floor of the turret. My ears ringing, it took a moment for my vision to stabilize, but when it did, I saw Anush pushing herself from her seat, climbing over the beach, and making her way to my commander's position.

"Hey!" I spat. "What are you doing? I'm not dead yet! Get back down there."

"Sorry," she said, shoving herself back down into her gunner's seat. "I thought I was just showing initiative."

"I'll make sure I put that on your commendation," I joked

without humor. "What the fuck just hit us? Someone give me a report, damnit."

"Looking for it now, boss," she said, the turret spinning toward the source of the shot.

I made my way back to my position and found my carbine missing, probably blown sky-high. "Suren, give me your carbine."

He finished loading another round, unhooked his weapon from the wall, and handed it to me. My head now sticking back out of the turret I could see the asshole that was gunning for us. A carrier equipped with a chain gun. It was a weapon meant for infantry support, not trying to kill tanks. It was punished for its stupidity when one of the other tanks scored a hit on its side, blowing straight through its body, splitting the carrier in half. Burning fuel and oil spilled out, causing the infantry around it to run for cover. Anush dispensed with them quickly via a burst from the coaxial machine gun.

Our line of tanks trundled on. The weight of our advance crushed the support structures of the enemy dugouts and trenches as we drove by them. Their walls crumbled and collapsed burying the dead, dying, and some of the straggling living in unmarked graves. As we went, we pumped cannon rounds into each bunker we saw.

Soldiers tried to run for cover but it was too late. Each touched off with a bright ball of fire. The burning shapes of men stumbled out of them, dead by not yet knowing it. I held my fire and watched them burn until they finally collapsed into the snow. Tanks rushed by us on either side, each excited with the intoxication of battle and the feeling of having the enemy on the run.

"Hold it together boys," Arthur said. *"We haven't won anything yet. Remember we need to hold them here for as long as possible. Stay on line."*

"Ah come on, Arshuni!" complained another tank commander

named Sarkis. *"We have them on the run! We need to run them down like the dogs that they are!"*

"Hold the damn line, Sarkis!" Arthur demanded.

"You regulars aren't the boss of me! Come on boys! Let's go!" Sarkis cheered.

His tank, the *Fire of Olympus* rushed forward, followed by two others.

"Get back here!" I ordered, but I knew I lacked any real authority.

"Damn idiots are going to get themselves killed," said Arthur.

The *Fire of Olympus* went up like a torch in the blink of an eye. Something had cleaved straight through its frontal armor, exploding the turret into the air like a cork from a bottle of champagne, propelled by a jet of flames.

"Son of a bitch!" I pounded a fist on the turret. "Davit, pull alongside him, we can't let these idiots kill themselves. We need them."

I flicked from internal comms to the network. *"Arthur, on me."*

"You know it."

The rest of the surviving tanks and I pulled alongside the dead *Fire of Olympus* in time to see the tank next to it, *Do What I Want*, have a hole punched through its turret. Flames blew out of the wound and I saw their loader jump away from the machine as it exploded behind him.

In front of them was a *Terra* pattern tank, dug into a fighting position. The front of its hull was completely covered by an earthen berm, showing only its fat, wide turret and flanks which had also been covered in additional armor plates.

"Holy shit!" Anush exclaimed, firing a cannon round directly into the enemy's turret.

It exploded, leaving only a scorch mark. The enemy tank fired again, its round sailed to the left of us, smashing into a tank called *By Her Name,* blasting an ugly wound into its front slope, an explosion gutting the driver's position and bringing the tank to a halt. A fire began to burn from the ruined hull and spread toward the turret, forcing the surviving crew to flee.

"Davit!" I screamed, my heart jumping into my throat. "Evasive action, break right. Suren, smoke it out!"

A cloud of thermal smoke shrouded the tank in darkness, but its turret kept moving, searching for targets.

"*Get away from that thing!*" Arthur said.

He fired, the round bouncing harmlessly off of the tank's earthworks. "*Its ass is exposed! We need to get around behind it!*"

"Davit, get behind it!" I repeated the order into my headset.

The tank jerked right and at the same time the enemy turret spun around to meet us, its ballistic computer onboard immediately began tracking us, preparing to launch a round directly into our side. I knew it was only a matter of time.

"Emergency stop!" I commanded.

Davit jacked on the brakes, the entire tank slamming to a total stop with enough force to throw me forward into the hatch. At the same time, the rebel tank fired, its gunner still assuming we would be moving forward. Its shot exploded harmlessly a few feet in front of us, if we hadn't stopped, we would have been killed instantly.

"Go!"

Davit gunned it, the tracks sliding on the snow and ice as Anush fired another round. This one was sent tumbling away, another victim of its countermeasures.

"Come on, damnit!" she cursed. "Goddess, if you're up there, give me something!"

"Up!" Suren shouted, arming the gun.

She fired again, this one went just a few inches too high, sailing off into the distance. She punched her fist against her controls in anger.

"You celestial bitch!" she hissed. "Bless me now you whore!"

Wrath fired again. The shot found purchase, exploding on the tank's exposed flanks but seemingly doing no real damage. Anush joined in, hitting the rebel tank on the side of the turret, but doing little other than blowing off one of its extra armored plates. Another *Wrath* shell took off an engine panel, sending it flying into the air. A thick cloud of smoke began to rise from the wound.

"Now we are talking!" I cheered.

But I had spoken too soon.

The enemy crew must have seen the one *Terra* model tank in the formation and knew it to be its most immediate threat, even if it hadn't been upgraded like the one they had. The turret swung over to where the *Wrath* was, it only took a few seconds, but soon Arthur was within its sights.

"Arthur reverse! He has you!"

"I got this rat bastard!" Arthur snarled.

Both *Wrath* and the rebel tank fired simultaneously. The bright flash forced me to look away, but only for a second. The enemy tank's barrel had been shunted off at a strange angle, smoke and fire rising from its gun mantle. *Wrath* crawled forward a few more feet before stopping. A hole had been punched through the side of its turret, molten metal dripped out of the fatal wound as fire began to lick out of the other side.

"Arthur!" I called out. *"Damnit, Arthur! Come in!"*

The hatches of the *Wrath* blew open, spitting out jets of fire. He was dead, they were all dead. Gone the second the rebel gunner had pulled the trigger. I pounded my fist on the turret and screamed. As I watched *Wrath* burn, taking with it the remains of its crew, I took solace in the fact that they had returned the favor to the enemy.

Then, the enemy's hatch moved. A few seconds later the tank commander's hatch was flung open. Smoke wafted out of the opening as a man appeared. The commander, clad in a grey jacket, his face covered in blood, scrambled onto the turret before reaching back down and hoisting up another man who looked unconscious.

"You want me to hose them, sir?" Anush asked.

I reached over and grabbed my carbine.

"No." I brought the weapon up into my hands, shouldering its buttstock. "I got this."

I flicked the switch from safe to automatic and yelled at the top of my lungs. "Hey!"

The commander stopped in his tracks, glancing over his shoulder, and locking eyes with me. They were wide and panicked. At that moment part of me wanted to tell him to put his hands up, to surrender. The other part of me commanded my finger to squeeze the trigger. The man was pitched off of the top of his stricken tank, three rounds punching into his chest.

I put a few more into the other wounded man just to be sure. "Okay, Anush. Go ahead."

The cannon recoiled as one final round slammed into the rear of the enemy tank. It pierced the weaker rear armor without slowing down, and the resulting explosion tossed its damaged turret off of the hull, landing upside down on the frozen ground next to its decapitated body. I sighed and slid back down into the warmth of the commander's chair.

"Hey, sir."

For a moment I thought I was hallucinating until I remembered we weren't the last tank left. Two others, the *Swallow's Fortress*, commanded by a sergeant named Serzh, and the *Black Garden*, commanded by another sergeant named Vazgen still survived.

"Sir?" the voice asked again.

I scrolled through the heads-up display in my mind until I saw the name of the sender, it was Serzh.

"Glad to see you're still alive, Serzh."

"You too, sir. Uh, I have a question. What do we do now?"

"I say we packed it up, pull back to camp," said Vazgen. *"We've done enough. If we stick around here it is only a matter of time before we get taken out."*

"If we pull back to camp, the colonel will have us swinging by the end a rope within the hour," I countered.

"We both know that is only true for one of us, sir." Vazgen retorted.

I never did like Vazgen. He was a slimy little gangster from the pits of Terra. That being said, he was right. If the colonel saw my face again I was sure he would make it the last time. If anyone else made a run for it they might catch a couple of dozen lashes, but would probably escape the gallows. At the moment, if I was them, I would rather take my chances with the gendarmes than the rebels.

"I think he's right, sir," Serzh said. *"What can three tanks do?"*

"Three tanks can do plenty," I said, my anger growing. *"Nayiri and her troopers must be in Barda Prime by now. She needs our support."*

"Sir, you can't seriously think that they are going to be able to complete their mission. You know as well as I do if they aren't already dead, they will be soon. If we leg it back to the camp, we might get there in time to make the evac shuttles when this whole thing goes sideways."

I didn't answer immediately. Instead, I sat there, my anger having turned to rage. I always knew the ties that bonded the Corps together were tenuous at best. Forged in mutual hardship and reinforced by an understanding that absolutely nobody cared about what happened to us. This wasn't an attitude supported by rank or organization as much as an implicit understanding that we were the only ones who cared about us. Without one another, we were alone in the universe. Listening to one of our own argue in favor of abandoning Nayiri filled me with an intense hatred I wasn't sure I had ever felt before.

"Uh, sir." Anush snapped me out of my internal monologue. "Whatever we are doing, we need to do it fast."

I looked through my sight and saw the initial shock of our advance was wearing off. The rebels were reforming and beginning to mass a short way away. They would be on us in minutes.

"We need to go!" Vazgen urged. *"If they attack us it'll be too late."*

I suppose an infantry officer could just shoot a mutinous squad leader, but that wasn't really my style. Not to mention impossible as we both sat in massive war machines. I wouldn't be able to compel him into fighting. His mind was already made up. The second we were distracted by the rebels he would make a run for it. It's what I would do if I were him.

"Guys," I said, finally. "I think we all know where this ends. The other tanks' commanders are talking about trying to make it back to camp. I can't go, if the colonel sees me again, I'm as good as dead."

"What are you talking about?" Anush asked, astonished.

"You could jump in with their crews, and get back to the camp. You might catch the lash, but you'd survive..." I tried to finish, but she wouldn't let me.

"Are you fucking stupid?" she spat.

I was staring down at my boots and didn't see her stand up, turn around and grab me by my collar. She forced me to look up at her.

"Didn't you pay attention to what we were talking about before we left?" She shook me, outraged. "We're family, just like Suren said. And if you think we are going to let you ride off alone toward Barda Prime, then you don't know us as well as I thought you did. Isn't that right?"

"That's right." Suren nodded. "Remember?"

He slapped the side of the turret. "This is our home and I'm not going anywhere."

"Well." Davit sighed. "I've seen your driving before sir, and I cannot in good faith leave *Daredevil* in your hands. She deserves better. So, I'm staying."

I bit my lip, feeling the tears in my eyes again. I could see the same in Anush's, but she was much better at masking it than I was. She let go of me and sat back down.

"Okay," I said, trying to gather my thoughts. "I think our best course of action is to break off from their line, we've done enough damage here. We should try to get to Barda Prime and support Nayiri the best we can."

"Then we should do it fast." Anush sniffed back her tears, hardly missing a beat. "Suren, give me a canister round. These fuckers are going to be coming at us and I want to show them that we are still here and kicking."

He quickly flipped the fat-headed canister shell around and punched it into the breach. The cannon boomed a second later and ahead of us dozens of rebels were evaporated by the hail of ball bearings.

"*We're going to help Nayiri. That's an order,*" I finally said.

"*You're insane,*" Vazgen scoffed, dismissively. "*We won't even make it to Barda Prime! You're on your own on this one. I won't be taking part in any suicide missions!*"

I bit my lip. He would be helping us whether he wanted to or not.

"Anush. Put a round into *Black Garden*'s tracks."

"You're kidding." She turned around in her chair, a look of incredulity on her face.

"You know, he's probably right," I admitted. "We probably can't outrun the rebels. But the rebels won't chase us if they are distracted. Any corpsmen that want to abandon their comrades and run is no corpsman to me. Fuck him."

"What about his crew?" Anush asked. "Not their fault their commander sucks."

"Davit will pray for them, isn't that right Davit?"

"Of course, sir."

"See?"

"Okay, fine." Anushed rolled her eyes.

I found the map in my heads-up display and transmitted the route to Barda Prime to Davit.

"Davit, reverse," I ordered.

The transmission clanked heavily and the tank took off backward. We moved without warning, catching the other tank commanders by surprise.

"Hey!" Vazgen called out. *"Where are you going?"*

"Do it, Anush."

She sighed, traversed the gun over to her new target, dropping the barrel low so as to only hit their tracks.

"What are you doing Haduni!" howled Vazgen.

Before he realized what was happening, Anush already fired. The shell slammed into their sprocket, blowing it off of the tank's hull and dropping the right track to the snow like a limp noodle. It was a good shot, there would be no way the crew would be able to fix that with any kind of speed.

"Sergeant Vazgen your new orders are to hold this position. Please, feel free to withdraw should the situation become untenable."

"You fucking asshole!" he snarled. *"I'll kill you!"*

"Careful now, Vazgen. It would be very hard to hold off the coming enemy without your cannon and I assure you that will be my gunner's next target."

As if on cue the approaching rebel forces began hitting us with small arms fire. A few rockets flew overhead and it was only a matter of time before their heavier weapons or vehicles showed up to the fray.

Serzh spoke up. *"Uh. Sir, I would like to accompany you to Barda Prime."*

"That would be acceptable, Serzh."

CHAPTER
TWENTY-SIX

THE SOUNDS of battle coming from the line began to fade as we left it behind us, the tank's engine putting out as much speed as it possibly could. I had no idea how long Vazgen and his crew would be able to hold out, but I assumed he would only give us a few minutes. My real hope was that the rebels manning the line would simply assume the rest of us had run off.

"How much further out are we?" I asked.

"Why don't you have a look for yourself, sir?" Davit answered.

I looked up into my sight and in the distance, I didn't see the skyline of Barda Prime, not yet. But I did see a towering column of smoke looming over the horizon. Certainly, that was not a good sign for Nayiri's mission.

"Holy shit." Anush whistled. "That entire city must be a warzone."

As powerful as our implants were, I still couldn't tap into Nayiri's network node. It could have meant she was dead. It could have also meant that the distance between the line and Barda Prime made my heads-up display useless.

"Are you guys still sure you want to do this?" I asked.

"It's a little late for going back at this point," she said. "I think that ship sailed when I put a shell into Vazgen's tank."

"If it makes you feel any better, I don't think he is going to be around to tell anyone," Davit pointed out.

I winced as my head hissed with static. I blinked and tried to shake the piercing sound away but it was no good. The empty static noise eventually began forming words, and as we got closer to Barda Prime, they began to get sharper.

"*Ando?*" came a distorted voice that I could hardly make out. "*Ando, are you alive? Is that you?*"

Through the garbled atmospheric mess, I was able to faintly make out Nayiri's voice.

"*Nayiri?*" I answered. "*Yeah, I'm here. I'm coming toward Barda Prime.*"

"*Don't come!*" Her voice fought through the waves of broken air. "*We couldn't make it to the strider development facility, we're pinned down!*"

She broke up again. "*We got bogged down in the city center, Mesrop Mashtots Street I think, and I'm pretty sure they have us surrounded. We have too many wounded to move. Just leave us, Ando.*"

"*You tried this before,*" I said, reminding her of when I towed her busted up carrier. "*I'm not leaving you. I'm going into that damn city, I'm going to break you out, and then we are going to destroy that facility.*"

"*Ando!*"

"*Spare me the whole 'I'm giving you an order' schtick, would you? Just hang on, we're coming.*"

"All right, everyone," I said, switching to internal comms. "Nayiri's detachment is surrounded at the city center. We are going in guns blazing to bail them out. Anush, stick to your coaxial machine gun unless you can be sure you're not about to hit friendly forces, understood?"

"Yeah, yeah."

"Serzh, are you tracking the plan?"

He laughed. *"Hell of a plan."*

"I'll take that as a yes, then."

After the incident with Vazgen, I was worried Serzh would try to make a run for it. However, it seemed he had simply resigned himself to his fate, even if he thought it was a particularly dumb fate that he was resigning himself to. In essence, it was the way of the Frontier Corpsmen.

The path to Barda Prime was exactly how it looked on the map: a wide-open wasteland of frozen nothingness. There were no roads or markers. Other than the smoke rising from the city that now showed its skyline over the horizon, there was hardly a hint of human habitation. The hints that I could see were those of war. Occasionally we drove by broken-down vehicles, carriers, and trucks. They had been damaged in the fighting before being abandoned.

It looked like my hope of slipping by had worked. The line, shattered by our surprise attack had quickly reformed. They must have been so busy counting the tanks that had been knocked out that they didn't notice that two had managed to escape and assumed that the attack had been thwarted.

As we got closer to the city, the sounds of battle could be heard. The crackle of thousands of rifles and machine guns was underlined by the dull thump of explosions. Signs of life, or what had once been life, pockmarked the area. A Frontier Corps carrier sat overturned and on fire. Elsewhere, small rebel checkpoints lay in ruin, hit by a cannon or missile of some kind. The tattered remains of its occupants sat, unmoving, in the snow.

A group of grey-uniformed soldiers milled around checking the burning hulk of the carrier. Their rifles were slung over their backs and they were laughing as they pulled the burnt and twisted corpses of the fallen corpsmen from the vehicle. Once they were done, they rifled through their pockets, taking what they wanted.

As we got closer the soldiers looked up from their duty at our coming tanks, exchanging words with one another. It was clear that out in the middle of the tundra they felt completely secure. Whatever was happening in the city must have been under control and the battle at the line had been decided. One of the soldiers waved at us as we approached. I felt Anush engage the turret and hydraulic fluid began to hum through the miles of cables that gave it power.

"Eat shit," she growled.

A burst of coaxial machine gun fire blew the men apart. One of the soldiers felt over and began crawling away, his legs being dragged behind him by their sinews. A second burst put him out of his misery.

I sighed. "We probably could have just driven by them."

"And why would we have done that?"

"So we don't alert the enemy in front of us!"

"And what are the odds that someone heard us in the middle of all of that going on in the city?"

"*Warning,*" Bitching Betty piped out. "*Deploying countermeasures!*"

The twisting smoke trail of an incoming missile curled through the air in front of us until it was blown up midair.

"Goddess damn you, Anush!" I spat.

My commander's sight flashed and enemy target reticles began to pop up on the horizon. It must have been a perimeter force, a series of positions to make sure nobody got in or out of the city. Machine gun tracers and rockets arced out of the positions, smacking off of our armor and exploding on the ground around us.

Swallow's Fortress' gunner replied first, sending a high explosive round into the distance. It found purchase in one of the perimeter positions, sending up a geyser of flame and destruction.

"Serzh, don't slow down," I said. *"We can't sit out here and slug it out with them. Push straight through toward Nayiri's position."*

"Aye, sir." Anush fired, filing the turret with the chemical stink of cannon propellant.

Her round impacted a building near its base. A plume of fire and smoke erupted on either side of it, collapsing the structure onto its defenders. *Swallow* fired again, hammering the building next to Anush's target, blowing a ragged hole in its side. At the sight of the coming assault, many of the soldiers were displaced, falling back into the city and abandoning the perimeter.

"Ha!" Anush hooted. "Run you cowards!"

I couldn't help but feel the rising excitement myself. Despite having us outnumbered and almost certainly outgunned, they had broken and run. On the boring duty of guarding the perimeter, then suddenly coming under attack, the soldiers probably thought they were being assaulted by a much larger force rather than just two tanks. My entire life I had always been told that the Imperial Army doesn't retreat. They were the stalwarts of the emperor and the spearhead of the advancement of humanity throughout the stars. Maybe they had lost some of their backbone by rebelling.

Then, my sight blinked with more target reticles amongst the cluster of buildings. The air crackled with energy, sounding like wild lightning strikes. Then, the ground around the base of the buildings began to shimmer. Steam rose up, gathering in a cloud above the city's perimeter. Before I could recognize the signs, I was blinded by a flash of light.

A solid beam of light lanced out of the city, cutting across the open ground between *Swallow* and *Daredevil*. The once-frozen ground split open with a deafening crack, a giant fissure threatened to swallow our tank as Davit coaxed *Daredevil's* engine to get us clear of it. The tracks spun uselessly on the ice but eventually grabbed onto the rock, pulling us free.

"Was that what I think it was?" I steadied myself as the tank struggled over the newly broken ground.

"I don't see anything!" Anush said, moving the turret to the left and right. "I don't think it's the strider. They wouldn't be able to hide that big bastard!"

I gritted my teeth. "What else could that have been?"

Amongst the smoking remains of buildings that had been hit by shells I saw a rising cloud of steam once again, its stark white sticking out against the pitch black.

"Look!" I highlighted the steam and sent the picture to Anush's implant. "Whatever the hell just hit us has to be putting out a lot of heat. Follow the steam back to its source."

As I thought to switch to the network and tell Serzh what I saw, the weapon fired again. The beam pierced the ground in front of the *Swallow* and raced directly toward it faster than its driver could evade. The super-heated particle energy beam sliced through the front slope of the tank before the driver, in his death throes, jerked the tank out of the weapon's path. The beam kept going, cutting to the right, before cleaving its track in half and stopping.

The front of *Swallow* had been cleaved in half as if by a celestial knife. The rest of the tank, propelled by forward momentum continued on, the severed driver's compartment falling away and catching fire.

"Serzh!" I yelled. *"Bail out!"*

But it was too late. The heat of the beam weapon had ignited the tank's fuel and hydraulic fluid lines. Fire ripped up from the nightmarish wound and leaped into the turret. Hatches flew open as the crew attempted to save themselves, but they were already lost. Their bodysuits were engulfed in flames and melted to their skin. They managed to pull themselves into the fresh air before the fire overtook them completely and they fell back down into the inferno below.

"Damnit!" I hammered a fist on the turret wall. "Davit get us into that city. Anush, that bastard is hiding in those buildings, take out its cover!"

Suren reached over and loaded an explosive round, as soon as he armed the gun Anush fired. The façade of a building ruptured, showering debris onto the city below. She fired again and again, and with each pull of the trigger another building was gutted by an explosion.

That was when I saw it. A carrier with a grotesquely oversized cannon grafted onto a turret. Strange looking wire nests looped from the carrier's body up to the cannon. They looked as if they had been crafted out of a leather-like material, a kind of dried-looking skin. The weight and length of the cannon bogged the carrier down as it tried to retreat from our barrage. Its tracks dug into the road and its engine struggled to move with any speed. As it reversed and attempted to turn the tip of the immense cannon slammed into the corner of a building, breaking through a wall before getting stuck.

"Found you!" Anush cheered, punching a sabot round into its flank.

The round cut through the carrier and exploded through the other side of it, continuing on through the building it was stuck in. The catastrophic damage caused a thunderstorm of energy to erupt from the converted troop compartment. The air began to shimmer again and uncontrolled, crackling red sparks leaped from the hole Anush had shot into its armor.

Finally, the thing exploded. It detonated with a powerful, incredible flash of light, touching off with such force it blew through the bottom of the carrier and leveled the entire block. The carrier at the center of it all was vaporized as it tumbled through the air. I watched through my thermal sights in horror and amazement as the city block glowed with pulsating fire.

The force of the explosion had laid waste to our approach to the city. Dozens of red enemy target reticles blinked out of existence, caught up in the uncontrolled surge of otherworldly energy that had swept through the area in an instant. The outburst of particle energy was unlike anything I had ever seen. Normal explosions would collapse a building, reduce it to rubble, and churn the people inside into something unspeakable.

The particle beam explosion flashed them from this plane of existence. The buildings simply ceased to be, rendered down to their foundations and the dirt around them turned to glass. Any trace of the humanity inside of them was gone, as was the carrier that held the cannon in the first place. Nothing remained of the city block. What kind of unholy weapons was the Ministry of Munitions working on that could do such a thing?

"All right," I said, pulling myself away from the destruction. "We're on our own."

"We only got that guy because he was focused on Serzh, if we run into another one of those things, we might not be so lucky." Anush's voice was lowered, almost wavering. "We thought we just had to be worried about one of those striders, but now they slapped that beam cannon on a carrier? Look what it did to *Swallow's Fortress*."

She moaned hopelessly. "What the fuck can we do?"

I kicked the back of her seat. "I thought you were the best gunner in the regiment?"

I wasn't sure if that was actually true, but she said it so often I just wanted to put the fire back in her belly.

"Sir, I think at this point I'm the only gunner in the regiment."

"I've known you for going on five years now. Never once did you let me forget that you were the best damn gunner the sixteenth had in its ranks. I don't care if it's by default, you better start acting like it. We need you Anush. Nayiri needs you. Don't give up on us now."

She took a deep breath, reached under her seat, and produced the Titanian whiskey once again. She flicked the cork off of the top with a thumb and took a swig.

"Don't count me out yet."

"Never would." I patted her on the shoulder and snatched the bottle from her hand.

I upended it into my mouth and felt its burning rush one last time. "How could I count out the best gunner in the regiment?"

"That's fucking right." She nodded, drumming her hands on her gunner's controls as her confidence began to return. "Did you see that damn explosion?"

She laughed nervously and slapped her chest. "That was me, baby. All me. Suren, give me a canister round with a high explosive on standby."

Suren amped himself up by slapping the turret walls, a smile slowly spreading across his face as he opened the blast doors and loaded another round.

I smiled. "That's the spirit."

I took a deep breath and through open my hatch, grabbing my carbine. I unhooked the bandolier of ammo and slung it around my shoulders so it hung in front of my chest. I had a feeling where we were going, I was going to need every bullet I could get.

"Davit, let's go."

CHAPTER
TWENTY-SEVEN

DAREDEVIL ADVANCED over the blasted grounds that had been annihilated by the particle energy explosion.

Barda Prime was like many settler towns. Easily constructed, prefabricated synthetic concrete buildings had been placed in a tight grid pattern lining public roads. Normally, these would be used for pedestrians and vehicle traffic but the harsh environment of Barda led to the construction of an insulated and sealed tube enclosed walkway and transit system that would bring people from one point to another.

The buildings, once slate grey and unadorned, had been pock-marked by gunfire and gutted by explosions. Nayiri's surprise attack into the city had hit it hard and once we were through the area leveled by the carrier, evidence of her bloody advance could be seen all over. Dead rebels, troopers, and civilians, littered the street. Windows were blown out, transit tubes had been destroyed, left in tangled and useless messes draped across the skyline. The occasional green jacket of a corpsman was visible amongst the carnage but it looked like she had given far more than she had got.

Since she had passed some time before rebel soldiers and civilians had begun to reappear to survey the damage. Civilians in thick winter jackets and face masks tended to piles of glass and debris while soldiers milled about, taking the toll of their dead. The shock on their faces was evident as we charged in, catching them in the open.

"Rules of engagement?" Anush asked.

I grimaced. "What do you think?"

It was rare for a world that rebelled against the Empire to not be put to the torch. The goal was always to make an example of them so that nobody else would ever try such a thing again. I knew here that wouldn't happen. Nobody would ever hear of Barda or the orbital strider. The security services and Ministry of Munitions would make sure of that.

"Just double-checking." Her coaxial machine gun clicked on and began hammering once again.

She swept the turret back and forth as she fired. The people who didn't run at the sight of us were cut down where they stood. Others came running to see what the noise was, weapons up and at the ready. She flicked the controls over to the cannon and pumped a canister round down the street. Thousands of ball bearings cut through the air, turning the already devastated area into a charnel house of flesh, bone, and industrial wreckage.

Consulting the Barda Prime map in my SEED, I immediately realized I was lost. The map I was looking at was that of not a city of hundreds of thousands, but a small settlement of maybe a few hundred. The map version of Barda Prime had only a few roads and a dozen or so of the prefab buildings. It looked to be about the size of Gandak.

The Barda Prime we were sitting in could not have been more different. The same prefab buildings stretched into the sky, the biggest I had ever seen since my time in school on Mars. It was enough to populate the city with more people than lived back on Sassoun Station. However, the bigger problem became evident.

"Hey, sir," Davit said. "None of these roads make any damn sense."

When Nayiri had sent me her location it had been plotted as a part of the map that had been provided to every SEED holder, myself included. That didn't do us any good as it became very clear that whichever map command had given us was not the actual map of Barda Prime.

"Shit," I spat. "I think they gave us the wrong map."

I stuck my head out of my hatch and took in the surrounding area, comparing it to my heads-up display. It was as if I was on a different planet.

"Isn't this place supposed to be top secret?" Anush asked. "Of course, they wouldn't trust us with real maps."

"It would have given away that this Goddess-forsaken ball of ice was hardly some far-flung mining outpost," Davit added. "Millions of people must live here. How do they keep it all under wraps?"

"These people probably aren't allowed to leave," I said. "You're from the third quarter, right? How easy is it for you to leave Terra?"

"I'm wearing this green rag, aren't I?" Davit pointed out.

"Only nobles and businessmen get off station visas in Sassoun," I said. "I imagine once you accept a post out here, you're not going anywhere ever again."

"Guys," Anush said, her words rising in urgency. "How are we going to find Nayiri?"

To our front, and in the crowded city cluster that had swallowed us, its defenders had begun to stir. Small arms fire began to spark off of the road and clang harmlessly off of the side of our armor. It was only a matter of time before they began wheeling up something heavy.

"Nayiri, are you still out there?"

"Despite their best efforts, yeah. Not sure for how much longer though.

"We can't use our map to find you, we have no idea where we are."

"We noticed that too. This entire place is one layer of secrecy after another, they don't even have maps available to the public. Only the rebel officers have access. Thankfully, one of our troopers managed to tap into their SEED network and steal one. I'll forward it to you."

I didn't want to think about what some poor trooper had to do in order to crack a dead man's SEED. Or maybe, they weren't dead. Some of the more brutal criminal types that filled the Corps had ways of making men talk. A chill went down my spine just thinking about it.

My heads-up display pinged with her message. I forwarded it to Davit's device just in time. A *Pilum* zipped over our heads and the force of its impact shoved me away from my open hatch.

I coughed as smoke filled my mouth. "Davit, update."

I expected to be assaulted with warning lights telling us that someone had finally scored a hit on our turbine or something else we needed. Instead, Bitching Betty remained silent.

"Nothing down here," he said, pulling the tank away and on a new path toward Nayiri's position.

I pulled myself back up to my seat and found the source of the explosion. The *Pilum* had missed us by only inches. A hole had been bored through my open tank commander's hatch. A hole large enough to fit my fist through, and the super-heated bolt of tungsten that made up the warhead had turned the area around the wound molten. The armor that used to make up my hatch begin to warp and drip down onto the top of the turret like candle wax.

As we drove through the city, I saw small groups of rebels gathering in alleyways and rooftops, waiting for their chance to strike out at the strange, lone tank that was attacking them. They would flash by in a second as Davit wrenched on the throttle, the turbine of the *Daredevil* screamed and howled as it powered us through the worst of it. Rockets, missiles, and grenades crashed and exploded uselessly at street level as Anush and I fired wildly at any momentary glimpses of grey that we saw.

Davit jerked the tank to the right, dodging a truck that had been parked sideways in the middle of the road. Rebels appeared from behind it, spraying us with gunfire. I ducked back into the turret as the rounds clattered off of the armor around me. Anush hosed them down with a spurt from her coaxial machine gun. In mere seconds, the outpouring of fire reduced the rebels and their truck to little more than smoldering junk.

As we left the ruined roadblock behind the enemy fire picked up. Rebels attacked us from windows, doorways, and rooftops. The boom of Anush's cannon would send them scurrying for cover but they would return only moments later. Leaning out of my ruined hatch, I fired at everything that moved with my carbine. As soon as I burned through one magazine, I quickly replaced it with a fresh one and kept firing. One of my bursts sent a rebel pitching off of a roof, splattering on the street below, before disappearing under our tracks.

"Suren!" Anush yelled over the din of combat. "Coaxials out of ammo!"

She was brushing empty brass and links away from her machine gun, finding the ammo chute empty. Suren looked around him for more ammo but found none. His loader's position had become a graveyard of empty shells and ammo boxes. Kicking them aside, there was no more machine gun ammo.

"We have more in the storage racks up top," he said, flinging open his hatch and climbing out of the tank without warning.

"Goddess above!" I cursed. "Suren, stay down or you're going to get shot!"

He scrambled onto the turret as hundreds or even thousands of shots rang out, sparking off of the armor all around him. I tried to cover him but my lone carbine was hardly enough to suppress all of the rebels who were shooting at us. Suren, ignoring everything going on around him calmly opened the left side storage rack and began digging around inside.

He seemed totally unaware of the fact that bullets were buzzing around his head like an angry swarm of hornets. He casually grabbed two more boxes of machine gun ammo and tossed them into the open turret. A burst of machine gun fire slammed into the spot he was just standing in as he slid back into the tank, closing the hatch behind him.

Davit chuckled. "The Goddess always favors the foolish."

"I'm not sure about the Goddess, but he better offer up a prayer to the neglectful god of marksmanship," I joked, punching several rounds into the back of a fleeing rebel.

Suren cracked open the ammunition box and fed a long belt into the coaxial ammo chute, locking it shut when he was done.

"About time!" Anush chided, letting a long burst rip through the street and sending a crowd of lightly armed rebels running for cover.

They were finished off when Suren loaded a high explosive round into the breach and Anush pumped it into the storefront they had chosen for a hiding spot. A shower of shattered glass and bodies rewarded her effort and she smacked her controls in excitement.

"*I think I hear you guys!*" Nayiri's voice poked into my mind. "*I can't believe this is working. I'm sending you a position, I think they are setting up one of those particle beam cannons there. If they get it up and running, we are as good as dead.*"

"Roger," I said. "*We ran into one of those mounted on a carrier on our way in. It killed our second tank.*"

"*Wait, you're alone?*" she gasped. "*Ando, get the fuck out of here, what are you doing?*"

"*Sorry, what's that? You're breaking up. I can hardly hear you,*" I lied.

"Don't you go getting yourself killed before I have a chance to slap you for being a damn idiot," she scolded.

"Yes, ma'am." My heads-up display blipped in front of my eyes, showing the highlighted position Nayiri had sent.

I forwarded it to both Davit and Anush. "Nayiri says they are setting up another one of their freakshow weapons there. We have to take it out before it they get it running."

Anush grinned. "With pleasure."

Davit turned the tank off the main road, our tracks tearing through the corner of the nearest building and sending the walls crashing to the ground. I ducked low behind my broken commander's gun platform as he brought the tank into an alleyway that was in no way big enough for us.

"Hold on, everyone," Davit said a bit too cheerfully as he gunned it, each side of the tank carved into the wall on either side of it.

Broken masonry and debris rained down on us and I cursed the lucky shot of the rebel that rendered my hatch useless.

"What the hell are you doing?" I complained as I was pelted by ragged hunks of brick.

"Shortcut." *Daredevil* emerged from the alleyway, skidding to a stop in a small courtyard.

In the middle of the courtyard stood a gaggle of rebels around the same kind of strange-looking cannon that had been strapped to the top of the carrier that we had destroyed. This time it was on a large trailer, outriggers supporting its girth, and they were attempting to angle the unwieldy thing toward where Nayiri and the others were holding out.

They recoiled in horror at our sudden appearance and Anush cackled like a manwoman at their obvious fear. Before they could drop what they were doing to make a run for it, she laid on the coaxial trigger. The turret glided back and forth as she did so, peppering the entire area with hundreds of bullets. I joined in with my carbine when some of them looked like they might get away.

Davit maneuvered around the cannon, careful not to touch it.

"Well, that is certainly one way to do that." Nayiri laughed, watching us emerge out of the courtyard.

"Once again, you're welcome."

Now in the city center, we saw the scout detachment's position. They had punched this far before eventually taking too many casualties to continue. Cornered and with no way out, they had pulled their carriers and trucks around in a loose circle in the urban opening. Grey uniformed bodies lay all around as did the burning hulks of various vehicles. The rebels had spared no expensive attempting to dislodge them but had so far failed to do so.

Anush pumped a round into the beam cannon now that we were clear of it, detonating the entire block we had just charged through. As the buildings and corpses of their defenders were warped and melted by the burst of particle energy, I could see the heads of corpsmen poking out from their defenses in the center. One of those taking in the show was Nayiri, waving us on from behind a carrier.

"Hell of a way to make an entrance," she greeted.

THE CITY CENTER had been transformed into a fortress. In the few hours since Nayiri's force had driven into the area and gotten stuck, they had done their best to dig their heels in. The vehicles that they rode into the city on had been torn to shreds. Carriers had fist-sized holes punched into their armor and fire charred their trucks. Useless as weapons of war, they were now the only barriers separating the detachment from the thousands of rebels that now swarmed the city.

Nayiri had set up a small command post at the center of it all. Tucked behind the broken ramp of her carrier, consulted maps and unit placement using her SEED as well as several different devices. Multitasking with a SEED was something I was never very good at and here she was, her eyes rolled into the back of her head scrolling through some menu as her fingers typed messages with either hand. I was starting to think there was more of a reason why I didn't get promoted than just the colonel hating me.

The carrier she was leaning against had been scored with countless impacts and the ground she was sitting on had been cracked and blasted away by explosions. It was obvious that the detachment had been fighting for their lives. The ferocity of which could be seen all around as rebels had been shot down well within their defenses. Their ragged, grey-uniformed bodies lay all over, intertwined with the green jackets of corpsmen who died in savage hand-to-hand combat.

Nayiri's eyes rolled back forward. "Welcome to the party."

"Looks like I missed out."

"Just missed out on freezing your ass off, by the looks of it." She nodded at *Daredevil*.

The poor thing was in a sorry state. Our charge through the city streets hadn't treated the old machine very kindly. Dents and dings were more consistent than its paint job and Davit's little shortcut had sheared off the storage compartment on our right side. I decided not to dwell on the fact that the right-side compartment was where I stored my personal belongings. In the grand scheme of things, it was better to have our compartment of extra ammo intact than my various dress uniforms.

"On the bright side, your little suicide charge seems to have put them on their back foot for the time being. We need to use that as an opening to break out of this mess."

She handed me a device where she had plotted the path from the city center to the research facility. "We should be able to load what troopers we have left either into or onto the vehicles and get to the facility. Your tank is the heaviest thing we have left, so it'll lead the way. How are you on ammo?"

"We should have enough. If not, we still have personal weapons. What about you?"

I nodded. "Our carriers have been out of chain gun ammo for hours. We aren't exactly loaded down for this kind of thing. Thankfully, the rebel friends dying all around us have given us a wealth of small arms ammo. Plus we still have enough explosives to give them a very bad day."

"So, we rush in, secure the facility, then what?"

"Don't worry your pretty little head about that," she said.

"Once we get there your job will to be park that tank of yours at the entrance while my guys handle the rest."

She held up a brick of explosives menacingly.

"I thought blowing the whole thing up was only a last-ditch effort?"

"At this point, I think last-ditch efforts are all we have left. After all of this—"

She held her hands out on either side of her. "—I'm not wasting any time. Our sappers get in there, blow the damn thing up, and we run as fast as we can."

"You've seen what those beam cannons can do." I motioned toward the blasted expanse that the last one had created. "If we blow up that facility, we will destroy this entire city, Nayiri."

"Frankly, Ando, I don't give a fuck anymore. Is that going to be a problem?"

"You're the boss."

"Good," she said. "We need to get out of here before they pull their shit together enough to press the attack. If we get bogged down again that'll be it for us. I'll get these troopers moving, you just make sure your crew is ready."

TWENTY-NINE

DAVIT WAS AN EMOTIONAL MESS. Not because he had just driven through some of the heaviest combat anyone could witness and still be alive. Rather, because the *Daredevil*, our beloved tank, had been damaged in almost every conceivable way.

He had the back deck of the tank opened, and was peering into the engine compartment and cursing loudly. Suren was alongside him, helping any way he could, or more likely, as much as Davit would let him. He had been relegated to handing tools down to the angry driver as he called out for them.

"How is she?" I yelled up.

Davit pulled his head out of the compartment, his face smeared with oil, engine fluids, and dirt.

"Where do you want me to start?" he complained. "I've had to fix so many fuel lines I think most of them are just electrical tape by now. The fluid leak in my compartment is so damn bad I am about to have to become aquatic just to survive down here. Oh, and the turbine took a hit from something, not sure what. It must have been a glancing blow or we would have been left burning out in the street like Serzh and his guys."

He held up a blade from the turbine, an ugly dent concaved it on one side.

"Can you make it work?" He placed his hands on his hips and eyed me like a scolding mother.

"Of course I can!"

"Good. You have five minutes," I encouraged.

The groan that emanated from him would have normally made me laugh but now it just made me shoo him away with my hands. He turned around, leaning back into the compartment to get back to work.

I climbed up onto the turret and found my damaged hatch had been removed and a mismatched replacement had been bolted into place. It looked like the kind of hatch normally used for a carrier. It wouldn't lock, but I could at least close it over me when things got a bit too hot and I had a feeling that they might.

Anush was inside, tossing out the various shells and brass that had accumulated on the turret floor. A cigarette dangled from her lips and she nursed heavily from the bottle of whiskey.

"Ammo?" I asked, leaning over, and snatching the bottle from her hand before stealing a drink.

"We'll be fine as long as we don't pull any more one-man charges into the city." She plopped down onto her gunner's seat, exhausted.

She sighed. "Hypothetically, let's say that is about to happen again."

"We have two boxes of coaxial belts left, about ten main cannon rounds, give or take. Then we are down to personal weapons and you are already using Suren's."

"He has the machine gun up top, too," I pointed out.

She shook her head. "It got taken out by a rocket. Blown clean off."

"Great," I moaned.

Down to a handful of bullets and a carbine is not a place any tanker wanted to find themselves. Suren dropped into the open loader's hatch, closing it behind him. The engine began to wind up, coughing and sputtering as it did so.

Davit cooed. "Come on, baby. Just a little further."

A strange smell of burning plastic filled the turret and I leaned over, flicking on the venting fans. They hummed and cleared the stink from the air.

"Should it smell like that?" I asked.

"It's fine," Davit insisted.

"It doesn't smell fine."

"I'm sure you don't smell very good right now either, sir, but you don't hear us complaining," Davit snapped.

I should have known better than to comment on the *Daredevil*.

"Ando, take the lead. The rest of us are following. Take it slow, I'm not sure how hard we can push some of these vehicles. They've taken a lot of damage," Nayiri's voice popped in.

"Roger." I turned back to my internal comms. "All right, Davit. Keep it slow, some of their carriers are barely holding it together back there."

As soon as we pulled out of the fortified city center we came under attack. Rockets and machine gun fire ricocheted off of our armor, crashing into the buildings around us.

"Hold your fire unless you can actually see what you're aiming at!" I cursed at Anush as she blasted a hole through a nearby apartment block with a high explosive round.

I held my carbine close to my chest, one hand holding the replacement hatch shut. The metal shook in my hand as it absorbed dozens of impacts.

"I can see them just fine!" she asserted. "It's not my fault if you can't!"

Suren rammed another shell into the breach and Anush sent it flying through the air, exploding into a rebel machine gun nest that had been set up on a balcony. The entire face of the building erupted and blew out, showering the street below with death and debris.

"Okay, fine I'll give you that one."

"Hold on back there," Davit said.

Looking through my sights I saw they had pulled more obstacles into the middle of the road in an attempt to keep us pinned in at the city center. Trucks, shuttles, and more than a few concrete blocks had been piled up. Davit revved the engine, pained to hear the once-mighty powerplant of the *Daredevil* struggle to get up to speed.

We crashed into the barriers, sending some flying off to the side while others were dragged under our tracks and crushed.

"*Haduni!*" called out a voice I didn't recognize.

The SEED had them labeled as 'Lieutenant Arame.'

"*Rebels on your back deck!*"

They must have waited for us to get too close to the buildings and jumped on top of us.

"Shit!" I spat. "I'm going up top!"

I flung my hatch open just in time to see one of them. A grey-uniformed rebel with a satchel charge slung over his shoulder. I unholstered my sidearm and fired twice into his chest, sending him tumbling over the side and splattering onto the road.

Something hit me in the back of the head, hard. It forced me forward, smacking my face off of the edge of my hatch. Hot blood ran down my face from the gash the blow opened across my forehead. Whoever else was on top of the tank had kicked my hatch into the back of my head and was pinning me in place. I could feel the metal edge of the hatch ring cutting deeper and deeper into my head. I screamed out in pain, unable to free myself.

Suren opened his hatch, throwing himself up onto the turret in one fluid motion using his immense upper body strength. A quick exchange of gunshots later, the pressure was lifted from the other side and I fell back into my seat, blood covering my face and stinging my eyes. Suren climbed back down into the turret, locking his hatch behind him. When he turned toward me, I saw his face had gone ashen white and blood oozed out of a wound in his chest. His eyes were wide in shock, as if he had only just realized he'd been shot.

"Suren!" I cried.

He mouthed something but only blood bubbled up. He slumped against the wall, slowly falling toward the ground. On the wall behind him, a thick smear of blood trailed his path downward. He tried to reach up, grabbing onto the breach, and pull himself back to his feet but it was no use.

I jumped from my seat, went to his side, and put my hand over his wound. Blood pulsed in between my fingers with each beat of his heart and I could tell from the look on his face that it was mortal.

"I'm sorry, boss," he managed to say, his voice barely audible. "I didn't mean to get shot."

"You saved my life, Suren," I said, putting my free hand around his shoulder and pulling him in close. "You stupid bastard. You saved my life."

The tank shook again, the smell of smoke rushed in only to be purged in seconds by the humming turret vents. Anush, tears pouring down her face yelled out at me.

"I need a damn round!" She sniffed and quickly shoved her face back into the gunner's controls so she wouldn't have to look at her fallen friend.

Suren's features had gone slack and his eyes locked onto something we couldn't see, not of this world. I hugged him one last time. I tried to remember back to what we were supposed to do with a body aboard the tank should one of us die. I hooked my arms under his armpits and pulled him into the small area under the breach.

"Sir!" Anush screamed. "Enemy tank!"

I managed to pull myself away from Suren's body, taking the time to close his eyes before I did so.

Officers go through cursory training at all of the positions of a tank before finishing school. However, it is normally only a few hours at most, not nearly long enough to make us particularly good at any one thing. This was only made worse by the fact I graduated from Armor School half a decade ago.

I hit the blast door switch with my knee and it slid open in a flash. The rounds were loaded in warhead first, meaning I couldn't tell which was which. Suren had developed a system where he marked each round on its end denoting the kind of shell it was. However, Suren, being illiterate, developed *his own* symbols to do this, rather than just writing "sabot" or "high explosive." I saw one shell that had a doodle of a badly drawn tank on it and figured that was good enough.

I hit the switch at the corner of the round that locked it into place on the storage rack. It popped out and I caught it in the crooks of my arms. The damn thing was heavy as hell and suddenly I had new, belated, respect for Suren's strength. He could fling the damn things around like they were nothing, here I was, barely staying upright with one in my hands. The tank lurched to the left before it was rocked by something hard. I stumbled, struggling to stay on my feet

"Hurry up!" Anush said. "He isn't going to miss a second time!"

I arched my back and heaved the round into the breach, punching it into place. The breach slammed shut automatically and I pulled the arming lever, gasping for air.

"Up!" I screamed, panting.

"On the way!" Anush called.

The breach recoiled only inches away from where I was standing, the force of which felt like I had been kicked in the chest.

"Hit!" she cheered. "Give me another one, it looks like he's still kicking."

I sighed, repeating the process. This time was a little smoother as I remembered some of the tips the instructors had taught us back in school. This time before, she pulled the trigger, I exhaled so the force of the cannon's recoil didn't knock the wind out of me a second time.

"Eat shit, you bastards!" she howled, stomping her feet on the ground. "That was for Suren!"

"Is it dead?"

"Oh, he's dead all right." She smiled before snapping back to the controls and firing off a burst from the coaxial. "Why won't these assholes take a fucking hint!"

I grabbed my carbine again, pushing my way through the loader's hatch. The area was slick with Suren's already frozen blood, the corpse of the man he had killed lay across the back deck of the tank. Suren didn't have a gun, so he had charged him, getting shot in the process. The rebel's neck was twisted at a gut-wrenching angle.

Rebels were pushing at us from all sides. Peeking out from alleyways, rooftops, and windows and firing with whatever they had. A grenade bounced across our turret before exploding harm-lessly on the front slope. I fired at everything I saw, but nothing was enough. When one rebel went down, two more appeared in their place. As we got closer to the research facility not even the terrifying buzzsaw of the coaxial was enough to keep them at bay.

One of the trucks behind us vanished in a burst of flames. Its chassis was thrown into the air by the force of whatever hit it, the burning remnants of humans raining down on the street in charred hunks of meat. Another rebel appeared, a *Pilum* over their shoulder but I shot them down before they were able to level against one of us.

In front of us, I could see the nondescript facility, as plain and unadorned as the rest of the city. A foreboding wall with guard towers overlooked a reinforced large metal gate. There was no sign that announced that we were entering a top-secret Ministry of Munitions facility, but it was clear we were in the right place.

I fired on another rebel that I caught attempting to sprint across the street in front of us. The last of my shots caught him in the leg, spinning him around and dropping him to the ground, howling in pain. The bolt of my carbine locked to the rear and as I reached into my bandolier for a new magazine, I saw it.

Three rebels in one of the guard towers, a *Pilum* launcher between them, staring right at us. The cannon was off to the left as Anush fired on other attackers and she couldn't see what was in front of us. My searching hand felt nothing but the empty canvas of the bag. I was out of ammo.

"Incoming!" I managed to yell as the *Pilum* flew through the air so fast it couldn't be registered by even our enhanced eyes.

The last thing I heard was the ear-piercing screech of tearing metal before everything went black.

CHAPTER
THIRTY

PAIN. Searing, horrible pain.

It was the first sensation that returned to me. First all over, then in pulsating waves. There was so much pain I couldn't pinpoint where exactly it was coming from. It felt as though someone had pinned me down and beat me all over. I tasted blood and smelled smoke.

Finally, after what seemed like an eternity, my ocular implants flickered back to life. My vision stayed black and white for a few moments before color returned. Slowly, my brain recognized where I was. I was on the floor of *Daredevil*. I was covered in blood, so much blood that it couldn't have just been my own.

Daredevil was freezing cold, colder than I ever remember it being. It was the coldest I had ever been in my entire life, piercing through the skin and stinging the bone. I looked down and saw my uniform and bodysuit had been torn, letting in Barda's frigid air.

"Anush?" I called out. "Davit?"

I got nothing in response. I tried to remember what had happened, but nothing came to me. We had been driving through Barda Prime, we were almost to the research facility, weren't we? Why was the tank so dark? Normally the interior lights at least kept everything slightly above pitch black. Davit was going to be pissed that something else in the tank had been broken.

That is when I saw a small ray, a pinprick of light, cutting through the darkness of the tank. A hole had been punched through the right side of the tank, right next to where the gunner's position should have been. Then I remember, we had been hit by a *Pilum*. I had to push myself up to my knees to see around the breach, that now hung at a strange angle.

The gunner's position had been vaporized. The ballistic computer bank was gone as were the sight and controls. Even the seat that Anush once occupied had been blasted beyond recognition. The area around it had been scared and stained a deep, crimson red that had become frozen to the walls and floor in a gruesome layer of ice. I didn't want to accept it, but I knew that this was all that remained of Anush. I wouldn't find anything else.

It didn't make any sense. If it had this power to simply annihilate any trace of Anush, it should have killed me too. The side of the breach facing the gunner's position looked like it had been worked over with a hammer. A massive divot had been bored into it with such heat and force that the several thousand-pound breech block had become warped and melted, hanging downward and would surely never function again.

The *Pilum* must have lanced straight through the turret and Anush. She wouldn't have felt a thing. I took an amount of comfort in that. Here one second, gone the next in the blink of an eye. After that, the *Pilum*'s armor-piercing spear had lost a certain amount of momentum before hitting the breach block. It didn't have the power to keep going and instead slammed into it, causing a mess of spalling that now riddled my body. I told myself not to worry about the wounds. If any of them were serious, I would have already died. This was just pain.

Where was Davit? Was he dead too? Could I have been the only one to survive somehow? I forced myself to climb onto the loader's seat and shove open the hatch. I was greeted by another blast of cold air. My carbine was gone, the only thing I had left was my sidearm with a half-empty magazine. I clutched it protectively in my hand as I got out of the tank.

The street had become a graveyard. All around *Daredevil* lay the smoldering wrecks of most of the rest of the detachment. Leading with our tank was a solid tactical plan, but when it had been knocked, it had created a roadblock for everyone behind us. Carriers and trucks had been surrounded and torched as they attempted to get by. Other troopers jumped off of their vehicles, running for cover in the city or toward the facility. A trail of green-jacketed bodies charted their progress.

I heard the faint sounds of gunfire coming from the direction of the facility. I wasn't the only one. I could tell from the fact that the entire city hadn't been leveled that Nayiri hadn't blown the strider up so she must have still been trying to complete the mission. I didn't know how, but I knew I had to help her. We had gotten this far, we couldn't stop now.

I lowered myself down to the front of the tank and found the driver's hatch open. Inside, surrounded by countless sun pendants, was Davit. It looked like it had been quick. The rebels had forced his hatch open with a crowbar by the looks of it and shot him before he could react. I leaned down and closed the hatch over him. I had a feeling that if he knew he was dead, he would have wanted to have been laid to rest inside of *Daredevil*.

I marched toward the facility in a staggering gait, struggling to hold myself up. Between the blood loss and the cold, my strength was being rapidly sapped. The pistol felt heavy in my hand and my feet were weighed down by bricks.

"*Nayiri?*" I reached out to the network.

It took every ounce of my remaining mental capacity to transmit. That wasn't a good sign. The cold was starting to effect my brain, or, had I lost that much blood?

"Nayiri?" I asked again. *"Are you out there?"*

"Ando?" came a pained, shocked voice.

Her words came through like a whisper. Hardly audible over my own mind and heartbeat that pounded in my temples.

"Ando..." Her voice fought to be heard. *"Run. We aren't going to—"*

Her voice faded away, broken up by my own tired, struggling mind. I tried to respond but I couldn't. I was too weak. The next thing I heard was a harsh hiss of static. The sign the network node had died. That Nayiri had died.

My legs wobbled, gave out, and I fell to my knees. I wanted to cry out from the pain, but nothing came. My throat was dry and ragged and only a wheezing cough came out. In front of me, I saw the grey shapes of rebels. They must have known I was dying as they closed in on me. They were moving carefully and had strange-looking weapons in their hands, but they were pointing them at me.

My vision was beginning to fail me again, but I knew what I was looking at wasn't human. They were wearing the grey jackets of the Imperial Army, but their motions were jerky, stuttering. Their skin was discolored and looked like something was rippling and pulsating just below the surface. They weren't holding their weapons. The weapons had been grafted onto their bodies with the vile tapestry of stitched-together skin. Bile rose up in my throat. I didn't know what I was looking at, but it made me wretch.

I tried to raise my pistol to shoot at the monsters that came close to me but it was immediately shot out of my hand by an expertly placed lance of plasma light. The pistol, and my hand, were flash burned out of existence. I cried out in pain before a second shot hit me, this time in the back. I didn't feel the pain this time as my lower extremities went limp and I crashed face-first into the street. I tried to right myself, but my legs wouldn't obey me. My arms moved only in soft, trembling motions. This was it, this was the end.

I waited for the final shot to come, but it didn't. Instead, one of them came up and grabbed me, their inhuman hand gripping the collar of my torn bodysuit. The smell coming off of them was a mixture of rotten flesh and the coppery tinge of blood. It made me retch once again and I vomited stomach acid into the street.

The rebel hoisted me up as if I weighed nothing, draping me across its shoulders like I was a particularly light duffle bag. The group of them began walking back toward the facility without saying a word but moving in such a manner that told me they could communicate flawlessly without them.

The path toward the facility was carpeted in the dead forms of corpsmen and rebels. The normal rebels, the human ones. Now, small groups of these warped, deranged monsters were searching among the dead, throwing them on their shoulders, and following us.

I was just glad the cold was beginning to ebb away and I didn't feel the pain anymore. I was just tired. The building in front of me began to blur, as the corners of my vision narrowed into nothingness and I slipped into a deep, warm, darkness.

THANK YOU FOR READING COLD STEEL

WE HOPE you enjoyed it as much as we enjoyed bringing it to you. We just wanted to take a moment to encourage you to review the book. Follow this link: Cold Steel to be directed to the book's Amazon product page to leave your review.

Every review helps further the author's reach and, ultimately, helps them continue writing fantastic books for us all to enjoy.

———

ALSO IN SERIES
FRONTIER CORPS
COLD STEEL
COFFIN TROOPERS

———

You can also join our non-spam mailing list by visiting www.subscribepage.com/AethonReadersGroup and never miss out on future releases. You'll also receive three full books completely Free as our thanks to you.

Facebook | Instagram | Twitter | Website (www.aethonbooks.com)

Want to discuss our books with other readers and even the authors? Join our Discord server today and be a part of the Aethon community.

———

Looking for more great Science Fiction?

A daring rescue. Interstellar war. Reality-shattering conspiracy...

In the midst of fighting a reignited war with the deadly Nimic, Lt. Commander Johnny Rangers of the Confederation of Aligned Planets is dragged into a rescue mission by mysterious agent Koya Nyrus.

With his best friend's life at stake, he finds himself on a restricted world full of secrets that could alter the course of the war.

Meanwhile, Rangers' father, Inspector Frank Branza of the Gravity City Police Force, sets out to uncover a vast conspiracy with plans to affect the very fabric of reality.

. . .

Little do the estranged father and son realize they're on the same deadly path that will change the galaxy forever.

Don't miss the start of the Gravity City series by CJ Valin and Artie Cabrera. Space will never be the same after this rip-roaring adventure across the stars!

Get Thieves of Destiny Now!

———

Kyle Washaki 'Wash' Williams thought his life couldn't get any more complicated. Then the aliens showed up...

After his mom died from cancer, Wash gave up his girlfriend and his dream of being a career Army officer to stay home and take care of his father, a former Special Forces soldier stricken with PTSD. Wash works three jobs just to pay the bills, and one of them is at the ranch of the man who's engaged to his ex-girlfriend, Jimmy Bonner.

Sound rough? He thought so too...until a portal to a hell-world of giant, insectoid aliens opens behind the ranch house, sucking Wash and Jimmy into the nightmare domain of the Hive Mind, a monstrous, underground blob of brain tissue that stretches across multiple planets through the Gate System.

It exists only to spread itself across the universe. And its next target is Earth.

Will Wash be able to defend the planet from conquest by a swarm of giant alien insects? And will Jimmy be able to put aside his rivalry with Wash to fight for Earth, or will he decide that an alien horde is the perfect tool to dispose of his old enemy?

The answer lies on the other side...of the Gates of Hell.

Get Gates of Hell Now!

———

Don't miss the Liberty of Death Box Set, featuring all three books in the explosive military sci-fi series perfect for fans of *Galaxy's Edge*, Rick Partlow, and Josh Hayes.

Vincent Solaris is a teenager drifting through life who manages to graduate Ethics School by the skin of his teeth. His unplanned future changes dramatically when he is arrested and charged with crimes against the Central Committee after a night of drinking.

While he escapes the gallows, Vincent is sentenced to three years of service in the Earth Defense Forces.

Vincent is sent off to train, thinking that he'll simply spend the next few years lazing away at the edges of Human controlled space. This idea is shattered when a mysterious alien army attacks.

On his way to the far-flung killing fields of war, Vincent meets Fiona, a Martian gangster serving a life sentence. Together, they must find a way to survive against the most terrifying foe that humanity has ever faced.

Get Liberty of Death

———

For all our Sci-Fi books, visit our website.